Murder with Macaroni and Cheese

A Mahalia Watkins Soul Food Mystery

A. L. HERBERT

KENSINGTON BOOKS
www.kensingtonbooks.com

KENSINGTON BOOKS are published by

Kensington Publishing Corp.
119 West 40th Street
New York, NY 10018

All Kensington titles, imprints, and distributed lines are available at special quantity discounts for bulk purchases for sales promotion, premiums, fundraising, educational, or institutional use.

Special book excerpts or customized printings can also be created to fit specific needs. For details, write or phone the office of the Kensington Sales Manager: Kensington Publishing Corp., 119 West 40th Street, New York, NY 10018. Attn. Sales Department. Phone: 1-800-221-2647.

Kensington and the K logo Reg. U.S. Pat. & TM Off.

eISBN-13: 978-1-61773-177-8
eISBN-10: 1-61773-177-3
First Kensington Electronic Edition: September 2016

ISBN-13: 978-1-61773-176-1
ISBN-10: 1-61773-176-5
First Kensington Trade Paperback Printing: September 2016

10 9 8 7 6 5 4 3 2 1

Printed in the United States of America

CHAPTER 1

"Someone needs to turn the heat down out there. I'm about to sweat my wig off," Wavonne says as she comes through the front door of Mahalia's Sweet Tea. "But it sure feels good in here." She leans her head and shoulders back, rolls her neck from side to side, and takes in the cool air pumping through the vents from three air conditioners toiling at maximum capacity on the roof above my restaurant.

"It is a scorcher." I look at my watch. "You were supposed to be here an hour ago and help us set up for lunch. We'll be busy today. People will want to get out of the heat and into the air conditioning. We'll go through iced tea like crazy."

"Speakin' of iced tea. What kind we got on special today? I need to get me a glass."

"It's strawberry. Laura brewed the syrup early this morning."

Laura is my assistant manager and, thankfully, a morning person. She usually gets in around eight a.m. and starts working with my kitchen prep staff to have us ready for our lunch opening at eleven. I generally come in after ten and stay until after we close. On weeknights it's often past eleven p.m. when I leave and usually later than that on Friday and Saturday nights.

"Strawberry! That's my fave!" Wavonne hurries toward the back of the restaurant where we keep the tea dispensers.

I stand by the bar as I watch Wavonne scoop some ice, drop it into a tall glass, add a big serving of homemade strawberry syrup, and fill the whole thing with sweet tea. For customers, we add the syrup to unsweetened tea—the strawberry flavoring is made from berries and plenty of sugar, so it adds a nice touch of sweetness to regular tea. But Wavonne likes her tea so sweet the straw practically stands up on its own.

"You *do* realize you are here to work, Wavonne, no?" I watch her linger by the drink station, alternating between sipping and stirring her tea with a straw as if she's a customer on a leisurely lunch break rather than a paid employee.

Wavonne is my significantly younger cousin and, after a troubled youth that involved only sporadic amounts of supervision from my alcoholic aunt, came to live with Momma and me when she was thirteen and has been a handful ever since. She's in her twenties now, but I still find myself reprimanding her as often as I did when she was a teenager.

"All right, all right. Slow your roll, boss lady." She pulls a lavender tie from her pocket and starts tying it around her neck. All my servers wear black pants, long-sleeve white shirts, and pastel ties. But all my servers certainly do not tell me to "slow my roll" or call me "boss lady." As a member of the family I allow Wavonne a certain amount of slack, and, knowing that I'll never fire her, she takes every bit of it. But, honestly, given her history, most days I'm happy that she manages to show up for work at all.

I'm about to ask Wavonne to make sure we have enough rolled silverware on hand for the lunch crowd when I see Saundra, my afternoon hostess, with the phone in her hand, motioning for me to come to the hostess stand.

"There's a call for you. I said I'd take a message, but she insisted on speaking with you now. She said she's Raynell Rollins's assistant."

"Raynell Rollins?" It takes a moment for the name to register. It's not a name I've *heard* in quite some time—I have, however, *seen* it all over town. I haven't been in touch with her since high school, but Raynell Rollins is a local real estate agent—you can hardly visit any of the better neighborhoods here in Prince George's County, Maryland, without running into one of her "For Sale" signs with her photo plastered on it. "Wonder what she wants," I say more to myself than Saundra, remembering how my friend Nicole, the only person from high school with whom I've kept in regular contact, gave me an update on Raynell a while back. She told me that Raynell married Terrence Rollins shortly after college when he was starting for the Washington Redskins. Nicole, who loves to gossip and has way more time to surf Facebook than I do, also recently informed me that Terrence, who has since retired from playing football, is now a sports anchor on a local station. I don't really follow sports, but I've seen him on the news a few times. Per Nicole, thanks to Terrence's past as a star football player and his current presence as an on-air personality, Raynell has managed to build quite the little real estate sales empire—mostly by tapping Terrence's network of broadcasting and professional-sport-player friends as clients.

I take the phone from Saundra and lift it to my ear. "This is Halia."

"Ms. Watkins?"

"Yes."

"My name is Christy Garner. I'm Raynell Rollins's assistant. She asked me to set up a lunch date with you."

"Really? Any particular reason? I haven't seen Raynell since high school." I'm considering adding that you can count on one hand the number of times Raynell and I spoke to each other while we actually were in high school, but I decide not to go there. Although I don't recall Raynell being a particularly nice person, it's not like there was any animosity between the two of us or anything like that—we just didn't run in the same circles.

"Ms. Rollins is scouting venues for her . . . and I guess *your* high school reunion. She would like to discuss possibly holding the event in your restaurant."

"I thought the reunion was going to be at Colony South Hotel. It's in less than two weeks, isn't it?"

I got an invite to the event months ago and sent my regrets. I rarely take off Saturday nights, and, aside from Nicole, who I already see all the time, there isn't really anyone who I'm terribly eager to reconnect with, so I decided not to bother attending.

"There was a water main break at the hotel. They won't have the event space repaired in time."

"Really? That's a shame."

"Raynell heard that you owned a local restaurant and thought you might be able to host the affair."

"I'd be happy to discuss it with Raynell."

I wonder why Raynell didn't just call me herself, but if memory serves me correct, Raynell was one for putting on airs—using an assistant as an intermediary is probably just one of those wealth and status things I don't understand.

"Why don't you ask her to come by for lunch tomorrow, and we'll talk about it?" I offer even though it's highly unlikely that I'll agree to host the event at Sweet Tea. Depending on how many members of our graduating class are attending, hosting the reunion might mean closing the whole restaurant for an entire evening to accommodate the crowd. I doubt the reunion committee has the kind of money I would have to charge to make up for a Saturday night's worth of lost receipts. Besides, I learned the hard way that closing Sweet Tea for a private event is not a great idea. A few years ago, for a hefty sum, I agreed to close the place to host a wedding reception for the daughter of the owner of King Town Center, which houses Sweet Tea. He agreed to more than cover any lost revenue and, when the man who can raise your rent come lease-renewal time makes a request, you think long and hard before saying no. I tried to get the word out to my clientele about the closure that particular night a few weeks prior to the reception. Among other things, I displayed a poster at the hostess stand and put a notice on our Web site. I even sent e-mails to patrons on our contact list, but my efforts proved to be of no avail. Customer after customer came through the front door wanting a table the night of the reception. Believe me, you have not seen *angry* until you've had to turn away mouths that were all set to bite into crispy fried chicken and fluffy waffles. And some of the customers I had to deny entry to seemed to take it as a personal offense and posted some rather unpleasant commentary on Yelp. I just don't feel like going through all that commotion again.

"Raynell is available at twelve thirty tomorrow afternoon."

"That would be fine. Please tell her to come by Sweet Tea then."

"Sure. I will likely accompany her, and she may invite Alvetta Marshall, who has also been involved in the reunion planning. If that's okay?"

"Of course."

Alvetta registers in my head—another one I haven't seen since high school. I'm sure she's referring to the girl I knew as Alvetta Jordan. I remember Alvetta being nicer than Raynell, and, although she was prettier than Raynell, she was definitely the "number two" girl at my high school. Raynell was the clear leader of the gang of "it" girls, and Alvetta was her primary minion. I think there were six or seven girls in Raynell's little squadron. They all followed Raynell around like newborn ducklings waddling behind their mother. Raynell said "jump," and Alvetta and the others said "How high . . . and in what kind of shoes?" I remember when Raynell got that horrible asymmetrical 'shroom haircut that was big in the eighties—next thing you knew, Alvetta and the other underlings were chopping one side of their hair and leaving the other side long to match their queen. Raynell bought an acid-wash denim jacket and, within days, it became like a new uniform for her girls. When neon was popular the whole lot of them wandered the halls like a walking advertisement for Day-Glo highlighters. I remember them going through a phase when each of them constantly sported a neon beaded necklace. They each had a different color—Raynell probably assigned them. I can't recall the colors the other girls wore, but I do remember that Raynell's necklace was bright green—only because the intense color reminded me of a St. Patrick's Day leprechaun. Raynell isn't much taller than a leprechaun, and seeing her roam the school halls in her colored necklace always made me picture her with a green top hat and pointy-toe green shoes with gold buckles on them. The image was always good for a laugh.

"Okay. I will confirm with Raynell, and we'll plan to see you tomorrow."

"Sounds good."

"Who was that?" Wavonne asks after I hang up the phone.

"The assistant to one Raynell Rollins. I went to high school with her—Raynell—not the assistant. Apparently, Raynell is on the reunion committee. Remember? I told you about the invite I got for it?"

"Yep. And I still don't get why you ain't goin'—all those former classmates who are likely eligible brothas. By the time people get to your age, Halia . . . you know . . . all old and creaky . . . half of them have been divorced and are on the prowl again."

I laugh. "You'll be in your forties one day, too, Wavonne. I hope to be there the first time someone calls you 'old and creaky.'"

She rolls her eyes at me. "You know some of those brothas have been beaten down by naggin' wives for years. They probably all damaged . . . ripe for the pickin'. If nothin' else, you could at least get a weekend fling out of it."

"Just what I need—a weekend fling with some man weighed down with more baggage than a bellman. Thanks, but no thanks!"

"Well then, don't you want to go just to show off? You own one of the most successful restaurants in town. If it were me, I'd go just to rub it in the faces of any nasty heifers who thought they were better than me in high school."

"What are you talking about?" I hear Momma say as she comes out of the kitchen into the main dining room. At seventy-four, she doesn't move as fast as she used to, but she still bakes up some mean desserts. She gets in early and whips up the cakes and pies for Sweet Tea. She's probably finished with her baking for the day and is about to head home.

"I can honestly say I have no idea, Momma."

"Halia was just remindin' me that she's skippin' her high school reunion."

"Why would you do that, Halia? Go. Mingle." Then she adds under her breath, "Find a husband . . ."

"What did you say?" I ask even though I heard her. Momma is forever trying to find me a love life.

"I said for you to go and mingle . . . and if you happen to find a potential romantic interest, so be it."

"You don't ever give up, do you, Momma?"

She ignores my questions. "Just go for Pete's sake . . . and think like a lion while you're there—wait until an eligible man is separated from the herd and then move in for the kill. Stick with the divorced ones. Anyone who's never been married by the time they reach your age must have something wrong with them." She notices the look on my face. "Except for you, dear. You've just been . . . well . . . busy."

"Not that it has anything to do with your badgering, Momma, but I may be going to the event after all. Apparently, there was a water main break at the hotel where they planned to have the reunion, and they need a new venue. I just got a phone call about it. One of my old classmates who is on the reunion committee wants to host the event here at Sweet Tea. She's coming by tomorrow to discuss it."

"Do you think that's a good idea, Halia?" Momma asks. "You don't need perspective suitors knowing you own a restaurant right off the bat. Men can be funny about dating women who are successful in business. Let them get to know you first," she adds as if my status as a restaurant owner is akin to a case of herpes or a prison record . . . or whatever else you wouldn't mention on a first date.

"I just agreed to meet with her. I didn't say I was definitely going to host it here. I'm not keen on shutting this place down for an evening . . . especially on a Saturday night. I think I'll make a few phone calls instead, and see if I might be able to se-cure another location. Then I can just cater the reunion. That way I can help out without having to close Sweet Tea for an evening."

"That sounds like a good idea," Momma says. "You can have staff supervise the catering, and then you can go as a guest. We'll get you a new dress—"

Wavonne cuts her off. "And maybe we can do somethin' with that hair of hers," she says to Momma, and then turns to me. "Let me give you a full makeover, Halia. I'll do your makeup and loan you a wig . . . one of the good ones with the European hair. I'll have you lookin' straight-up pimp in no time."

"I don't think 'straight-up pimp,' whatever that means, is exactly my style. But thanks all the same, Wavonne."

"Suit yourself, but that Eddie Bauer/L.L. Bean getup you got goin' on is not goin' to get you noticed."

"I'm on my feet and moving around this restaurant all day. I like to be comfortable, Wavonne."

"Fine. Be comfortable. But you ain't gonna land no man at your reunion lookin' all frumpadump."

"Whatever, Wavonne. My 'frumpadump' self has work to do, and so do you." I turn to Momma. "And isn't it time for you to get on out of here?"

Momma looks at her watch. "Why, yes. It really is. I've got to run, girls," she says to Wavonne and me before focusing her eyes on just me. "I do hope you attend the reunion, Halia. And remember what I said: you're the lion, and the single men are the gazelles. As soon as one lags behind—"

My back is already turned to her as I cut her off on my way to my office to make some calls and see about finding a venue for the reunion. "I know, Momma: 'Move in for the kill.'"

CHAPTER 2

"Wavonne! If I catch you doing that one more time . . ." I let my voice trail off as we both know whatever I say is no more than an empty threat. She just used a glass to scoop herself a cup of ice out of the well instead of the metal scooper. She does this all the time, and last year, in the middle of the dinner rush, she broke a glass in the process—we had to pour hot water in the well to melt all the ice and make sure we didn't miss any shards. Then restock the whole thing.

"My bad, my bad." Wavonne dumps the ice back into the cooler and uses the scooper to fill her glass before placing it under the sweet tea dispenser. "What time your high school friends comin' over?"

"They should be here soon. And I wouldn't call them 'friends.' They are just former classmates. We barely interacted in high school at all."

"Oh . . . so they were the *popular* girls?"

"What makes you think I didn't hang out with the popular girls?"

"'Cause you were probably always cookin' with Grandmommy or had your nose buried in some book."

Murder
with
Macaroni
and
Cheese

Books by A. L. Herbert

MURDER WITH FRIED CHICKEN AND WAFFLES

MURDER WITH MACARONI AND CHEESE

Published by Kensington Publishing Corporation

"So what if I spent time in the kitchen as a teenager and liked to read? I turned out okay."

"How about the chicks you have comin' in here? How'd they turn out?"

"I don't really know. I haven't seen them in over twenty years."

"What are their names again?" Wavonne pulls out her phone.

"Raynell Rollins and Alvetta Marshall. Why?"

Wavonne starts typing on her phone. "Here's Alvetta." She places her phone under my nose.

"Ah . . . the magic of Facebook." I take the phone, click on Alvetta's main photo, and watch it enlarge on the screen. "She looks good . . . *really* good."

Wavonne grabs the phone back from me and looks herself. "She's all right . . . considerin' she's like forty-somethin'." She clicks on her phone again. "Says here she's First Lady of Rebirth Christian Church."

"Is that so?" I ask. "I guess that mean's she's married to the pastor. Rebirth is one of those mega churches, isn't it? With a few *thousand* members?"

"Yeah. It's not too far from here . . . over in Fort Washington."

"Didn't we just have a bunch of Rebirth members in here last Sunday?"

"Yep. The ones who hoarded three tables for over two hours."

"They do tend to be some of our lesser-behaved after-churchers." I don't know exactly when we started simply referring to them as "after-churchers," but the folks who come in here after services for Sunday brunch are one of the prime reasons I have the rare thought of getting out of the restaurant business. Diana Ross herself could walk into Sweet Tea wearing a diamond tiara, and I bet she'd be less demanding than some of the after-churchers. The ones who come from the gigantic mega churches like Rebirth are typically the worst.

Now don't get me wrong—I'm a Christian, and I'm all for giving God his due on the infrequent Sunday that I can get away from Sweet Tea to attend service—but some of these mega churches just leave a bad taste in my mouth. Momma attends one in Camp Springs. The few times I've gone with her, the collection basket went around more times than a tip jar at a strip club, which wouldn't be so bad if I didn't suspect that half the money deposited in the basket was going toward the pastor's Mercedes G-Class or to keep his wife, who, like Alvetta, refers to herself as the "First Lady," in all the latest fashions from Saks and Neiman Marcus.

"Those Rebirthers were here forever last Sunday. They about ran Darius and me ragged with special requests. Thank God you implemented that tip policy, or we'd have been left with their usual five percent tip."

Wavonne is not one for math, but it wasn't long after she started working at Sweet Tea that she learned how to calculate percentages—working for tips will do that for a person. People really should leave at least twenty percent of the total bill for good service, and no server likes to get less than fifteen percent. But if Wavonne is on the other side of a five or ten percent tip, we all know to batten down the hatches. Even with her poor impulse control she knows better than to chase after a customer who's stiffed her. So instead, she complains to no end to whichever staff member is within earshot. Usually words like "project ho" or "thot" are involved.

"I hated to do it, but I had to do *something*." I'm referring to the Sunday brunch tipping policy I implemented last year that automatically adds an eighteen percent gratuity to all parties. We've always added gratuity to parties of six or more, but some of our less refined customers started breaking up into smaller parties to avoid the charge, and it was becoming a particular problem on Sundays. Most of my customers are decent tippers, but certain after-churchers see it fit to leave well below the industry standard tip amounts. And I'm all for spreading God's word or what have you, but I'm sorry, religious literature left on the table after a customer departs does *not* constitute a tip and is certainly not going to pay my servers' rent or their car payments.

"Let's see what else we can find out about her." Wavonne starts tapping on her phone again.

I'm about to lean my head over and see if she's found a profile for Raynell when I spot a slick black Hyundai Equus glide into a parking space in front of the restaurant. I move closer to the door, and, as the car comes to a stop, I see one of those clear stickers on the back window with a drawing of a church outlined in white. I lean toward the glass to make out the writing underneath the sketch—it says *Rebirth Christian Church*.

"I guess the *First Lady* has arrived."

"Think she's upset that we ain't got a red carpet?" Wavonne asks, walking toward me.

I chuckle. "Maybe so. I guess a tall glass of iced tea will have to do."

CHAPTER 3

Wavonne stands next to me as we watch the door to Alvetta's luxury sedan open. My eyes are initially drawn to her towering pink heels as they make contact with the pavement. I follow them up to a lovely floral dress paired with a short light blue jacket—a bolero jacket, I think it's called.

"Oh *hail* no!" Wavonne says. "I just saw that outfit online."

"The dress?"

"It's not just a *dress,* Halia. That is some *Oscar de la Renta.* Costs like two thousand dollars. I bet those Blahniks on her feet were another thousand, easy."

One of Wavonne's favorite things to do, often when she should be waiting on customers, is to look at high fashion online, snap screen shots of what she likes, and then try to find lookalikes at T.J. Maxx or Ross.

"I guess I'm in the wrong business. Clearly religion is much more lucrative than owning a restaurant."

"You ain't kiddin'. If I'd known landin' a minister would get me all up in some de la Renta, I'd go to church with Aunt Celia more often."

"Oh you would, would you?" I ask as I open the door to greet Alvetta.

"Halia Watkins!" Alvetta calls to me as she carefully navigates her heels on to the raised sidewalk in front of Sweet Tea.

"Alvetta!" I smile. "You look amazing. The picture of summer," I add, eyeing her dress of pastel flowers. And, considering it's nearly ninety degrees today, being dressed for sunshine is certainly appropriate.

As she makes her final approach toward the door, I'm reminded of how beautiful she was in high school . . . and still is. She has the same long legs and hourglass figure . . . the same dewy brown skin, high cheekbones, and full eyelashes framing her hazel eyes. Clicking her heels along the sidewalk with her long black hair pushed back with a pair of oversized white sunglasses, she looks like she's about to board a private jet bound for some exotic location.

"Thank you." She leans in, grabs both my hands, and gives me a kiss on each cheek.

"It's so nice to see you. Please. Come in."

"It's great to see you as well." She steps inside Sweet Tea and begins to look around. "What a lovely place. I'd heard you'd become a successful restaurateur. I can't believe I've never been here . . . especially considering I only live a few miles away."

"That is a shame, but we'll make up for it today. We'll indulge you with the finest soul food in town." I notice Wavonne hovering next to me. "This is my cousin, Wavonne. She works as a server here."

"Nice to meet you."

"Please. Let's have a seat." I gesture for Alvetta to follow me as I walk toward a four top by one of the front windows.

"What would you like to drink? A cocktail or a glass of wine? Or we have a watermelon mint iced tea on special—it's perfect on a hot day like this."

"That sounds delightful."

"Wavonne, could you get us a couple of glasses of the watermelon mint tea?"

Wavonne, who followed us to the table, finally diverts her envious eyes from Alvetta's attire, nods, and heads toward the drink station.

"So, how are you? What have you been up to?" Alvetta asks.

"This." I look around me. "Keeping this place running leaves little time for much else. How about you? I heard you married a church pastor." I figure that sounded better than telling her Wavonne and I were just snooping around on Facebook for details about her.

"Yes. My husband, Michael, is the pastor of Rebirth Christian Church in Fort Washington. We have a congregation of more than ten thousand. It keeps both of us very busy."

"I'm sure it does."

"You should come to service sometime. I'll reserve you a seat in the Pastor's Circle."

"The Pastor's Circle?"

"It's the seating area closest to the stage. The seats are reserved for special guests and VIPs."

"How nice," I reply, even though the idea of a VIP section seems more appropriate for a nightclub rather than a church. "I'd love to, but it's hard to get away on Sunday mornings. Preparing to feed church attendees after the service doesn't give us much time to actually attend ourselves."

"Well . . . when you can get away, I hope you'll come."

"Of course," I respond before switching gears. "So. The reunion?"

"Yes. I'm so excited. It will be a real treat to get the old gang back together again." She seems to be saying this as if I were part of the "old gang." By no means was I part of the "Whitleys," a named bestowed upon Raynell and Alvetta's gaggle of snooty girls in honor of Whitley Gilbert, the spoiled elitist character played by Jasmine Guy on *A Different World,* the spinoff of *The Cosby Show* that was popular back in my high school days. I'm not sure Raynell and Alvetta ever knew that the Whitleys is what they were called by most of the school. It wasn't a name *necessarily* used in a derogatory fashion, but it was always said with a hint of distaste by those of us who were not part of the exclusive clique. I was reasonably popular in high school, but more in a studious "class president" sort of way rather than the fast-partying, latest-fashion-wearing way of the Whitleys.

"I'm sure it will be a fun night. I've lost touch with most of our classmates. Occasionally, some alumni I recognize will come in here for lunch or dinner, but Nicole is the only former classmate I'm still in regular contact with."

"Nicole Baxter? How is she?"

"She's good. She's planning on attending. She lives in Bowie now. She—"

Wavonne interrupts me. "Here we go." She set three glasses of tea down on the table. I'm curious who the third glass of tea is for until I see her grab a chair from a neighboring table, slide it over, and plop herself down on it. "Your other friend who's comin' over . . . you said her name was Raynell Rollins?"

"Yes."

"I thought that name sounded familiar. Then I was pourin' the tea, and it came to me—*Raynell Rollins.* She wouldn't happen to be the wife of Terrence Rollins?"

"Yes," Alvetta responds. "That's her."

"Get out?! She's the wife of *Terrence Rollins?* Former wide receiver of the Washington Redskins?"

Alvetta smiles. "Yes indeed. He retired from the Redskins years ago. He's a sports anchor on the local news now. I'm sure you've seen him. He's on every night at six and eleven."

"I've seen him," I say. "He certainly is a nice-looking man."

"Do you really think Raynell would have it any other way?"
I laugh. "No, I guess not."

"I think that's Raynell now." Alvetta directs her eyes over
my shoulder.

I turn around and look out the window at a white Cadil-
lac Escalade easing into the parking space next to Alvetta's car.

"Great. We can start figuring out a plan for the event." I
turn to Wavonne. "Is there something I can help you with?"
I'm wondering why she is still sitting with us when we had
arranged for her to be the server for this table, not to mention
the two or three other tables she should be waiting on at this
very moment.

"Nope. I'm good."

"Wavonne, you are supposed to be serving this table—not
sitting at it. And you have other tables that need tending."

"I got it covered. Darius said he'd look after my tables for a
few mins." She leans in and whispers to me. "You need to
hook me up with this Raynell sista. She and her husband may
be my ticket to finding a professional sports playa boyfriend."

I don't want to have an argument with Wavonne in front
of Alvetta, so I just nod at Wavonne and get up to greet
Raynell. As I watch her step out of the SUV I'm reminded of
how short she is, even in the high heels she's sporting. I often
remember women like Raynell—woman with big personali-
ties and bigger egos—taller than they actually are. Absent her
stilettos she barely clears five feet.

Unlike Alvetta, Raynell, with her wide nose and square
jaw, is not a natural beauty. You wouldn't call her obese, but
words like "stout" or "solid" come to mind when you look at
her. She doesn't have much of a waistline. Somehow she manages to be plump without having curves—her figure is more in
line with . . . say a tree trunk rather than an hourglass. But you
have to give the girl credit for doing the best she can with what
God gave her. As she gets closer to the door, I can see that her

hair and makeup are meticulous, and her lavender pantsuit flatters her less than curvaceous figure as best it can.

Raynell's power never did stem from her looks. It was always her confidence and authoritarian manner that made her the empress of my high school. And I'm guessing it's those same traits that landed her a handsome rich husband.

Raynell's boxy stature is made even more apparent when a petite, much younger woman rounds the corner from the passenger side of Raynell's SUV, carrying what appears to be a very heavy bag in one hand and an iPad in the other.

The pair reaches the door, which I open for them, and, as Raynell's eyes meet mine, I suddenly remember how she was sort of a bitch in high school. I wonder if she still is.

I welcome her, and she extends her hand in a fashion that makes it seem as though I'm supposed to kiss it rather than shake it. Confused, I decide not to do either and just say, "Hello, Raynell. It's good to see you again."

"You too, Halia." She turns her head from left to right, looking around Sweet Tea. "Such a cozy little . . . little lunch counter you run here," she says of my restaurant, which seats nearly two hundred customers and regularly makes local top restaurant lists. She then looks me up and down. "And who can blame you for putting on a few pounds . . . who wouldn't, working in a restaurant."

Yep, still sort of a bitch.

CHAPTER 4

"Alvetta," Raynell says as we approach the table. "How are you?"

"I'm just fine. You?"

"Trying to survive this heat. You know how I *hate* summer." Raynell reaches into her designer bag, pulls out a handkerchief, and dabs at her forehead. The brief walk from her car to the restaurant was enough to make her faintly perspire in the August warmth.

"Please have a seat," I say to Raynell and her companion. "Raynell, this is my cousin, Wavonne, one of the servers here at Sweet Tea."

Wavonne stands to greet her. "I'll be helping with the reunion planning."

"You will?" I ask. This is news to me.

"Of course. You know how I like to help out as much as I can around here."

I let out a quick laugh before I can stop myself. "Of course." I figure this is a better response than "Since when?"

Raynell gives Wavonne (and her poufy wig, heavy make-up, and tight clothing) a once-over and apparently decides she is not worth a handshake or a hello. She just offers Wavonne a quick smile as she sets her purse down, slides into a chair next to Alvetta, and plops a gaudy gold and sparkly-stone Michael Kors keychain on the table. "You sit over there," she says to the young lady with her, who I assume is the assistant who called me to set up the lunch date, but I can't be sure as Raynell hasn't introduced her to any of us.

"Halia Watkins." I extend my hand toward the young lady. "And this is Wavonne."

She gives my hand a shake and nods politely in Wavonne's direction. "Hi. I'm Christy. Raynell's assistant." She's a pretty girl with a tiny frame, light brown skin, and short black hair. I'd be surprised if she were over twenty-five.

"She can take notes or make calls . . . or whatever needs to be done while we talk," Raynell says.

"Great. That will be a big help."

"Alvetta, sweetie. Are you using that eye cream I gave you? The bags under your eyes don't look much better than the last time I saw you," Raynell says as I sit down next to Christy. I guess I shouldn't be surprised. I didn't spend much time with them, but I observed the girls enough to recall that Raynell worked overtime at destroying Alvetta's self esteem in high school. Why should things be any different now? Alvetta doesn't have so much as a hint of any bags under her eyes, but the ends of her hair were not split or frayed either back in high school when Raynell convinced her she needed to cut her hair.

It was always clear that Raynell was jealous of Alvetta's good looks and seemed to go to great lengths to convince Alvetta she was an ugly duckling when the exact opposite was true. I can't be sure of her motives, but Raynell was queen bee of the Whitleys, and my guess is she wanted the status of having the prettiest girl in school as her best friend, but, at the same time, was afraid Alvetta would challenge her authority if she was actually aware of what a knockout she was.

I don't recall the complete details, but from what I remember, Alvetta came from *very* modest roots. She was the daughter of a single mother who served as a live-in housekeeper for a more fortunate family. The rumor around school was that Alvetta actually shared a room with her mother in the employer's home.

My high school was largely made up of students from working-class and middle-class families. There were certainly poor kids at my school, but many parts of Prince George's County were more affluent in the eighties than they are now. Being so close to D.C., many of us, including Raynell, had parents who made healthy incomes as government employees or by working for government contractors. Andrews Air Force Base (now Joint Base Andrews) in Camp Springs, not far up the road from my school, was also a big employer.

It had to be hard for Alvetta to be the daughter of a maid who didn't even have her own home. But two things kept Alvetta from being derided—her good looks and her friendship with Raynell. At some point, while Raynell was assembling her little empire of fashion conscious she-devils during the early part of our freshman year, the two of them became inseparable. Raynell's cronies consisted of a whole gaggle of girls, but Alvetta was her closest friend—Raynell's most loyal and trusted subject. Raynell protected Alvetta from jeering based on her upbringing (no one dared cross Raynell Spector—she was known by her maiden name in high school), but, at the same time, she made a hobby out of criticizing Alvetta herself in a constant effort to remind Alvetta who was in charge.

"You look lovely, Alvetta," I say before she has a chance to respond to Raynell's rude question. "You haven't aged a day." Raynell looks momentarily annoyed with me for complimenting Alvetta. "I can say the same about you, Raynell," I offer, trying to make a quick save. And Raynell really hasn't changed that much, either, but, in her case, that's not necessarily a good thing—in high school her features, and really her whole demeanor, reminded me of a bulldog, and they still do.

"This menu is killer," Alvetta says. "I want to try everything."

"It's nice," Raynell chimes in. "You know, for a *casual* dining establishment. I had so wanted to hold the event at a different . . . a different *type* of restaurant . . . some place high-end with white tablecloths and palette-cleansing sorbet between courses. But, considering many of our classmates may be . . . how shall I put it . . . 'financially challenged,' we booked the Cotillion Ballroom at that raggedy little motel in Clinton. And then they go and let a pipe burst, leaving us in quite a lurch."

I'm familiar with the venue she's referring to, and, while Colony South may not be the Four Seasons, it is a quaint little hotel (not motel) with a small conference center and nice amenities. To hear Raynell talk, you'd think it was Red Roof Inn with bedbugs.

"Do you think you can accommodate us here, Halia?" Alvetta asks.

"I did give it some thought, but I don't think I can shut down Sweet Tea for the evening; however, I spoke with a friend of mine who books the ballrooms at that Marriott in Greenbelt. They have availability and can accommodate up to two hundred guests . . . and I'd be happy to give the reunion committee a deal on catering."

"That sounds like a viable plan," Alvetta says.

"I don't know," Raynell groans. "Marriotts are so . . . so *ordinary*."

"The space may be ordinary, but I can assure you the food will not be. I can put together a stellar menu for the event and work with your budget."

"And I'll help with all the arrangements. I can keep an eye on the buffet while Halia's busy minglin' with all her old class-mates," says Wavonne.

Raynell just glares at Wavonne as if she is not keen on her involvement. "I suppose we don't have much choice at this point," she says. "Christy, make a note to call the Marriott and make the arrangements."

"I can call my contact there if you'd like. They don't usu-ally allow outside caterers, but she owes me a favor and—" I'm about to continue with my offer to make the arrangements myself when Raynell interrupts me.

"Christy can do it," she says as Christy types a note on her iPad.

I'm about to talk menu options when Darius shows up at the table looking hurried.

"Hello, everyone." He starts refilling the three glasses on the table with more iced tea. "What may I get you two ladies to drink?" he asks Raynell and Christy.

"What's that?" Raynell points to Alvetta's glass.

"That's our watermelon mint iced tea."

"I'll have one of those, but, given it's past noon, slip a shot of vodka in it for me," Raynell says. Christy requests the same minus the octane.

"Sure, but before I get those drinks, let me tell you about our specials today. We have soft-shell crabs dusted with a Cajun cornmeal batter and lightly fried. They're served with twice-fried French fries and coleslaw. We also have butter-baked chicken. There's barely a need for a knife and fork—the meat practically falls off the bone for you. We serve that with macaroni and cheese and collard greens."

"Thanks, Darius," I say. "We'll let the ladies look at the menu a bit more thoroughly, and then I'll ask Wavonne to take their orders and serve the table." I turn to Wavonne. "And the two other tables you've punted off on Darius."

"How am I supposed to help you with the reunion if I'm not at the table to hear the deets?"

"I'll give you a complete rundown on everything we discuss. Now *get.*"

Wavonne moans before slurping down the rest of her iced tea and getting up from the table.

"She's quite the character," Raynell says. And, while this is true, there is a condescending tone in Raynell's voice when she says this that I don't appreciate.

"She's a good kid, but she tests me sometimes," I say with a laugh. "She's lived with my momma and me since she was thirteen. My aunt, her mother . . ." I'm about to give them Wavonne's backstory, but then I decide it's none of their business. "Let's just say she had a complicated family situation before that."

"How sweet," Raynell says. "You still live with your mother."

"I guess we do still share a house. Momma needed my help when she became Wavonne's guardian, so I moved back in. These days I'm rarely home at all. This place keeps me very busy." I'm finding myself on the defense. Maybe I'm reading too much into it, but Raynell seems to be saying, "Oh so you're a spinster with no man and live with your mother . . . how pathetic." Rather than continue to justify my living situation, I decide to move on. "So, the reunion. Sounds like we have the place nailed down. Why don't we talk menu?"

"Fried chicken and waffles, catfish, spare ribs, pot roast," Alvetta says, running her finger down one side of my menu as she reads out loud. "It all sounds so good. I don't know where to begin."

"There are a lot of choices." Raynell looks casually disinterested. "But everything is laden with calories. We'll need some options for those us who haven't let our bodies go completely to hell since high school and—" Her cell phone ring interrupts. As it continues to chime, she looks at the screen and hands the phone to Christy. "It's Gregory. Handle it."

"Of course." Christy takes the phone from Raynell, gets up from the table, and bypasses Wavonne as she heads toward the hostess station to take the call.

I watch Christy walk away and then return my attention to Raynell, who's chattering on about the fat content of some of the selections on my menu. I try not to laugh as her stout self blabs to Alvetta and me about how she'd have to double her treadmill time if she were to eat most of the items we serve. But from the looks of Raynell's thick middle, I suspect doubling her treadmill time wouldn't require that much exertion—after all, doubling zero minutes still nets you zero minutes.

I find myself barely paying attention as she blathers on. I think more about how some things never change—Raynell is just as bossy, unpleasant, and condescending as she was in high school. And then, as if she can read my mind and wants to confirm my thoughts, she takes a quick breather from relentlessly critiquing my menu before she shoots her mouth off again.

"So, Halia," she says. "Your hair's almost the same as it was in high school. All this time and you never thought about updating it or switching to a more stylish cut?"

CHAPTER 5

"One watermelon mint tea with a kick," Wavonne says as she sets a glass in front of Raynell. After she places a second glass in front of Christy, who has returned to the table after "handling" one of Raynell's phone calls, she lifts a black cast-iron pan from the tray it shared with the drinks and places it in the center of the table.

"What's this?" There's a touch of excitement in Alvetta's voice.

"It's *just* cornbread," is Raynell's response.

"It smells heavenly."

"And that's coming from the wife of a minister." I smile at Alvetta. "It's my grandmommy's sour cream cornbread." I cut into the pan of golden goodness and place a slice on everyone's plate.

Alvetta takes a bite. "Oh my. That is some *good* stuff."

"It's not bad," Raynell says before taking a second bite, and a third, and then polishing off the whole slice with one last chomp.

"Are you ready to order?" Wavonne asks.

"I'll have the chicken," Raynell barks.

"The butter-baked chicken on special?"

"No. The roasted chicken. With green beans . . . no oil, and a baked potato . . . no butter or sour cream. I'm watching my figure."

"Got it."

"I'll have the pot roast with mashed potatoes and gravy," Alvetta says.

"Oh . . . get the butter-baked chicken, Alvetta," Raynell says. I bet you'll like that better."

"Um . . . okay."

Some things never change, I think to myself yet again. *Once a loyal subject—always a loyal subject.*

"And for you?" Wavonne asks Christy. Before she can answer Raynell pipes up. "Bring her the soft-shell crab special. That sounds good, Christy, right?"

"Sure . . . of course."

I pause for a moment before giving Wavonne my order, wondering if Raynell is going to tell me what to have as well. "Bring me the butter-baked chicken too, please."

Wavonne nods and turns from the table.

"So back to the menu for the reunion," Raynell says, cutting off a second large slice of the cornbread and bringing it to her lips. For something she called "not bad" a few moments ago, she sure seems to be scarfing it down.

"What if we went with some eighties-themed foods?" Alvetta asks.

"That's silly." Raynell offers her standard look of disapproval. "What are we going to serve? Capri Sun and Fruit Roll-Ups?"

"Actually, that doesn't sound half bad," I joke.

"Back then, lunch sometimes consisted of an order of fries and a Diet Coke . . . and maybe some Ho Hos for dessert. I'd slice a finger off to have that metabolism back again," Alvetta says.

"You and me both," Raynell agrees. "It sounds so cliché, but those really were the days."

"You know it. The clothes . . . and the hair."

"The acid-wash jeans, the big earrings, oversized sweaters . . . and those stupid Dwayne Wayne flip-top sunglasses the brothers wore . . . thought they were fly as hell in those things," Raynell says.

"I remember when Lee Trainer walked into school wearing that suit with the stripes and a pink tie like he was Rico Tubbs," Alvetta says

"Please. You thought . . . *we all* thought he was *all that*," Raynell says.

"Remember the rolled-up jeans?" I ask.

"Not just rolled up," Raynell corrects. "They had to be folded over at the bottom before you rolled them up. That way they set nicely on your high-top Air Jordans."

I chuckle. "I didn't have Air Jordans. I had the Converse Weapon. Boy, did I think I was something else in those things. I remember getting those shoes for Christmas along with a new Walkman." I turn to Christy, who has been quiet up to this point. "Do you even know what a Walkman is?"

Christy smiles. "Yes. Those portable cassette players."

"We're probably boring you to tears. I'm sure the eighties are long before your time."

"She's fine," Raynell says before Christy can respond. Even by Raynell standards she seems to treat this Christy girl pretty bad.

"I am. Really. It's fun to watch you guys reminisce."

I doubt she meant it, but if Christy was telling the truth, we decide to give her a rocking good time and launch into a series of chats about everything from Lisa Lisa and Cult Jam to Salt-N-Pepa to the hair bands the white kids listened to. We are deep into a discussion about Brenda K. Starr and "I Still Believe," which Christy admits to knowing only as a Mariah

Carey song from her teen years, when Wavonne and Darius show up with our entrées.

I see eyes go wide as Wavonne sets the butter-baked chicken down in front of Alvetta and me. Raynell appears unimpressed when Darius serves her the roasted chicken, but I can't say I blame her. It's a nice dish, and the chicken is tender, but it's really just one of a few items I added to the menu with little enthusiasm to meet the occasional requests we get for lighter fare. I'll be the first to admit that much of the food we serve at Sweet Tea is not for calorie watchers or people monitoring their cholesterol, but we do offer a few dishes for the more health-conscious. In addition to Raynell's roasted chicken, we have several salads, a low-calorie but flavorful steamed shrimp dish, a grilled fresh fish that changes daily, and we'll (albeit grudgingly) broil our crab cakes rather than fry them upon request.

I turn to Christy and see her eyeing her soft-shell crabs curiously and recall how Raynell essentially forced her to order them.

"Where are you from originally, Christy?" I ask as if I'm just trying to get the conversation rolling again.

"I grew up outside of Hartford."

"Connecticut? So that explains why you're looking at those soft shells so apprehensively. Soft-shell crabs are definitely a Maryland thing. I don't imagine they were terribly common in New England."

"No. I've never had them before."

"You'll like them." Raynell reaches over and breaks off a crispy batter-coated claw from one of the crabs on Christy's plate.

"Do you want to switch?" I ask her. "How about you take my chicken? I'd love to have the crabs." Soft-shell crabs are one of those "love 'em or hate 'em" foods. If you were brought up on them, there are few things better than a Maryland blue crab freshly caught just after shedding its hard shell, seasoned, battered, and fried-up golden brown. And if you really want to eat it like a local, you'd slip it between two pieces of soft white bread. But if they are unfamiliar to you, the idea of biting into what looks like a giant deep-fried spider can be less than appetizing.

"Are you sure?" She seems to look at Raynell for her approval.

"Of course." I go ahead and switch the plates before Raynell has a chance to offer or decline to give her blessing.

"That's very nice of you," Christy says.

I sense Raynell is about to reprimand Christy for not eating what she ordered when her phone rings for the second time since she arrived.

"It's Gregory again." She hands the phone to Christy. "Tell him I'll meet him after lunch in about an hour and a half."

"Mr. Simms. Hello," I hear Christy say as she steps away from the table with Raynell's phone.

"Clients. They expect you to be available twenty-four seven."

"That's the price of being one of the top real estate agents in all of Prince George's County," Alvetta coos.

"Not *all* of Prince George's County, Alvetta," Raynell says, and then looks at me. "I only work Mitchellville, Fort Washington, and Upper Marlboro . . . sometimes Brandywine," Raynell says, spouting off the names of Prince George's County's nicer neighborhoods. "Occasionally, I'll accept some clients in Accokeek or University Park. And, of course, I take listings at National Harbor," she adds, referring to the luxurious waterfront community in Oxon Hill.

"Yeah . . . she don't work in none of the Heights," Alvetta says with a laugh.

"You ain't kiddin'," Raynell replies as she pokes her fork onto Alvetta's plate and scoops up some macaroni and cheese.

Jokes about the "The Heights" are commonplace inside and outside of Prince George's County—made mostly by people who don't live in them. The Heights refer to various communities in Prince George's County with "Heights" in the name: Marlow Heights, Capitol Heights, Hillcrest Heights, District Heights . . . People like Raynell and Alvetta, who, like me, grew up just south of most of the Heights themselves, stick their noses up at these areas, which tend to be poorer and have higher crime rates than the more uppity "outside the Beltway" locales in the county. The Heights are generally the areas of Prince George's County that are being referred to when you hear lame jokes about PG County standing for "Pistol Grip County" or "Poor Ghetto County."

"Mmm-mmm!" Raynell crows before she has a chance to stop herself . . . and before her fork, once again, finds it way over to Alvetta's macaroni and cheese. "Girl, this is *good!*"

The compliment surprises me, and I think it surprises Raynell as well.

"It's my grandmother's recipe. Cheddar cheese, heavy cream, and butter. How can you go wrong? And adding cream cheese makes it extra smooth."

"What's this crispy stuff on top?"

"Bacon and panko bread crumbs. Grandmommy used cracker crumbs, but I think the panko crumbs give it more of a crunch. That's the only change I've made to the recipe. Back in the day, I helped my grandmother make it every weekend for Sunday dinner."

"Are you going to leave some for me?" Alvetta teases as Raynell pilfers more mac and cheese. I look on as Raynell starts helping herself to Alvetta's chicken as well, and without thinking, I find myself pushing my own plate closer to me before Raynell starts pilfering my lunch too.

CHAPTER 6

"Where is that waitress? Wavy? Wolfie?"

"Wavonne," I correct her, before signaling for Wavonne.

"We're going to need another order of this," Raynell says after Wavonne approaches the table.

"Another order of what?" Wavonne asks as Raynell points to an empty spot on Alvetta's plate.

"Bring Raynell a side of mac and cheese, Wavonne, would you, please?" I ask.

"Mac and cheese?" Wavonne asks, eyeing Raynell. "I thought Sasha Fierce here was watchin' her figure."

"Wavonne!" I reprimand as Alvetta lets out a quick laugh—a laugh she immediately halts when Raynell's disapproving eyes dart toward her.

"Not for me," Raynell says. "For the table to share."

"One mac and cheese comin' up."

As Wavonne heads to one of the terminals to put in the order, our conversation returns to high school memories—football games, dances, the McDonald's on Stuart Lane where so many students hung out after school and loitered in the parking lot on Friday and Saturday nights to watch the occasional brawl or find out who had parents out of town and a keg tapped in the backyard.

Long after the à la carte order of mac and cheese arrived, and we've finished our meals . . . and Raynell has helped herself to half the food on everyone else's plate, Wavonne returns to the table. "How about dessert? My aunt Celia has made a mean coconut custard pie. We also have her famous chocolate marshmallow cake and banana pudding."

"I couldn't possibly eat another bite," Alvetta says.

"Me either," I hear Christy say next to me.

"I don't really have much of a sweet tooth," Raynell says as she grabs a spoon and scraps the last bits of macaroni and cheese from the metal casserole dish. "And I've got to run for a meeting."

"Just the check then?" Wavonnne asks.

"No check, Wavonne," I say. "The ladies were my guests today."

"Thank you, Halia. That's very nice," Alvetta says

Wavonne is about to walk away when Raynell stops her. "What was it you said about a chocolate marshmallow cake?"

"It really is a lovely dessert," I say, before Wavonne has a chance to describe it as "dope" or "straight-up pimp." "Momma makes all the desserts here. Her marshmallow cake is one of my favorites—it's a very rich chocolate cake topped with a fluffy marshmallow frosting."

I see Raynell's lips involuntarily part as I describe the cake.

"Not for me, but I'd love a slice to take to my husband."

"Of course." I turn to Wavonnne. "Wavonne, honey, why don't you box some desserts for each of the ladies to take home."

"Oh, that's not necessary," Christy says.

"I'm happy to do it. Take it home. Enjoy it with a nice cup of coffee," I insist.

"Thank you."

"Yes, thank you, Halia," Alvetta says. "For everything."

So many thank-yous today, but not a single one from Raynell, I think to myself as I catch her looking at her watch, which I noticed earlier had the word "Rolex" on it.

"I really do have to get moving," Raynell says. "It doesn't look like we got that much planning done for the reunion—too much talk of Jody Watley's big hoop earrings, and Jane Child's nose ring/chain thing . . . and Kid's hi-top fade. We still need to discuss the menu for the evening." She turns to Christy. "Christy, set up another meeting for us."

"Why don't I put a menu together with some prices? I can e-mail it to you."

"I'd really like to discuss it a bit more," Raynell says as Christy scrolls through Raynell's calendar on her iPad. "Christy, what have I got open tomorrow or early next week?"

"You're pretty booked. You're showing properties to Gregory all day tomorrow and—"

"I have an idea," Alvetta interjects, and seems to look to Raynell for permission to share it. Raynell nods at her, and she continues. "Why don't you come to service on Sunday, and then we can meet in the café afterward and discuss the final details."

"That would work for me," Raynell agrees.

I hesitate for a moment. "It's hard for me to get away from here on Sunday mornings, but let me check with my assistant manager. I may be able to sneak off for a little while."

"Great, I'll reserve you a seat in the Pastor's Circle."

"Two seats," I hear from behind me as Wavonnne returns to the table with three brown bags with the Sweet Tea logo on them. "If I'm going to help Halia with the event, I should be there, too."

"Two seats it is," Alvetta says.

"Let me call you later today to confirm," I say to Alvetta.

Wavonne hands a bag to Alvetta and one to Raynell, who also snatches the bag meant for Christy out of Wavonne's hand.

"Get the car and cool it down, would you?" Raynell hands her keys to Christy. It seems odd to me that Raynell would ask Christy to retrieve her car like she's a valet given that Raynell parked in the front of the lot, but then I remember how Raynell was perspiring just from the short walk into the restaurant. If she stepped into her Escalade after it's been sitting in the August afternoon sun, she might just melt altogether.

We get up from the table, say our good-byes, and my guests head toward the exit with Christy scurrying ahead of Raynell and Alvetta. Wavonne and I linger behind and watch Raynell and Alvetta hover next to the door, waiting for Christy to cool down Raynell's car.

"For her *husband*," Wavonne says, eyeing the bags Raynell has in her hand with Momma's cake packed in them. "You know her husband's gonna come home to nothin' but a crumpled bag, an empty Styrofoam container, and a chunky wife with marshmallow breath."

RECIPE FROM HALIA'S KITCHEN

Halia's Macaroni and Cheese

Ingredients

1 pound large elbow macaroni
8 slices of bacon
1 garlic clove, minced
3 tablespoons all-purpose flour
3 cups whole milk
1 cup half-and-half
1 teaspoon hot pepper sauce
½ teaspoon salt
½ teaspoon black pepper
4 cups sharp cheddar cheese (grated)
1 pound softened cream cheese
1 cup panko (Japanese) bread crumbs
3 tablespoons melted butter

- Preheat oven to 375 degrees Fahrenheit.

- Boil pasta with a pinch of salt for 7 minutes, or according to package directions. Drain. Set aside.

- Fry bacon in a large frying pan until crispy. Remove bacon from pan, blot with paper towels, and chop into thin strips. Set aside.

- Add three tablespoons bacon grease to large saucepan. Add minced garlic and sauté over medium heat for 1 minute. Slowly add flour while constantly stirring mixture until a roux or paste forms.

- Add milk, half-and-half, hot sauce, salt, and pepper. Continue stirring until sauce thickens (8–10 minutes).

- Remove pan from heat and drain sauce through sieve (to remove any lumps) into large glass or metal bowl. Add cheddar and cream cheese. Stir until sauce is smooth.

- Add cooked pasta and blend. Transfer to well-greased 13-by-9-inch baking dish.

- Mix bread crumbs with butter and chopped bacon and sprinkle over macaroni and cheese.

- Bake until bread crumbs are crispy, about 30 minutes.

Eight Servings

CHAPTER 7

"Oh my," I say as traffic stalls and I realize we are likely not headed toward a typical church service—cars don't come to a near standstill before the building is even in view at a typical church service.

"Ain't he fine," Wavonne says from the passenger seat next to me about one of the police officers directing traffic. "We should have brought some of your honey butter, Halia . . . put a little on him and eat him right up!"

"Wavonne!" Momma calls from the backseat. "We're heading to *church*, for goodness sake."

"Sorry, Aunt Celia," Wavonne says. "I'll ask the minister to bless the butter first."

I chuckle as we're guided through a maze of orange cones. As the van creeps forward, we eventually round a corner, and Rebirth Christian Church comes into view. The land in the general area is flat, which makes the enormous circular-shaped church resemble Ayers rock rising from the Australian outback.

"It looks like the Verizon Center with a steeple on it," Momma says.

"That is one big place. I bet they could host the BET awards in there."

"The parking lot . . . or should I say *lots* . . . look completely full," I say as our forward motion comes to yet another halt.

Momma lowers her window. "Excuse me," she says to one of the men directing cars. "What's causing the delay?"

"It's like this every Sunday, ma'am. You need to wait for the current service to wrap. The parking spaces will open up when the nine a.m. worshippers start to leave. Then we'll get you moving."

Momma thanks the man and puts the window back up.

"All that parking." I'm eyeing the vast lots surrounding the church. "And there still isn't enough to ease this backup."

"Says here more than ten thousand people attend services here every Sunday," Wavonne says, staring down at her phone. "Ooh, let's check out the pastor." She taps on her phone. "Mmmm . . . not bad for an older guy." She turns her phone toward me.

"He's a good-looking man."

"Let's see what they say about Ms. Thang." Wavonne taps a few more times. "Well, la-te-da." She turns the phone toward me again.

I view the photo of Alvetta in a conservative navy blue suit and white blouse. She's accented the outfit with a simple strand of pearls. "She looks nice, and I have to hand it to her, if she was going for a 'minister's wife' look, she nailed it."

"Says here she's a graduate of Howard University, where she received a bachelor's degree in psychology, which she's found to be an asset when called upon to counsel church members," Wavonne reads aloud from Alvetta's bio. "Oh lawd—girlfriend's a headshrinker."

"Since when did an undergraduate degree in psychology qualify you to counsel people?" Momma asks. "Don't you need at least a master's degree or a PhD?"

"I suspect just being the wife of the pastor qualifies you for all sorts of things."

We wait a few minutes longer, and departing church attendees finally start to make their way out of the lots and traffic begins to move. When we eventually secure a spot in Lot D to the left of the church I text Alvetta to let her know we are here.

Momma and I walk toward the building, moving slowly in an effort to let Wavonne keep up as she tries not to tumble over in the ridiculously high heels she's wearing.

I examine the crowd as we approach the entrance. I was expecting to see worshippers dressed to the nines—especially the women. I was anticipating regal suits and big showy church hats. But, while most of the people walking toward the church are smartly dressed, women in full suits are in the minority. I don't see a single hat, and some people are dressed rather casually in slacks or even jeans.

We step through the main entrance and see nothing even reminiscent of the churches I'm used to attending. While Momma now attends another mega church across town, she came from a Methodist background, and Daddy was Catholic, so we dabbled between the two religions when I was growing up. I'm used to dimly lit, almost somber interiors . . . stained glass windows, organ music, uncomfortable pews, and people talking in a whisper if they are talking at all.

Rebirth is designed like a sports arena with a brightly lit wide corridor that appears to circle the perimeter of the building. To the left of the vast hallway, which is lined, trade-fair style, with various booths and tables promoting church activities, I get a peek through some double doors into the . . . I'm not sure what to call the area where the service is actually held—the terms "theater" or "stadium" come to mind, though. We're about to start perusing the various promotional stalls when I see Alvetta walking toward us.

"Halia!" She strides forward on a pair of exquisite pointed-toe pumps. "So glad you could make it." As usual, she looks flawless in a close-fitting skirt somewhere between pink and peach and a white silk blouse.

"Me too. You remember Wavonne, and this is my mother, Celia Watkins."

"Yes. Of course. Hello, Wavonne." She turns to Momma. "Alvetta Marshall." Alvetta extends her hand to Momma. "Welcome to Rebirth Christian Church."

"Thank you. I'm looking forward to the service. I'm the only regular churchgoer in this bunch." Momma casts disapproving eyes on me and Wavonne. "Good luck with these two heathens."

Alvetta laughs. "How about I show you around?"

We follow Alvetta down the main walkway.

"This is the Grand Hall. It loops around the worship center. As you can see, our ministries set up tables to recruit new members before and after the services. We have over a hundred different ministries." Alvetta starts pointing to various tables. "That's the artist ministry, the fitness ministry, the photography ministry . . . over there is the magazine ministry—"

"Magazine ministry? Can I get me a free copy of *Us Weekly*?" Wavonne asks.

"Afraid not. The magazine ministry produces the church's monthly magazine. It's full color and has a readership of over twenty thousand people."

"Full color? That sounds expensive," I say, thinking of how much money I've spent on color printing for the restaurant.

"Not at all. We sell advertising that more than covers the costs of production and distribution."

As we continue to walk through the Grand Hall Alvetta smiles and waves at the other churchgoers. She even stops to hug or offer a quick kiss on the cheek to some of them. She has a confidence about her as her heels click along the pristine hardwood floors that was absent when she was at the restaurant with Raynell a few days ago.

"Let me show you the kids' area."

We follow Alvetta a few more steps down the hall, make a right through some doors, and I swear we've fallen through a hole into Wonderland or a Smurf village.

"Damn." Wavonne looks around and catches sight of the cartoonish-looking artificial tree in the center of the room. Its painted leaves go up to the high ceiling and continue outward, creating a canopy over the room that is dotted with oversized multicolored mushrooms, rabbits, deer, and other woodland creatures. The forest theme is continued on the walls in the form of a vibrant mural. There is a reception area on the far side of the room where parents are checking in their children.

Wavonne leans in and, oddly, exercises some discretion by lowering her voice. "Forget the service. I bet some of them be droppin' the little rugrats off here for some free baby sittin' and headin' to the mall."

"This is quite something," I say to Alvetta, hoping she didn't hear Wavonne's comment.

"This is just the play area. We have six classrooms behind the reception desk. Volunteers teach bible class to the older kids, and we offer supervised play for toddlers and babysitting for infants."

"I've never seen anything like it. I mostly went to a Catholic church growing up. Our plan for children involved parents hurriedly taking them to the back of the church if they starting misbehaving during the Mass," I say.

"Our children's program lets parents focus on their worship. It's very popular." Alvetta signals for us to follow her yet again. We step back in to the main hallway, and Alvetta continues the tour. She whizzes us past a fully equipped gymnasium, several coffee kiosks that seem to be as well outfitted as any Starbucks I've been in, a spacious book and media retail store with long·lines at the registers, and a surplus of multi-purpose meeting rooms before guiding us up two flights of steps that lead into what she calls "the control room." From the view through the floor-to-ceiling glass in front of us I can see we are behind the back wall of the worship center just above the balcony seating area.

"I bet the control room at CNN doesn't look much different than this," Momma says, watching the multitude of video monitors, microphones, and switch panels operated by five people wearing headsets at their respective stations.

"We control all the special effects from up here," Alvetta says. "The lighting, sound, fog, the curtains . . . there's a button for everything."

"Well, I'll be . . ." is all I can muster. I look through the panes of glass and feel like I'm backstage at a Bruno Mars concert. Church attendees are starting to file into their seats on both the main level and the balcony. A few minutes later, men and women in weighty burgundy robes begin their procession into the seats behind the main stage. I do some quick calculating and determine that the choir loft alone seats more than two hundred people.

"We should head back downstairs. The service will be starting shortly."

"Sure," I say, surprised to find myself excited for the service. After getting a tour of the building and an insider's look at the control room I'm eager to see how everything comes together for the main event. Something tells me we are not in store for the kind of sleepy church service I grew up attending. Other than it likely being grand and maybe theatrical, I'm not really sure what to expect or how the whole thing will unfold, but given the over-the-top nature of everything else I've seen this morning, I can't wait to find out.

CHAPTER 8

Wavonne, Momma, and I briskly follow Alvetta down the stairs and eventually enter the worship center. Alvetta continues to offer quick waves and hellos to the people she passes as she leads us to a small seating area directly in front of the stage.

"This is the Pastor's Circle. We reserve it for special guests."

Unlike the rest of the seating in the worship center, the chairs in the Pastor's Circle have a significant amount of leg room and side tables next to them—each one equipped with a bottle of water, a crystal glass, a small bible, a church bulletin, and some mints.

"Girl, we flyin' first class," Wavonne says as we all take our seats, and I must admit it is fun, for the first time in my life, to be in the VIP section of *something*. "Look at all those jealous heifers givin' us the eye. That's right, hookers, we in the Pastor's Circle! How you like that?"

"My God! We can't take you anywhere," Momma whispers to Wavonne.

"Isn't that the truth," I agree. "Now settle down and behave yourself, Wavonne."

Wavonne raises her eyebrows at me before looking toward Alvetta. "Where's Omarosa Manigault-Stallworth? Won't she be joining us?" Wavonne says this in a hoity-toity voice, as if she's Tina Turner on one of her British accent kicks. I wonder who she's talking about, but Alvetta doesn't seem to have the same trouble.

"Raynell will join us after service. She doesn't really *do* mornings," Alvetta responds.

Thinking about how there are probably all sorts of things Raynell doesn't do, I grab the church bulletin on the table next to me and start skimming it. There are notices about group meetings, church finances, and community events. There's also a column called "The Word" by Pastor Michael Marshall. It strikes me as clever that he writes it in longhand, and the church publishes it "as is" rather than typing it up. The cursive writing sets it apart from the rest of the word-processed text and gives his message a very personal tone. I'm about to give "The Word" a read when there's a dinging noise over the speaker that apparently is a signal for everyone to stand. As Momma, Wavonne, and I follow along with the crowd and rise from our chairs, we see no fewer than ten people take their seats on the left side of the stage and pick up their instruments . . . guitars, horns, saxophones . . . you name it. Growing up, my church had Mrs. Tebbler . . . and *only* Mrs. Tebbler, who played the organ at the nine- and eleven-o'clock services. Rebirth appears to have a full orchestra. We continue to look on as six people, two men and four women, all dressed in black, take their places behind as many microphones in front of the choir loft.

The orchestra begins to play an up-tempo melody, and the singers in black with *their own* microphones (I can only imagine what kind of church politics are involved in getting one of those coveted spots) begin to sing. It's not long before the entire choir, more than two hundred members strong, joins in, and the worship center fills with music emitting from a state-of-the-art sound system.

I'm not sure this type of over-the-top service is for me, but

I can't help but feel . . . feel *something* with the sound of a few hundred stellar voices, accompanied by a talented orchestra, going at full volume.

"Sing it, girl!" Wavonne calls out as one of the vocalists dives into a solo.

I look around and see people swaying to the music—some with their arms raised like Eva Peron on the balcony of Casa Rosada. And, just when I think my senses of sound and sight have received their delights for the day, a team of women march in from all sides with glittery flags. They take positions at various spots around the main level and begin twirling the flags every which way to the beat of the music. I must say, the effect is striking. Alvetta catches me marveling over the whole grand display and beams with pride as if to say, "I may be the illegitimate daughter of a maid, but look at me now, presiding over one of the biggest congregations in the state of Maryland."

When the music quiets we take our seats, and Michael steps forward from the back of the stage. He's more handsome than his photo online led us to believe, and he's only a few words into his address, when I realize why he packs them in by the thousands every Sunday. He's a gifted speaker with a deep baritone voice and immediately sets the crowd at ease with some self-deprecating humor. He moves about the stage with a headset microphone rather than speaking from behind a podium. Calls of "Preach, Preacher, preach!" and "Amen!" boom from behind us when he makes key points during his sermon. He talks about the heat of the summer and how everyone sweats . . . and then makes a joke about how he misspoke, and everyone but his lovely wife, Alvetta, sweats—"Alvetta's skin," he says, "just gets more dewy and lustrous." A silly joke, but it works because of his good looks, charisma, and command of the stage. He goes on to speak about how we really sweat when faced with temptations from the devil, and

I'm not quite sure how he did it, but he uses this segue to seamlessly request that attendees give generously today to keep the air conditioning flowing in the building.

When the collection basket comes around Momma drops in ten dollars, Wavonne passes it to me without making a donation, and I, mindful of Alvetta's eyes right next to me, drop in forty dollars, and wonder if it's enough. *Should I have done fifty? A hundred?*

After some additional singing from the choir and some general announcements about the church's ministries and classes, the service wraps with a final hymn. As I listen to the choir, I make a mental note to try and come back to Rebirth over the holidays. I don't think I'll be joining as a tithing member any time soon, but I'd definitely be up for a return visit in December—I bet this choir puts on a Christmas concert the likes of which I've never heard before.

At the close of the service, Michael descends the stage, walks toward us, and takes Alvetta's hand.

"We'll just be a few minutes," Alvetta says as she steps away from her seat and joins Michael at the foot of the stage where they stand in a makeshift receiving line. Most of the church attendees are exiting the worship center from a number of doors on all sides, but a handful come down the walkways toward Michael and Alvetta, who graciously greet them with hugs and handshakes. Wavonne and I watch for a few moments as the two of them interact with church patrons like a well-oiled machine—an extremely good-looking well-oiled machine.

"If you two want to walk around for a few minutes while Michael and I finish up here, feel free," Alvetta says after excusing herself from her adoring fans. "I'll meet you in the café in about twenty minutes."

"Sure," I reply, and, just before our little trio starts to make our way out to the main hall, we catch a glimpse of Alvetta returning to Michael's side. He's talking to two young ladies, both wearing short skirts and heels that might be even higher than Wavonne's. But, even in the towering pumps, the girls still look up at Michael, who stands at about six foot four. You can see the infatuation in their eyes as they listen to whatever words of wisdom he's sharing with them.

As we turn to leave, Wavonne leans in. "So which one of those thirsty hos you think he's cheatin' on Alvetta with?"

CHAPTER 9

Once we're out in the Grand Hall we meander around, scan the various booths, and eventually stumble upon a large table promoting a retreat. The banner hanging along the front of the display says: POINT AND CLICK YOUR WAY TO THE LORD: USING TECHNOLOGY TO BRING US CLOSER TO GOD. We're about to continue walking right on past the "point-and-click" table when Wavonne gets a look at the man behind all the promotional materials—a nicely built thirtysomething brother with an angled razor part on one side of his neatly cropped Afro.

"Hold up." Wavonne stops in front of the table. "I need to check me out this retreat." She looks the young man up and down. "What was it Salt-N-Pepa said about bein' *stacked and packed?*" she mutters to me.

"Shoop!" I say with a laugh. The upcoming reunion sparked me to pull out an old Salt-N-Pepa CD. I've had it going in the van lately as Wavonne and I drive to the restaurant.

"Hello, ladies," the young man says to us.

"Hello yourself," Wavonne replies as Momma and I stand behind her.

"I'm Rick Stevens. I'm part of the church's Retreat Ministry. We still have a few openings for next weekend's session if you're interested."

Wavonne shamelessly looks him up and down a second time. "Oh, I'm *interested,*" she coos. "Tell me more."

"We'll be spending the weekend at The Williamsburg Inn. It's really an impressive hotel." He hands Wavonne a hotel brochure, and she begins to look through it. "There's a welcome reception on Friday evening, seminars throughout the day on Saturday, and an early breakfast on Sunday. We'll be discussing, among other things, the church's strategy to expand our outreach via social media. We'll be holding classes for members about how to effectively use Facebook, Twitter, Instagram, and such to promote God's word and attract new members to the church."

"Mmmm . . . fancy," Wavonne says as she continues to thumb through the brochure. I look over her shoulder and see photos of the hotel—lots of wainscoting, colonial furniture, and heavy drapes. "Will you be attendin', Rick?"

"I will. I'm leading a focus group about the church's Web site. We'll be reviewing the site in detail . . . determining what works well, and what can be improved."

"I know all about Web sites," Wavonne brags. "I help my girl Jereme with her blog. It's called 'Real, Wig, or Weave?' We put up photos of celebrities, and viewers post commentaries about whether Beyoncé or Viola or Mary J . . . or whoever are sportin' their own hair, a weave, or a wig. We've got hair-care tips and let readers know about specials on products. You should check it out."

"Sure."

"I think I'd like to attend this retreat. How much does it cost?"

"The church subsidizes some of the expenses, so it's only five hundred dollars for the weekend, which includes your hotel room, a complimentary breakfast on Saturday and Sunday morning, and access to all the classes, seminars, and discussion groups. And it's a great way to meet other church members."

"Halia." Wavonne turns to me. "Loan me five hundred dollars, would ya? So I can go on this retreat with Rick and help him with the church's Web site . . . and *anything else* he may need some help with."

Knowing that one, Wavonne has no interest in the helping with the church's outreach via technology and just wants to go to Williamsburg to get all up in Rick's business, and two, that "loan" and "give" mean the same thing to Wavonne, I respond, "Umm . . . no."

"Come on, Halia. Tell her, Aunt Celia, I'll be doin' the Lord's work."

"Not getting involved," Momma says.

"We have the reunion next weekend anyway, Wavonne. You promised to help me with that."

I watch as Wavonne tries to determine if her time will be better spent chasing Rick around at a retreat in which she has no interest or tagging along with me to my reunion where she can spend some time with a retired professional football player who may be able to introduce her to some real live Redskins.

"That's right." She puts the brochure back down on the table. "I need Raynell's husband to set me up with some football. . . ." She lets her voice trail off as she notices Rick looking at her. "With some *footballs* . . . yeah, some footballs . . . to give to needy kids."

"Yes, we all know you are all about helping needy kids." I try not to roll my eyes as I say this.

Wavonne glares at me before turning back to Rick. "How about I leave you my phone number, and you can call me if you ever want to talk Web sites . . . or whateveh."

"Sure. Of course." Rick taps a few times on his phone and

hands it to Wavonne. She grabs it from him, enters her contact information, and gives it back to him.

"Whatever happened to a pen and paper?" Momma asks, looking on.

Rick extends his hand to Wavonne. She shakes it and then holds it a tad longer than is really appropriate before I remind her it's time for us to meet Alvetta in the café.

"There's a bible-study group meeting now," Momma says, looking down at the bulletin as we walk through the hall. "I'll check that out while you two discuss reunion plans with your friends."

"Okay. Why don't we plan to meet in front of the book-store in an hour?"

Momma nods and goes looking for the bible-study group while Wavonne and I continue to walk the lengthy perimeter of the church in search of the café.

CHAPTER 10

Wavonne and I reach the café, and as we step inside, we realize the *café* is really more of a full *cafeteria* with a long line of
people making their way through the serving area.

"Over here," Alvetta calls to us from a table along the wall.
Raynell is seated with her. Michael and another man who I
recognize from TV as Terrence are standing next to the table.

"Hello again," I say to Alvetta as we reach the table and
turn and smile at Raynell. "Hey there," Alvetta says. "This is
my husband, Michael, and Raynell's husband, Terrence."

"Halia Watkins." I shake their hands. "And this is my
cousin, Wavonne Hix."

The gentlemen smile, and we exchange a few words. I tell
Michael how much I enjoyed his sermon, and how beautifully
I thought the choir sang. Then I chat a bit more with Michael
about how impressive the church is while Wavonne cozies up
to Terrence.

"So, you're a former Redskins wide receiver?" Wavonne
asks him.

Terrence is slighter than I imagined. By no means is he a
little guy, but when I think "football players" I think of big
burly men—Terrence is built more like a baseball or soccer

player. I'm guessing he stands at around six feet tall, and I wouldn't put him at any more than one hundred and eighty pounds or so.

"Yes," Terrence says. "Guilty."

"What a career. Three hundred and one catches for 5,220 yards and forty-one touchdowns."

Wavonne knows less about football than I do, which is almost nothing. Clearly, she's been studying up on Terrence.

Terrence laughs. "Very impressive."

"I've followed your career since you started with the Skins in ninety-five," Wavonne lies. She was probably scanning his Wikipedia page when I saw her sneaking looks at her phone during the service.

"Ninety-five? You had to have still been a child."

While Wavonne laughs and curls a strand of synthetic hair, Raynell, who has barely acknowledged us thus far, decides it's time to put the kibosh on Wavonne's flirting. "I hate to break up Wendy's little rehash of my husband's career, but—"

"My *name* is *Wavonne.*"

"Yes. *Wavonne,*" Raynell says, then looks at her husband. "Aren't you and Michael due in the theater for the big football game?"

"It's just a preseason game, but I guess we are," Terrence says.

"Theater?" I ask

"It's more of a large media room," Alvetta clarifies. "It has a big projection screen . . . seats forty people . . . leather recliners . . . it's quite nice."

"It was good to meet you." Terrence shakes my hand again and then Wavonne's.

"You too," Wavonne says. "Before you jet, let me axe you somethin'. Do many Redskins players attend church here? Ever have any . . . any meet and greets?"

"We actually do have quite a few players on the rolls here.

Meet and greets? Hmm . . . we don't have anything specific planned with the players at the moment, but if you join some of the church's ministries and come to service regularly, you're bound to run into some of them."

Raynell rolls her eyes at Wavonne's obvious attempt to gain some introductions to professional sports players. "Terrence. Get!" she says. "We have reunion plans to discuss."

Terrence smiles and looks at Michael. "Guess we better do as the boss tells us."

"Pleasure meeting you," Michael says before he and Terrence make their exit.

"Please have a seat," Alvetta says, and Wavonne and I slide into the booth across from her and Raynell. We've barely gotten settled when a lanky young man wearing an apron appears at the table.

"Good morning, Mrs. Marshall," he says to Alvetta while setting down a coffeepot, a bowl of creamers, various sweeteners, and a carafe of orange juice. "What may I get for you and your guests?" He fills each of our mugs with steaming coffee and pours orange juice into four crystal glasses.

"Why don't you just fix us a few plates with the works?"

"Of course, Mrs. Marshall."

As the young man steps away I see Raynell discreetly elbow Alvetta.

"Kenny," Alvetta calls. "Extra bacon please for Mrs. Rollins."

"For the *table*. Not just for me," Raynell says. "So, let's talk reunion plans. Is everything all set at the Marriott?"

"Yes. My connection there gave the committee a very nice rate, but that's about all I know. Christy was managing the details."

"Where is Christy?" Raynell asks no one in particular, irritation in her voice. "She was supposed to be here by now."

"There she is," Alvetta says as Christy hurriedly makes her way to the table.

"Sorry, Raynell. Traffic getting into the parking lot was crazy."

"What's the latest on the venue for the reunion on Saturday?" Raynell says, not bothering to greet Christy properly or even reprimand her for being late.

Christy grabs a chair from a neighboring table, sits down at the end of the booth, and pulls a manila folder from her bag. "It's all set. We have the Grand Ballroom reserved. Twenty-five round tables. Each table seats eight people. Standard centerpieces and candles. The buffet tables—"

"Fine, fine." Raynell cuts Christy off. "Sounds like it's under control. You've confirmed the deejay?"

"Yes."

"The staging area for the silent auction?"

"Yes. There's a small conference room next to the ballroom. We'll display the items there."

"Silent auction?" I ask.

"Yes. I thought it would be a good idea for classmates and some local businesses to donate items. All the proceeds will go to the Raynell Rollins Foundation for Children in Need."

"It's a great charity. Raynell raised sixty thousand dollars last year." Alvetta beams.

"Well, you know, I'm a giver."

"You are, Raynell. You do so many good things."

I stifle a laugh while Wavonne leans in and whispers in my ear. "Was Alvetta this far up Raynell's ass in high school?"

I ignore her question. "So, Raynell. Tell us more about the charity."

"We focus outreach on children in the D.C. metro area, but it's open to everyone. We identify children of unfortunate means and provide funds for virtually anything that might improve their situation: food, clothing, school supplies, scholarships, summer camps, you name it."

"Sounds like a great resource." I can't help but notice the way she looked directly at Alvetta when she spoke of "children of unfortunate means."

"It is. The silent auction at the reunion will be the perfect way for us to raise funds," Raynell says. "You'll have to donate an evening at your restaurant. What's it called again? Salty Tea?"

"Sweet Tea," I correct. "Of course, I'd be happy to donate a gift card."

"Great. We've collected several donations so far." Raynell looks to Christy. "Remind me of some of the items."

"Everything from free dry cleaning to a complimentary oil change at Middleton's Garage . . . to a dozen roses from Sienna's Floral Arrangements in Oxon Hill. One of your classmates donated a sculpture, and John Thomson, who owns a photography studio, donated a free portrait setting. Another classmate—"

"Meh," Raynell groans. "Such paltry items. Meanwhile I'm donating an antique desk worth a couple thousand dollars."

"Not everyone is as successful as you," Alvetta says. "And the reunion is still a week away. I'm sure more donations will come in."

Alvetta is about to continue reassuring Raynell when Christy's phone rings.

"Raynell Rollins Real Estate. This is Christy. How may I help you?" Christy is silent for a moment before she nicely asks the caller to hold. "Raynell, it's Gregory. Confirming you are meeting him to show properties at two."

"Yes. Tell him I'll meet him at the Brandywine location."

As Christy passes on Raynell's words to the gentleman on the phone, I realize I haven't once heard her use the word "please" or phrase anything as a question when she speaks to

Christy. Everything she says to the poor girl is simply a command.

"Like I was saying," Alvetta interjects when Christy wraps up the call. "Michael and I will make some donations, and while I doubt we'll get anything as valuable as the desk you contributed, as some of our former classmates who live outside the area arrive for the event, I'm sure they'll check in and make some donations."

"I hope so. I'll have Christy make some more calls this week . . . shake a few trees," Raynell says, her eyes suddenly pointed in my direction. "Speaking of the desk. I was going to hire someone to take it to the hotel to display at the reunion, but it's not that large and, surely, you must have a van or a truck or something for that little lunch counter of yours . . . no? Would you mind picking it up on Saturday and taking it over to the hotel?"

"Um . . ." I'm not sure what to say. She already has Christy and Alvetta acting as her lackeys. I'm really not eager to add my name to the list, but it is for charity and, honestly, I'm a little curious to see Raynell's house. "I guess so. I'm sure we'll be running back and forth to the hotel a few times on Saturday anyway to get the catering set up."

"Great. Christy, write the address down for Halia."

As Christy writes Raynell's address down on a piece of paper, the young man who approached the table earlier returns with two others, and the three of them, all holding trays, begin laying down plates. While I watch people who were in line at the counter when we first stepped inside the cafeteria continue to wait for their turn at the serving station we enjoy table service—the perks of being guests of the First Lady I suppose. Dishes loaded with eggs, bacon (pork *and* turkey), sausage, English muffins, pancakes, and oatmeal land in front of us. They're accompanied by containers of whipped butter, syrup, and a selection of jellies.

We enjoy our breakfast and begin discussing the menu for the reunion. I present Raynell and Alvetta with a list of options for appetizers to be passed around during the cocktail hour, main and side dishes for the buffet, and desserts. I also suggest that I whip up a few pitchers of our house cocktail to be served at the cash bars.

Generally this approach works well when planning a menu for catered events—customers review the options, make a few selections, and we wrap things up. Such is not the case with Raynell Rollins, though. Alvetta is mostly agreeable to my suggestions, but Raynell doesn't like any of the appetizer recommendations. She wants to know if I can arrange for chilled shrimp cocktails, but when I inform her of the cost of quality fresh shrimp and the effect it will have on my catering price, she lets it go. She's decided she doesn't want fried chicken on the buffet as "fried chicken has no business at a formal event." But apparently macaroni and cheese does have every business at a formal event because she insists that it be part of the menu. She goes on like this for about an hour, and I politely explain why most of her requests (e.g., a staffed raw oyster bar, chocolate soufflés, Kobe beef sliders) are not feasible within the available budget.

I think she believed she was going to be able to bully me into taking a loss on the event and preparing dishes way beyond what my fee would cover. I might have been a little timid around Raynell in high school, but I'm certainly not afraid of her now. I'm not looking to make money on this catering job, but I'm not going to lose money, either. So, after a lot of hemming and hawing, we eventually finalize the menu and come to an agreement over a nice selection of appetizers, entrées, and desserts. And, if I do say so myself, come Saturday night, my old high school classmates are in for a real treat when they get a sampling of some of my tastiest recipes.

CHAPTER 11

"Those look divine," I say to Momma as she starts popping chocolate cakes out of their pans. She's been at Sweet Tea since five this morning. It's eight now, which is actually early for me to be at the restaurant. I'm generally here until well after we close, so I try not to start my workday too early. Coming in during the late morning also allows very little overlap between Momma's time in the Sweet Tea kitchen baking all of her delicious goodies and my time in the Sweet Tea kitchen supervising the rest of our creations, which, believe me, helps keep the peace around here. Momma usually starts her baking at six a.m. and wraps about four hours later, but like me, she came in early today to get a jump on the catering order for the reunion.

Raynell's husband (at least Raynell said it was her husband) loved Momma's chocolate marshmallow cake so much that Raynell asked . . . well, more like insisted, that we serve it as the featured dessert for the reunion.

Momma has twelve layers of chocolate cake cooling on the counter—enough for four cakes. As the smell of rich cocoa reaches my nose, I have to fight the urge to press my hands on them just to feel their warm velvety texture.

As there's always an occasional freak . . . yeah, I said it . . . an occasional "freak" who doesn't like chocolate, to supplement the chocolate marshmallow cakes, we'll also be serving sour cream coconut cakes. And that's just the desserts. We'll be starting the affair with mini corn muffins and fried chicken salad tartlets during the cocktail hour. These will be followed by a full dinner buffet of herb baked chicken, salmon cakes, and host of yummy sides. Of course, this spread is way beyond the budget of the reunion committee, but I agreed to offer a substantial discount. I'll barely break even with this job, but I guess it's okay considering it's for my alma mater.

"Let me get started on the frosting while they cool. Wavonne, start opening those jars of marshmallow cream, would you?" Momma calls over to Wavonne, who couldn't have been any less helpful since she arrived with me a few hours ago. She's currently sitting on a stool with her head against the wall and her eyes shut.

"Wavonne!" I call to wake her up.

"Huh?" She slowly opens her eyes.

"Help Momma with the frosting, please."

"I'm so tired." She sluggishly lifts herself from the stool. "Why'd we have to come in so early? I was up late watchin' a *Basketball Wives* marathon. Those sistas live the life, Halia. They got it all—money, big houses, cars, clothes, jew-reys . . . everything. That's the life I was meant to have . . . not being up at no damn six a.m. to make cakes. Now I just need Raynell's husband to hook me up with a football player, and it will be me on TV covered in bling when they launch a show about football wives."

"You know, Wavonne. Has it ever occurred to you that maybe you could earn your *own* money and have your *own* career to pay for all those big houses and big cars . . . and all that other stuff?"

Wavonne looks at me like I have horns. "What kind of fool would work when she can land a man to pay her bills?"

"The kind that knows she might not ever find that rich brother."

"Oh, I'll find me a rich brotha all right."

"Well, until such time, you need to earn your keep around here." I nod toward the jars Momma asked her to open.

"She doesn't have it *all* wrong, Halia," Momma chimes in, and I'm reminded of why I prefer not to share the kitchen with her. "A little less career and a little more husband hunting isn't the worst idea in the world."

I sigh. "Yes, Momma."

"Don't moan at me. This reunion is a perfect opportunity for you to get out there. There must be an old high school flame . . . or someone who's recently divorced . . . or someone . . . *anyone* for you to connect with."

"Halia had a flame in high school?" Wavonne looks up from the jars toward me. "Ooh girl, gimme the deets."

"There are no old flames, Wavonne. Other than the occasional homecoming or prom date with guys who were usually more friends than boyfriends, my high school years were pretty devoid of romance."

"So, in other words, your love life was as borin' then as it is now."

"My love life is not that bad," I protest. "I date."

Momma lets out a loud dramatic laugh. "Since when?"

"I went out with Jeremy Hughes just . . . well, okay . . . it was like a year ago. And there was Timothy Jenkins."

"That was even before Jeremy, and we all know that was more a bidness meetin' than a date. You just wanted to get a discount on some kitchen equipment," Wavonne says. "And as for Jeremy . . . any man who wears more foundation and concealer than I do . . . and who takes you to a freakin' *Sound of Music* sing-along at Wolf Trap is hardly husband material."

"I tried to set her up with Stan, the UPS driver," Momma says to Wavonne as if I'm not in the room. "But she didn't move fast enough, and now he's dating that mousey little thing who manages the Walgreens."

"Martha Brennen? That tiny lil' rodent?" Wavonne, who is always combing the aisles of the Walgreens next door for cheap makeup or accessories, asks. "That ho-bag follows me around whenever I go in there like I'm gonna steal somethin'. I don't know what that little Polly Pocket thinks she would do if I did take anything—she barely comes up to my rack. Even Halia could take her in a fight," she adds, turning to me. "Run down there and fight for your man, Halia. Go on."

"Stan is hardly my man." I laugh. "Why don't you both focus on your own love lives, which, if I recall correctly, are no more existent than mine."

"That may be, but I'm gonna get that Raynell to set me up with a Redskin. Then I won't have to be all up in here at the butt crack of dawn makin' cakes."

Momma takes the jars from Wavonne and scoops their contents in a large metal bowl she's already filled with softened butter, secures the bowl into one of my favorite kitchen gadgets, my five-quart stainless steel Hobart N50 mixer. I just up-graded to it a few months ago. It cost a mint, but it works beautifully. Some people get excited over the Audi A6 and the BMW 500 . . . or Versace and Ferragamo. But if you want to see me light up, let's talk about the Hobart N50 mixer or the Kolpak P7-068-CT Walk-In Cooler . . . or the Duke E102-G Double Full Size Gas Convection Oven. Some girls dream of fancy cars and jewelry—for me, a freshly sharpened Misono 440 Molybdenum Santoku knife makes me positively giddy. I'm a sucker for a freshly seasoned Tomlinson cast-iron skil-let . . . and don't get me started on the Manitowoc QM-30 Series Self-Contained Cube Ice Machine that's been on my wish list for a couple of years now.

Momma starts the mixer and begins to whip the frosting. As the butter and marshmallow cream blend together she slowly adds powdered sugar to the whirling bowl. When the icing has creamed together nicely, she adds a touch of vanilla, gives it a final mix, and *voilà*, we have Momma's famous marshmallow frosting.

"Yeah . . . good luck with that, Wavonne. From what I know about Raynell, she isn't keen on helping anyone but Raynell. Not to mention she doesn't seem to be terribly fond of you in particular."

I grab two serrated knifes from the knife block, hand one to Wavonne, and we both help Momma slice the small domes off of the tops of the cake layers, so they will lay smoothly on top of each other.

"My knees are not what they used to be. Give them an eye-level look and make sure they are even," Momma asks me.

"Let me do that for you two old hens," Wavonne offers. "Drop it like it's hot," she says as she squats down to get her face level with the cakes. "Perfect."

We've helped Momma enough with her baking to know the drill from here. We take four circular pieces of plywood that I've already covered with decorative purple foil and lay them on the counter. These will function as the serving platters. We place four strips of parchment paper on each platter, so they lie just underneath the edges of the cakes to keep icing off the foil while we work. We then place a dollop of frosting on the center of the boards to anchor the cakes before we flip a moist chocolate layer onto it.

"Now, you girls be careful," Momma says as she goes down the line with a pastry brush and sweeps away any loose crumbs so they don't get in the frosting.

"That's too much, Wavonne!" Momma calls as she watches Wavonne haphazardly plop a glob of frosting onto one of the layers. "These are for Halia's former classmates. We want them to be perfect."

Wavonne removes some of the icing with her spatula and starts to spread it around. "I wanna slice up one of these for breakfast, Aunt Celia," she says as we begin on the second layer. "Girl, hook me up with a slice of this cake and maybe a caramel flan latte, and I'd be like a pig in—"

"Don't even think about it, Wavonne. We need four for the reunion, and that's all Momma's made."

" 'Bring me those jars.' 'Too much icing.' 'No cake for you,' " Wavonne mutters under her breath, mimicking Momma and me. "That Russian woman who runs the prison kitchen on TV barks fewer orders."

Momma and I ignore her as we continue to pull the cakes together. When we finally get all three layers assembled and frosted, Momma, ever the perfectionist, slips a thin spatula in hot water, quickly dries it, and uses the heated tool to carefully smooth out the cakes.

"You can tell people you made them, Halia," Momma says as we stand back and admire our finished work. "If these cakes can't land you a man, nothing can."

CHAPTER 12

I can't believe I'm pulling up in front of Raynell's house to pick up the desk she's donated to the silent auction like I'm some sort of moving service. I'm already catering the reunion at zero profit. You'd think that would be enough. I guess I could have just said no and told Raynell to make other arrangements, but she's a hard person to say no to. Besides, I did want to see her house, which I now see I correctly assumed would be quite impressive. And yes, I thought of asking Wavonne to make this run, but my understanding is that this desk is an antique and might be fragile. Wavonne can be careless, and I'm sure I'd never hear the end of it from Raynell if the desk ended up being scratched or otherwise damaged in transit.

Oh well . . . I guess it's for a good cause—at least I hope the Raynell Rollins Foundation is a good cause and not one of those charities with operating expenses sucking up all the donations before they get to the people they are actually supposed to help. For all I know, the donations go to subsidize Raynell's salon appointments and first-class vacations.

I step out of my van and take in the sheer size of Raynell's home. My first thought is *damn, that's a lot of windows*. I start counting them—fifteen windows along just the front of the house and three more in the rooftop dormers overlooking the expertly landscaped yard. Most of houses in newer suburban neighborhoods have brick facades in the front, but the sides and rear are generally covered in siding to save on cost. But this is not the case for the residence of Mr. and Mrs. Terrence Rollins. I can't see the back, but both sides are brick from the roof to the ground.

I walk toward the double front doors, and, based on my experience shopping for wooden tables and chairs for the restaurant, I suspect they are mahogany.

I press the doorbell and hear it chime inside the house. A moment later I'm surprised to see Raynell open the door. I was sure it would be a housekeeper.

"Halia. Hello." Her eyes veer past me toward the driveway. "Gosh. The neighbors are going to wonder who's here in that ramshackle thing," she says of my van, which I'll admit is no Mercedes, but it's only five years old with a few minor nicks on it. "Come in."

I step inside onto gleaming hardwood floors and look up at the foyer ceiling that goes clear to the top of the house. A large window above the front doors carries beams of light onto a mammoth contemporary chandelier dripping with a few hundred thin rectangular crystals. To the left I see a formal dining room with yet another smaller, but no less exquisite, chandelier hanging over a shiny dark wood table (also mahogany I believe) that seats ten people. To the right is a formal sitting room with lush carpet and contemporary furniture.

"The desk is in the family room."

I follow Raynell as we walk alongside the staircase to the kitchen, which opens into a two-story family room with exposed beams and a stone fireplace. The entire wall along the back of the kitchen and the family room consists of floor-to-ceiling windows. I remind myself to lift my jaw back up as I examine the kitchen. It's better equipped than some of the commercial kitchens I worked in earlier in my career. It's a regular utopia of rich wooden cabinets offset with metal hardware, stainless-steel appliances, and glossy granite countertops. There's a large island in the middle and a long glass-top table in the dining area in front of the windows. I guess you might call the area with the table "the breakfast nook," but that term doesn't seem to do it justice.

"I love your kitchen."

"We never use it," Raynell says with zero enthusiasm, and continues walking toward the adjoining family room.

I want to shout what a crime that is—to let such a lovely well-appointed kitchen go to waste—but I keep my mouth shut and follow Raynell.

"Here it is."

I look down and see an ornate piece of furniture . . . what you might call a "period piece." While quite handsome, it is decidedly out of place among all the modern furnishings in Raynell's home. It hosts a bunch of cubbies and drawers and stands on thin legs that descend into claws—I think they are called ball-and-claw Chippendale legs. It's adorned with metal pulls and outlined with a trim that looks like a detailed wooden rope.

"It's lovely," I say. "How old is it?"

"I had it appraised a few weeks ago. The appraiser thought it was at least two hundred years old. I gave Christy the paperwork with the details. She put together a description that we can display with the desk at the auction. It's valued at more than a thousand dollars, so I've suggested twelve hundred as the minimum bid. We'll see who of the trifling fools we went to high school with has that kind of money."

"That's nice of you to donate it," I say, wondering what her angle is. Raynell is not the kind of person who does things out of the goodness of her heart. Maybe she's tried to sell it and can't, or maybe she's lying about its worth . . . who knows.

"It's nothing. And honestly I'll be glad to have it out of my house. I'm all about clean lines and modern furniture. This thing just clashes with my whole decorating theme."

"What made you buy it if it's so dissimilar to the rest of your décor?"

"Oh, I'm always picking up things that I think might have value—not necessarily to keep. One of the perks of being a real estate agent is I often get first dibs on the possessions divorcing couples are trying to get rid of. They put their house on the market after the divorce papers are filed. Often one of the spouses will sell me things below market value just to be spiteful—the stories I could tell. There's less drama on an episode of *Scandal* than in some of my business dealings with couples who've decided to separate." She looks to the right of the desk. "I bought that painting from the same client who sold me the desk." Raynell points to what can only be described as a stunning portrait of a young black woman in a lovely one-shoulder evening gown. She's poised in front of an old-fashioned microphone. The painting manages to capture her both singing and smiling at the same time. It immediately makes me think of the 1940s . . . or maybe the early fifties.

"Wow," I say. "What a beautiful painting . . ." My voice trails off as I realize that beautiful doesn't really do it justice. "Exquisite . . . it's truly exquisite," I add as I think about what a shame it is to see it just sitting on the floor leaning against a bookcase rather than being displayed on the wall.

"Meh," Raynell says, unimpressed. "It's worthless, and I overpaid for it. I'm not sure if I'll keep it."

"Who is the painting of? She looks familiar."

"Sarah Vaughan. Apparently, she was a jazz singer or something back in the day."

"Sarah Vaughan!" I exclaim. "My mother played her version of 'Send in the Clowns' when I was a kid. She had an amazing voice. I remember Momma referring to her as 'The Divine One.'"

"I thought her heyday was more in the forties and fifties."

"Her career spanned decades. I only know because Momma is a big fan. 'If You Could See Me Now' was another big song of hers—that's a really old one I think . . . from the forties, maybe."

"Well, apparently she's dead."

"She must be dead for more than twenty years now."

"You'd think that would make the painting worth something—even if it isn't a Keckley."

"Keckley?"

"I thought the painting might be an original Keckley. Arthur Keckley was a well-known black artist who painted portraits of performers at the Lincoln Theatre on U Street in D.C. during its prime. He painted all the greats: Duke Ellington, Pearl Bailey, Ella Fitzgerald, Cab Calloway, Billie Holiday . . . and I was hoping that this one was the rendition he did of Sarah Vaughan."

"It's not, I take it?"

"No. I had Christy find me an appraiser. He evaluated the desk as well. I was actually more excited about the painting, but it turns out only the desk has any real value. And even that is only worth a couple of thousand dollars. The painting is just one of many copies of the Lincoln Theater portraits that were done by unknowns. I could probably sell the painting for a few hundred bucks. But, really, I guess it's not half bad. I'm thinking of switching it out of the antique-looking gold frame into something more modern. Maybe then I'll hang it and see if I want to keep it.

"You should keep it. It's rich with history even if it's not an original."

"History shmistory. Show me the money."

I'm about to offer to buy it from her, thinking that Momma would love it, or that it might be a nice addition to the artwork at Sweet Tea, when there's a faint knock on the front door.

"Hello?" we hear Christy call out.

"In here," Raynell responds.

Christy walks into the family room. "Hi," she says to me.

I'm about to say hi back, but Raynell starts running her mouth before I have a chance. "Christy's here to help you move the desk. I would lend a hand, but I just had my manicure done. Doesn't it look nice? OPI's Vampsterdam." Raynell holds up one hand with nails done in a deep reddish brown polish.

"Yes." Somehow the color fits her—much like Raynell, it's sort of dark and witchy.

"Christy will also help you transport it and unload it at the hotel. I need to stay back and get ready."

I guess she assumes I don't need any time to get ready, or that I'm planning on showing up to the reunion in a garbage bag and a pair of Birkenstocks.

Christy looks at me, nods, and we both grab a side of the desk from underneath the top. Raynell watches as we lift it out of the room and past the staircase toward the front door.

"Careful," Raynell says as she opens the front door for us.

Christy and I carefully descend the front steps with the desk, maneuver it out to the van, and set it down for a moment while I open the hatch. We take a breath, manage to raise it level with the floor of the vehicle, and slide it inside. As I close the hatch I see Raynell disappear back into the house, and think it's rude of her to not even say good-bye or thank you, but then again, it's Raynell.

Christy and I walk around to the front of the van, get inside, and buckle up.

"I hate to ask, but since you have the van, Raynell wanted

me to see if we could swing by my place and pick up a few more items your classmates have donated."

"Why is the stuff at your place?"

"Raynell didn't want people bringing things here. I believe her words were something to the effect of, 'I don't want those trifling fools I went to school with coming here. They're liable to case the place and rob me blind when I'm not at home.'"

"Sure. No problem."

I'm about to drive off, when, once again, it dawns on me how out of character it is for Raynell to be donating a desk worth more than a thousand dollars to charity. I'm still wondering what's in it for her when I see her scampering out of the house holding a glossy poster the size of a large pizza box.

"Be sure to display this on the desk," she says as Christy opens the door and accepts the sign. It has an inappropriately large (and heavily Photoshopped) photo of Raynell and her contact information, and reads "Donated by Raynell Rollins, Realtor. Please contact Raynell for all your real estate needs in the finer neighborhoods of Prince George's County."

Raynell heads back into the house, and after reading the sign I look at Christy. "Well, I guess it's better than saying, 'Donated by Raynell Rollins. I don't work in none of the Heights.'"

RECIPE FROM HALIA'S KITCHEN

Celia's Chocolate Marshmallow Cake

Chocolate Cake Ingredients

2 cups all-purpose flour
1 teaspoon salt
1 teaspoon baking powder
1½ teaspoons baking soda
1¾ cups sugar
¾ cup unsweetened cocoa powder
½ cup whole milk
½ cup sour cream
1 stick of butter (½ cup)
3 eggs
1 teaspoon pure vanilla extract
1 cup strong hot coffee

• Preheat the oven to 350 degrees Fahrenheit.

• Generously grease and lightly flour two 9-inch round cake pans.

• Sift flour, salt, baking powder, baking soda, sugar, and cocoa into bowl. Mix on low speed until combined.

• In another bowl, combine milk, sour cream, butter, eggs, and vanilla. With the mixer on low speed, slowly add the dry ingredients to the wet until well combined.

- With mixer still on low speed, add coffee and mix until well combined.

- Pour batter into the prepared pans and bake for 25–35 minutes, until a toothpick comes out clean.

- Cool in the pans for 30 minutes, then turn out onto rack and cool completely.

Marshmallow Icing Ingredients

4 sticks of butter, softened (2 cups)
2 cups powdered/confectioners' sugar
1 teaspoon vanilla
2 jars marshmallow creme (14 ounces total)

- Cream butter in a mixing bowl with an electric mixer on medium speed until soft and fluffy.

- Gradually beat in powdered sugar.

- Beat in vanilla extract.

- Add marshmallow creme until thoroughly incorporated.

Eight Servings

CHAPTER 13

"Would you come on," I say to Wavonne as we approach the hotel from the parking lot. As usual, she's moving at a snail's pace as she tries to balance her Rubenesque frame on a pair of heels that clearly value form over function.

We've just stepped out of Momma's Toyota Avalon—it's not exactly a Mercedes, but it's better than showing up to the reunion in my aging utilitarian minivan. I had some things to take care of at the restaurant and was then running behind getting ready for the event, so we are later than I had wanted us to be. My catering team has been onsite for more than three hours setting everything in motion, but I had hoped to be here at least an hour ago to supervise the final food and serving preparations. I'm technically a guest at this event, but I'm sure I won't be able to help myself from checking in on the food here and there.

I don't like to think of myself as one of those women who cares what former classmates she hasn't seen in more than twenty years think of her, but I have to admit I made way more of a fuss over my appearance tonight than I have in a long time. Wavonne and I went for hair and makeup at my friend Latasha's salon this afternoon, and I bought a new outfit from Nordstrom last week—an Adrianna Papell purple lace overlay dress. It's lovely and a bargain at less than two hundred dollars. The sales lady in the Encore section even talked me into a Spanx waist and thigh shaper. It was quite the devil to get on, and it's not the most comfortable thing in the world, but it does help smooth out my curves. I think it even gives my caboose a lift. I thought it might help me squeeze my size fourteen frame into a size twelve dress, but I guess even Spanx has its limits. I've paired the dress with some low-key gold hoop earrings and simple black pumps. Tomorrow I'll be back in my khakis and no-slip unisex kitchen shoes, but, I must say, it does feel nice to be gussied-up like a real woman for the first time in a long while.

"These shoes are made for posin', Halia. Not walkin'. When Terrence tells all his football player friends about me the description needs to be off the chain."

I guess my pumps would be considered high heels, but I'm managing a more hurried pace as mine are maybe two inches or so compared to the five- or six-inch beasts Wavonne has shoved those canoes of hers into. I don't even know how to describe them. I think Wavonne called them "platform booties." They are bright yellow and, with no fewer than six straps, one wouldn't think they'd need a zipper in the back, but apparently they do. The outlandish shoes are an appropriate match for her dress—an ankle-length fitted sheath of a thing with a multi-colored zigzagging pattern and a wide scoop neck that shows off Wavonne's ample cleavage.

"How do I look?" I ask Wavonne when we reach the door to the hotel lobby.

"Dope as hell. You might just get lucky tonight, Halia."

I laugh. "Okay. Let's do this."

We walk through the main entrance and down the hall, and I immediately recognize my friend Nicole Baxter sitting behind a welcome table in front of the main reception room.

"Halia!" She hops out of her chair, shimmies her full-figured self around the table toward me, and wraps me in her arms. "You look gorgeous!"

"Thanks. So do you."

Nicole, who's white, was one of a handful of students, like myself, who crossed the racial divide at my high school. While the student body there is now almost exclusively African American, back in the late eighties there were still a fair number of white kids on the rolls. And, by and large, the black kids socialized with the black kids and the white kids socialized with the white kids. The few Asian and Hispanic students were generally lumped in with the white students. Outside of class, we mostly only crossed paths through student activities and sports. Off-campus outings and parties were not known for their racial diversity. But Nicole and I were both joiners with no athletic ability, so we served together on the debate team and the poster club and the drama club . . . and the student council . . . and who can remember what else. Nicole is naturally very social and, while I'm not exactly shy, her gift of gab was a good match for my somewhat reserved personality. We both share a sharp (some may say "caustic") sense of humor. We became fast friends, and she's actually the only person from my senior class that I'm still in regular touch with. And, if there's one person to still be in touch with, it's Nicole.

Nicole married well, doesn't work, and has no kids—all of which leaves lots of time for collecting gossip. She knows the skinny on all our former schoolmates. A few days ago she and her husband came to Sweet Tea for dinner, and I got an earful about how Candy Bennett and John Moore are now engaged, but only after a torrid affair in which they were sleeping together while still married to other people. I learned that Tim Bell, who is not expected at the reunion, is now Tina Bell, an advocate for transgender rights. Nicole also told me that Sasha Montgomery probably won't make it to the reunion, either, as this soon after her surgery even the best concealer won't cover the scars along her hairline.

"You look lovely as well, Wavonne." Nicole hugs Wavonne and starts shuffling through the name tags on the table before handing one to each of us. Mine has my senior photo on it, while Wavonne's simply has the word "Guest" under her name.

"Go on in. I'm going to staff the table just a bit longer. I'll find you."

"Okay."

As I pin on my name tag, I see Wavonne shove hers in her purse. "I'm not pinnin' nothin' on this dress. I'm takin' it back to Gussini tomorrow and gettin' my nineteen dollars back."

I take a second look at the dress and, even at nineteen dollars, I suppress the urge to tell Wavonne that she overpaid. One look, and you can see how poorly the stitching has been done around the neckline, and the fabric is so sheer that . . . well, let's just say I'm glad Wavonne has Spanx on as well. The shapewear is performing double duty tonight—not only is it smoothing out all of Wavonne's lumps and bumps, but it's also keeping certain anatomical parts from being visible through the thin material.

We walk through a set of double doors into the ballroom and see that the party is already in full swing. We stop by the bar and order two servings of Sweet Tea's signature drink, Mahalia's House Cocktail, a refreshing blend of my homemade berry syrup, Sprite, grapefruit vodka, and lemon juice (Check out *Murder with Fried Chicken and Waffles* for the recipe. ☺). As I take a sip of my drink, I'm pleased to see my servers, dressed in black pants, crisp white shirts, and pink ties, making the rounds with the hors d'oeuvre trays.

"Hi, Joslyn," I say to one of the servers who approaches as soon as she recognizes us. "How's it going?"

"Good. We're passing out the appetizers now and dinner preparations are in progress."

I take a moment to examine the selections on her tray and admire my handiwork. My team and I were up late last night preparing the finger food. While I do love the peapods' stuffed cheese filling and the smoked salmon deviled eggs, I decide to taste test one of the fried chicken salad tartlets while we are still on the sidelines of the room. I take a bite and am reminded why they are such a favorite of mine—shredded fried chicken (seasonings, breading, and all), a bit of mayonnaise, sour cream, some sliced seedless red grapes, and a touch of salt and sugar— all mixed together, delicately placed into crispy mini-tart shells made from Grandmommy's pie crust recipe, and topped with a sprinkle of chopped candied pecans.

"That is *good!*" I say as Wavonne takes a napkin from Joslyn and begins to pile it with a hefty sampling of items from the tray.

"All the starters seem to be going over very well with everyone."

"Great. I'll check in with the kitchen in a little bit."

Joslyn steps away, and I take a moment to give the ballroom a once over. I know it's more than two decades since graduation, but you'd think I'd recognize more than just a handful of faces. I see Beverly Wolfe, who was on the debate team with me, and Matthew Dyer, who I remember routinely getting shoved into his locker by some of the school bullies . . . and Tisha Hammond, who sat next to me in home economics and was completely worthless when it came to cooking. I'm still scanning the crowd when Alvetta, who is standing with Raynell and two other women, catches sight of us and waves us over.

I approach Alvetta and Wavonne toddles behind me as best she can given her snug dress, steep shoes, beverage glass, and napkin full of food.

"Hello, ladies," Alvetta says when we reach her little gaggle. "Halia, the appetizers are exquisite."

"Yes," Raynell chimes in, and almost spills her cranberry-colored cocktail on me when she leans in and gives me a quick air kiss. "This bunch does seem to be enjoying them. Perhaps the more sophisticated cuisine I suggested on Sunday would have been wasted on this crowd after all. Your . . . how do I put it . . . 'down home' vittles seem to be more their speed."

"*Down home vittles?!*" Wavonne questions. "You gonna let her talk about your food like that?" Alvetta and the other girls suddenly look uncomfortable. I vaguely recognize them as former Whitleys, and, no doubt, they are not used to people who don't shamelessly cater to Raynell.

I laugh. "Oh, Wavonne. Raynell is only . . . well . . . being Raynell." I give Raynell a little wink. "I'm glad everyone is enjoying the food."

"Halia," Alvetta says. "You remember Tamika and Nesha." She nods toward the two ladies standing next to her.

"Of course." I extend my hand to each of them, and we exchange greetings. "This is my cousin, Wavonne. She's my date for the evening."

Raynell looks at Wavonne and then me. "Your date? I guess the man shortage is affecting so many these days."

"Speakin' of men," Wavonne says to Raynell. "Where's yours?" Wavonne looks around the room.

"Terrence couldn't make it tonight."

"He and Michael are at the church retreat this weekend," Alvetta says. "They are both leading some discussion groups, and Michael is giving the keynote address at the main reception tonight. They wouldn't have known too many people here anyway. They would have been bored."

"What do you mean Terrence ain't here?" The disappointment shows in Wavonne's voice.

"He's away for the whole weekend," Raynell says. "Sorry,

no football player introductions tonight. Walter, over there," she adds, pointing toward an overweight bald man popping a deviled egg in his mouth, "is an appliance salesman. You'd probably stand a better chance with him anyway."

I can sense Wavonne about to counter Raynell's catty comment, so I pull her aside, excuse us, and take her for a little walk to the other side of the ballroom before she has a chance to really start something with Raynell.

"That stubby little oompa loompa be trippin', Halia. I got a mind—"

"Let it go, Wavonne. She's not worth it," I advise. "Why don't we go check out the auction room?"

Wavonne lets out a long groan before responding. "Fine . . . as long as it's a ho-bag-free zone."

I begin to lead the way out of the ballroom with Wavonne following. "I can't make any promises with regard to ho-bags, Wavonne, but let's hope for the best."

CHAPTER 14

"I see Raynell snagged the best spot to display her desk and all her real estate promotional crap," Wavonne says as we step into a room about a quarter of the size of the one we just left.

"Wow. She really is shameless." I eye the desk, which, of course, is exhibited closer to the ballroom entrance than any other item. Christy and I displayed the poster that Raynell gave us when we were leaving her house earlier today on one side of the desk, but, since then, it has been joined by a multitude of business cards, brochures of homes Raynell is listing, and promotional magnets, calendars, and notepads.

"Some retoucher worked overtime on that." Wavonne takes note of Raynell's oversized photo on the poster. "Who ever did it should get an award. She almost doesn't look like a Rottweiler."

"Almost," I agree. "Let's see if this desk has gotten any bids." I find the sheet of paper where people write down their bids among all of Raynell's marketing paraphernalia and review the numbers. "So far, the desk has only fetched two bids: one for five hundred dollars and one for five hundred fifty dollars."

"That's not even the minimum bid. Sista girl is not gonna be happy about that."

"I'm not sure she cares what the desk fetches. Clearly her donation was just a vehicle for marketing her business."

We step away from the desk and begin perusing the other items on display and find there is quite a variety. Leonard Durey donated a certificate for complete auto detailing at his car wash in Marlow Heights. Jamie Stacks (who is apparently a massage therapist these days) is giving away a sixty-minute massage. Karla Sable is offering a dozen cupcakes from her bakery to the highest bidder, the list goes on and on. . . .

"Here's yours," Wavonne says when she comes across the display for the one-hundred-dollar Sweet Tea gift card I donated. It includes the gift card (unactivated in case some fool tries to steal it) and a Sweet Tea menu. "Look, it's already reached ninety dollars."

"Really?" I walk over and take a look. I'm pleased to find that seven people have bid on it already.

"Who are the dummies who've bid a bunch of money on this tacky-assed T-shirt?" I hear Wavonne say a few steps ahead of me. I look up and see her bent over to take a better look at the shirt. "The bidding is up seventy dollars."

I join her in front of the table and smile. "Oh my God! I have not seen one of those in forever." I take in the white T-shirt featuring a black Mickey and Minnie Mouse decked out in FILA sportswear with the words "Yo Baby, Yo Baby Yo" across the top and "Mickey & Minnie, Good to Go" across the bottom. "These shirts were all the rage back in the day." I laugh thinking about it. "Everyone had one. I think Disney ended up suing whoever made them." I lift the shirt from the table. "This looks brand new . . . like it's never been worn."

"Probably cause it's butt ugly."

"We didn't think it was ugly in the eighties."

"No, we sure didn't," I hear a voice behind me say.

I turn around. "Robin Fillmore."

I wouldn't have called Robin and I great friends. She was more of a partier than I was, but she also had a studious side and served in the student government with me, so we were sort of casual friends.

"Hi, Halia. So good to see you again."

"You too."

"I was just telling my cousin Wavonne here about how popular these shirts were when we were in high school."

Robin smiles at Wavonne. "Believe it or not, she's telling the truth. They were just one of many stupid things we took a liking to in the eighties." She looks back at me. "Remember those horrible jelly shoes . . . and stirrup pants . . . sneaking out to an M.C. Hammer concert . . . driving down to freakin Waldorf to cruise the parking lot at Waldorf Shoppers World?"

"I had forgotten all about that." It wasn't something I did often as I really was pretty straightlaced in high school, and cruising Waldorf Shoppers World was mostly a white-people thing, but I did partake a time or two.

"Cruise Waldorf Shoppers World?" Wavonne asks.

"We'd just circle . . . and circle . . . and circle the parking lot of a strip mall down in Charles County. On the first loop you might notice a guy you like the looks of in another car, make eye contact with him on the second loop, maybe exchange a few words with him on the third loop. People did it for hours . . . often until the police came and cleared us all out."

Wavonne looks at us, decidedly unimpressed. "You circled a parking lot to get dates?"

"I guess we did," I confirm. "We didn't have iPhones back then, Wavonne. We couldn't just fire up Tinder and start swiping through photos."

Wavonne rolls her eyes. "Life in the olden days."

"If we weren't cruising and no one had a party we were

usually at The Oak Tree drinking and smoking . . . and doing God knows what else."

"I don't think I ever went," I say to Robin, but I do remember hearing about the infamous tree. It was a big tree in a field that everyone just called The Oak Tree . . . over in Cheltenham I think . . . where a lot of the area high school kids would converge to blare boomboxes and party. The field was down a hill, so drivers couldn't see it from the road.

"Really? Why?" Robin asks.

"Because, just like now, she's a stick in the mud," Wavonne says.

"I wasn't . . . *am* not a stick in the mud, Wavonne." I turn back to Robin. "But I didn't really run with the kind of crowd that hung out at The Oak Tree."

"I wonder if that tree is still there."

"I doubt it. That field is probably a tract housing development by now," I say, and Robin and I continue to chat as we move along to the next display table with Wavonne.

"This is nice," Robin says when we come upon a small painting of a farm scene. It's an oil painting of a pasture with a big red barn in the distance. There are some animals grazing in the field—a horse, two cows, some chickens, and a pig. "It's quite well done. The artist perfectly captured the feeling of early evening with the sun setting behind the barn."

I took an art class in high school, and I remember being taught how to capture light using yellow and orange paints. I was never good at it, but I do recall sitting next to a girl who was good at it—*very* good, actually.

I leaned over to read the place card describing the donated painting, and, as I suspected, it was painted by my former painting classmate. "Well, look here." I say. "Kimberly Butler painted it."

"Really?" Robin asks as the three of us take a closer look at the canvas.

"Yes. She was in painting class with me. She definitely had an artistic talent back then. It looks like she's really continued to develop it. The painting really is lovely," I say, but as I continue to look at Kimberly's work something about it is bothering me—I can't put my finger on what it is, but there is just something odd about the painting.

We give the painting a last look before continuing to peruse the rest of the auction items. Before too long we reach the end of the rows of display tables, and Wavonne and I decide to make our way back to the main ballroom while Robin stays behind to place a few bids.

"You ain't goin' to bid on anything?" Wavonne asks me.

"No. Nothing really interested me," I say as we rejoin the party. "Now just try to have a good time and stay away from Raynell. You two seem to bring out the worst in each other. There are plenty of other people to talk to." And no sooner have the words left my lips when a striking woman with flawless medium-brown skin moves toward us. She's wearing a "barely there" red strappy slip dress that shows off a near perfect figure.

"Halia? Halia Watkins, right?" the woman says to me.

"Yes." My eyes linger on her face. I look for a name tag, but she's not wearing one. "I'm sorry. Offhand I don't recognize you."

"Kimberly. Kimberly Butler."

"Oh my gosh! We were just talking about you. We saw your painting in the auction room. It looks lovely . . . and so do you, I might add. Really, you look amazing," I say, and actually mean it. "What a difference from when we were . . . I mean you looked nice back then, but *now* . . ."

Kimberly smiles. "Thank you. I guess it just sort of happens . . . one eventually fills out."

And "happen" it did indeed. In high school Kimberly was shapeless and dowdy. I remember her hiding her flat chest and

nonexistent behind under heavy sweaters and baggy cordu-
roys. The white girls could get away with boyish bodies, and
some of them actually dieted themselves down to boney petite
frames, but a black girl without curves—that had to be a tough
pill to swallow.

"You look great as well, Halia."

"That's sweet of you," I say. "Kimberly, this is my cousin
Wavonne. I'm actually catering the event tonight, and Wavonne works at my restaurant with me. She came to help me
keep an eye on things, so I could enjoy being a guest."

Kimberly greets Wavonne, shakes her hand, and then turns
back to me. She looks at me awkwardly for a moment before
speaking. "While I have a chance, Halia, I just want to say
thanks."

"For?"

"I don't know . . . for being one of the nice ones. I know
we weren't exactly friends, but at least you were never mean to
me. Let's face it—I wasn't the most popular girl in school to
say the least. Hell, I hate half the people here . . . especially the
women. The only reason I came is to show these bitches that
I turned out pretty well in spite of them and their nastiness."

I'm about to agree that she did turn out pretty well and
maybe compliment her on her dress when a male classmate on
his way to the bar, unlike me at first, actually does seem to recognize her. He taps her on the arm and begins to engage her
in conversation. He ignores Wavonne and me.

"*Rude,*" Wavonne says as the man continues to pay us zero
attention and keep his focus on Kimberly and her voluptuous
figure. She really seems to shine these days, and it appears Wavonne and me are getting lost in her light.

"Come on, Halia. We ain't gonna stand here bein' treated
like no Kelly and Michelle." Wavonne grabs my arm and pulls
me a few steps back.

It actually works out well that we've put a little distance

between us and Kimberly, so I can give Wavonne a little back-story on Ms. Skimpy Red Dress. I'm about to tell her how homely Kimberly looked in high school and what a dramatic transformation she's made, but before I do, I catch Kimberly's eyes scanning the room as her companion speaks to her. As he's going on and on about God knows what, I see Kimberly's pleasant expression suddenly evaporate. I wonder what the gentleman she's speaking to said to make her look so abruptly agitated, but then I realize that it wasn't something she *heard* that distressed her. I can tell from her eyes that it's something she *saw* . . . something she's *seeing* at this moment. I turn around to find exactly who or what her line of vision is fixed on, and, let me tell you, if I could draw a line from Kimberly's eyes to the focus of her hostile attention, it would run straight as an arrow to one Raynell Rollins.

CHAPTER 15

Wavonne also notices the unsettled look on Kimberly's face. "What's wrong with her? Why's her face all gnarled up all the sudden?"

"Her demeanor went sour when she spotted Raynell."

"Well, that would make anyone's demeanor go sour."

"Yeah . . . well, she and Raynell have a *history*."

"Ooh, girl, I smell me some gossip. Lay it on me."

"Hmm . . . where to begin?" I pause for a moment. "Like I said, Kimberly wasn't much to look at in high school. She was sort of gawky, and boy, was she shy."

"So, the type of girl Raynell ate for lunch?"

"You've got that right. People like Raynell have a homing device on girls like Kimberly. They seek them out to use and abuse—that whole search-and-destroy dynamic. Actually, I don't remember Raynell paying much attention to Kimberly during the first couple of years of high school. It wasn't until later when Kimberly made the mistake of developing a crush on whatever buffoon Raynell was dating at the time—I think it was Eddie Wicks . . . yeah, it was Eddie . . . he was on the football team and played whatever position requires the big hulky brothers. He was built like a refrigerator and, if I recall correctly, about as dumb as one. It's all coming back to me now—he and Kimberly were thrown together as chemistry lab partners. He needed a lot of help from Kimberly, and she took a liking to him. Poor girl made the foolish error of telling someone—I can't remember who—about her feelings for him. Well, whoever she told was a blabbermouth, and you know how quickly word gets around a high school cafeteria."

"You ain't lyin'. A girl borrows one pair of Chanel sunglasses from someone's locker without axin', and, next thing you know, the whole school be callin' her a thief."

I give Wavonne a look.

"Don't be judgin' me, Halia. Turns out they weren't even real Chanel . . . and I was gonna give them back . . . I *was* . . . especially after I found out they were bobos."

"*Anyway*. Word quickly got around that Kimberly had a thing for Raynell's boyfriend. Everyone, including Raynell, knew that Kimberly never stood a chance of snagging Eddie, but bullying was a hobby for Raynell, so it didn't take much for her to go on the attack.

"She took Kimberly's crush as a license to kill. She would bark like a dog at Kimberly in the hallway, get others to hold their noses when she walked by, and even spread rumors about Kimberly having a tail. Everyone was afraid to cross Raynell, so no one stood up to her or told her to knock it off. As if the harassment wasn't enough, Kimberly became an 'untouchable' on top of it—other students kept their distance from her for fear of becoming a Raynell-target themselves. And while I never participated in any of the bullying, I'm sorry to say I never made an effort to stop it, either. I guess I was as afraid of Raynell as everyone else.

"The worst was when Raynell switched Kimberly's shampoo after gym class with Nair hair removal cream. I wasn't in the locker room when it happened, but I heard the story—the whole school heard the story of how Raynell stood laughing as Kimberly emerged from the showers in tears with patches of hair missing. Kimberly wore a head scarf to school for the rest of the year."

"Her hair looks pretty good now," Wavonne says as we watch Kimberly's new admirer give her a kiss on the cheek before continuing on to the bar.

"That was Brian Clarke," she says, re-approaching us. "He sat behind me in homeroom two years in a row and never said so much as hello to me. Now he's asking for my number and wants to have dinner while I'm in town."

"What did you say?" I ask.

"I gave him *a* number . . . not mine, but if he needs a pizza delivered it will come in handy."

"Ooh, I *like* you," Wavonne says.

Kimberly laughs. "That guy was a tool in high school, and he's still one now. We only talked for a few minutes, and he managed to slip in something about his BMW and how he only wears Hugo Boss suits. If only having money could make up for being a jackass."

"He has money?" Wavonne shifts her eyes toward Brian, who is in line at the bar. "Excuse me, ladies. I think I needs me a cocktail."

As Wavonne saunters toward the bar I continue to engage Kimberly in conversation. I tell her all about Sweet Tea and my years in the restaurant business, and she gives me the scoop on what she's been up to since graduation. She tells me that after high school, she attended the Pratt Institute in Brooklyn and stayed in New York after college. While working a series of odd jobs she slowly made a name for herself as an artist. She beams with pride when she tells me about the early years after college that she spent banging on doors trying to get galleries to show her paintings. And how, now, after much persistence and hard work, New York's finest galleries approach her and outbid each other by reducing their commissions for a chance to show her work.

"Congratulations," I say. "That's really impressive. Maybe I can see more of your work sometime. Your paintings are probably out of my price range, but I occasionally switch out the artwork in Sweet Tea to keep things fresh. Who knows—I might buy something to hang in the restaurant."

"Sure," Kimberly says. "Let me give you my card." She retrieves a glossy full-color business card from her purse and hands it to me.

I give it a quick look. "That's a lovely photo of you."

"Thanks. It has my contact information and a link to my Web site. I'll be in town for a couple more weeks if you'd like to talk about some of the pieces I have available . . . or even commission an original."

"An original? Wouldn't that be fun." As I drop the card in my purse I see Raynell hurriedly making her way toward us—her cranberry cocktail replaced with what appears to be a sour apple martini. I notice Kimberly stiffen when she catches sight of her.

"Halia, I think it's about time we open the buffet. Hopefully the main course will go over as well as the appetizers. Clearly, these people have no experience with fine dining, so it should be okay."

"Sure. Let me check in with my team," I say, before I bring up the uncomfortable topic of money. I usually require at least half my catering fee up front with the outstanding balance due the day of the event, but given that this job was for my own reunion I agreed to forgo the deposit and collect my full fee today. "Do you have the check for the catering?"

"I was in such a rush today I forgot all about it. Christy's my chauffeur for the evening. I'll write a check when we get back to my house tonight, and give it to her. She can drop it at the restaurant for you tomorrow."

"Why don't I just swing by your house in the morning and get it?"

"Oh God, no. Get it from Christy. Let her get up early."

While I grudgingly agree I notice Kimberly still standing next to me, glaring at Raynell. "Um, Raynell . . . this is Kimberly. You remember her? Kimberly Butler?"

Kimberly and I wait for a flood of recognition and maybe an outpouring of apology—we get neither.

"Yes, yes, of course," Raynell says, but you can tell from the look on her face that she doesn't remember her. She extends her hand while giving Kimberly a good once-over. "You were on the cheer squad, right?"

"Yes," Kimberly lies. "Go Hornets!"

I laugh quietly, knowing full well that Kimberly was never a cheerleader, and she's just screwing with Raynell.

"I wonder why we didn't hang out more?" Raynell says, clearly confused as to why someone as attractive as Kimberly was not part of the Whitleys.

"Oh . . . I wasn't really into the whole skanky slut thing," Kimberly says with a laugh and just the right amount of inflection, so you can't quite tell if she's serious or joking.

Bewildered, Raynell decides to laugh it off. "So what are you up to these days, Kimberly?"

"I live in New York. I'm an artist . . . oil paintings mostly, but I also work with watercolors, and I've been experimenting with an airbrush lately just for fun."

"How nice," Raynell says with a condescending tone. "Sounds like a fun hobby."

"I thinks it much more than a hobby," I say. "Kimberly's art has been shown in galleries all over New York City."

"Really?" There's a change in Raynell's demeanor—the sort of change that happens to Raynell-types when they realize the person they've been talking to might be of use to them. "So you're really a pro?"

"I would like to think so. My last painting sold for more than twenty thousand dollars at the Leslie Miller Gallery in Chelsea."

"Hmm." Raynell puts her finger to her chin. "Do you know much about appraising art? I have this painting of Sarah Vaughan . . . you know, the famous jazz singer. I recently purchased it. I thought it might be a Keckley. Arthur Keckley was—"

"The famous painter who did renditions of singers who played the Lincoln Theater back in the day. Yes, I know who he is. His originals are worth a hefty sum."

Not one who's used to being interrupted, Raynell stammers for a moment. "Um . . . yes. That's him. Unfortunately, I was told by one appraiser that it's not an original, but I'd love to get a second opinion just to make sure."

"I'm not an art appraiser by any means, but I may know enough to be able to tell you if it's real. Maybe we can set something up while I'm in town."

As I watch Kimberly hand Raynell a business card, I wonder what she's up to. I can't imagine she has any real interest in helping out her high school tormenter.

"Thanks." Raynell turns her head and yells to Christy, who's a few feet away chatting with Alvetta. "Christy. Give Kimberly here my contact information. She's going to come by and give me a second appraisal on the Sarah Vaughan painting," she says, takes a last sip of her martini, and departs for the bar to get a refill.

Christy rushes over looking exhausted, which isn't surprising. She's been here all day getting the silent auction set up and helping out with other details.

As Christy digs for a card in her purse, I take a moment to excuse myself to make sure the buffet is ready to make its debut. I start to walk away when I notice a hush come over the ladies I'm leaving behind—all their gazes fixed in the same location over my shoulder. I look behind me to see what all the fuss is about, and there *he* is—a brother so fine, it's no wonder conversations have stopped and all eyes are on him.

CHAPTER 16

"Gregory Simms," I hear coming from behind me. I flip around and see Nicole. "The man you and the rest of this room are staring at—it's Gregory Simms."

"Really?" My eyes are still fixed on his handsome face. He's wearing a snug pair of dress pants that outline a behind you could set your drink on. I suspect he decided to forgo the suit and tie that most of our former gentlemen classmates are wearing as the tight polo shirt he's sporting shows off an impressive chest. "The Gregory Simms that always had his nose in the book? The one all the jocks made fun of because he couldn't even do one pull-up in gym class?"

"From the looks of those biceps now, I bet he can do a hell of a lot more than one pull-up these days."

"Who's that?" Wavonne has returned from the bar with a fresh drink. She must have decided to ditch Brian to head back over here and get some details on Gregory.

"The man who looks like he just stepped out of a cover of *GQ*?"

"Uh-huh."

"That's Gregory Simms," Nicole answers. "He was in our

class—a quiet academic type back then. I doubt he weighed more than a buck thirty in high school."

"Now that is a *man*," Wavonne says.

"He lives in Miami now," Nicole extols. "I got the skinny when he checked in at the welcome table. He owns a chain of gourmet burger restaurants called South Beach Burgers—handmade burgers, fresh cut fries, shakes . . . all that stuff."

"Really? A fellow restaurant owner."

"And a successful one, too." Wavonne's already tapped on her phone a few times and must have found her way to the South Beach Burger Web site. "Twelve locations from Florida stretching up to North Carolina."

"Well, good for him," I say. "He was always a nice guy. I'm glad he's doing well."

"Doing well is right. That's a Burberry polo he's got on, and those pants are Moschino. That's more than a thousand bucks in clothes right there. Factor in those Ferragamo loafers, and you're looking at another five or six hundred bucks."

"How does she know the designers of everything he's wearing?" Nicole asks me.

"Hell if I know. She can't remember that table three wants another iced tea, but ask her to name the designer of a blouse some random woman across the street has on, and she'll get it right every time."

"Don't worry," Wavonne says, looking at Nicole's dress. "I don't do Kohl's designers."

"Really?" I say. "This from someone who bought her dress at Gu—"

"Guess," Wavonne lies, glaring at me before I can finish the word "Gussini." "I bought this at the Guess store . . . the one in Montgomery Mall."

"No one cares where you bought your dress, Wavonne," I say. "Certainly not me or Nicole anyway."

"Why are we wastin' time talking about clothes anyway? Take me over there and introduce me," Wavonne says to Nicole.

"Me? If anyone should do the introducing, it should be Halia. She's the one who went to prom with him."

"What you mean, she went to prom with him?!" Wavonne turns to me. "You mean to tell me you got all up in *that?*"

"All that was not . . . well, *all that,* in high school. We were in honors English together. He needed a date. I needed a date. We were just friends. I don't even think there was a good-night kiss."

"Wait . . . wait. He's the guy who looked like Urkel with you in that photo Aunt Celia has on the bookcase . . . where you're wearin' that poufy pink Puerto Rican bridesmaid's dress?"

"That was the style back then, Wavonne. All the prom dresses were poufy in the eighties."

"You looked like a big pink balloon. I'm surprised nobody tried to pop you."

"Don't worry, from what she's said about her and Gregory that night, nobody did," Nicole says with a laugh.

"Very funny, Nicole," I say. "Come on, let's go say hello."

Kimberly lingers behind and as Nicole, Wavonne, and I begin to make our move, or as Momma said a few days ago, "move in for the kill," I notice that Gregory has caught Raynell's attention as well. I see her also making a beeline toward him. We speed up our gait accordingly to beat her to the target, but Raynell takes notice of our ascent toward Gregory, and picks up her pace, too. For a stout sister, the girl can move when she wants to.

"That thirsty heifer's tryin' to move in on my man," Wavonne says.

We speed up some more. Raynell speeds up some more. You can almost hear the movie chase scene music playing in the background. Me, Wavonne, Nicole, Raynell—anyone watching all these thick ladies moving at top speed probably thinks the buffet just opened.

I continue to scurry as I look back and see Wavonne struggling in her heels.

"Leave her," Nicole says. "She's dead weight."

I laugh but fail to heed her words. I give Wavonne a chance to catch up, which, unfortunately, causes us to lose the de facto race. By the time we reach Gregory, Raynell is already giving him a hug.

"Did you ladies just get out of prison?" Raynell asks once she's released Gregory from her embrace. I detect a slight slur in her words. Her affinity for colored cocktails seems to be catching up with her. "It's like you've never seen a man before."

"Look who's talkin'. You're the one who beat us over here," Wavonne says. "And ain't you got a *husband?*"

I ignore both Wavonne and Raynell. "Hello, Gregory."

"Halia Watkins!" Much to Raynell's dismay he leans in and gives me a long hug. "It is *good* to see you."

"You too." I have to admit I'm smiling from ear to ear. It *is* good to see him. "This is my cousin, Wavonne, and you know Nicole."

"Yes, yes," Gregory says, and shakes Wavonne's hand. "Pleasure to meet you."

"Let go of his hand, Wavonne," I say as she continues to clasp Gregory's palm with seemingly no intention of releasing it.

"Wavonne and Halia are our caterers for the night," Raynell says as if we're the hired help. She catches Gregory taking a quick peek at Wavonne's cleavage and adds, "Wavonne's a *waitress* at this little hole-in-the-wall Halia runs." She says waitress with the tone someone might use when saying the word "prostitute" or "drug dealer."

"Oh, I know of Mahalia's Sweet Tea. It's hardly a hole-in-the-wall. I hear it has the best fried chicken and waffles south of Sylvia's in Harlem."

"I'm flattered you've heard of it."

"Of course I've heard of it. I'm in the business as well. Correct me if I'm wrong, but I believe I've seen Sweet Tea on some of the local top restaurant lists."

"We've made the *Washington Post* and *Washingtonian Magazine* lists since we opened," Wavonne brags.

"That's all very nice, but I have a little business I'd liked to discuss with Gregory if you'd excuse us," Raynell interrupts.

When she says this it dawns on me that Gregory Simms must be the Gregory she was getting some calls from when she was at Sweet Tea, and, then again, when we met her at church on Sunday.

"It can wait, Raynell," Gregory says.

"I'm helping Gregory find some retail space." Raynell interlocks her arm with his in a way that seems a tad inappropriate for a married woman to be doing. "He's looking to expand his restaurant and add locations in Maryland. His restaurant is a *chain,* Halia, with multiple locations . . . not just one."

"Why would you want to discuss business tonight with a *real estate agent.*" Wavonne mimics Raynell's earlier tone when she condescendingly referred to Wavonne as a waitress. "Tonight should be about having fun. Let's get you a drink? I bet you're a Cîroc man."

"I'm good right now," Gregory says politely. "I really don't need a drink, and I guess if I'm going to talk business with anyone, it should be with Halia, a fellow restaurateur."

Gregory's comment makes me smile. It's funny to see Raynell hanging off Gregory on one side, and Wavonne trying to put the moves on him on the other. They are both working him hard, but, if I didn't know better, I'd swear the one he has eyes for is me.

CHAPTER 17

"I'd be happy to talk shop with you anytime," I say to Gregory.

"Gregory, are you sure you don't want to hear about some of the new locations I've found for you?" Raynell asks. "And *Halia,* aren't you supposed to be opening the buffet?"

"She's got staff here to do that," Wavonne says.

"Aren't *you* part of that staff? Isn't there some macaroni and cheese or *something* that requires your attention?"

"Come on, Wavonne," I say, trying to diffuse yet another war of words that's about to erupt between her and Raynell. "We really should check on the food."

"I'd love to come along and see what you've prepared," Gregory says.

"What about the potential restaurant sites?" Raynell continues to play tug-of-war with us.

"He can go over those with you later," Wavonne says. "Right now, he's comin' with us . . . and, besides, I think you need to visit the little ho's room and fix your weave . . . some tracks are showin'."

"Wavonne!" I shriek.

"I'll have you know there are no tracks on this head."

Raynell starts running her fingers through her hair, lifting sections up to reveal nothing but scalp. "This is all *mine*. I doubt you can say the same."

"Well smack my ass and call me Janeka," Wavonne says, her disdain for Raynell abruptly transforming into genuine curiosity. She sidles closer to Raynell and leans in to inspect her head. "That is some *good* hair. What's your secret?"

"Girl, you have to condition, condition, condition." Raynell's own dislike for Wavonne seems to be temporarily sidelined as well. I guess a compliment about one's hair can soften even the most ferocious of women.

As the ladies continue to suspend their mutual distaste for one another over a discussion of holding sprays and pomades, I notice Kimberly. She's lingering by the bar, eyeing the two of them. She watches as Raynell tosses her hair to show Wavonne its volume. I can only imagine what Kimberly is thinking while Raynell, the woman who so cruelly robbed her of her hair in high school, stands showing off her flowing mane to Wavonne.

"Shall we check out the food?" Gregory says to me while Raynell and Wavonne are still distracted with hair talk.

"Sure."

"I had some of the appetizers. Were those your doing as well?" Gregory asks as we walk toward the serving tables.

"Yes."

"Those deviled eggs were killer. I wouldn't have thought to pair smoked salmon with deviled eggs, but it definitely works."

"Thanks! That's one of the things I like about catering gigs—they give me a chance to try out some new recipes."

When we reach the buffet I see my team putting out the last of the chafing dishes.

"So we've got the salad station over there." I point to the

far end of the line. "Then my famous sour cream cornbread and some dinner rolls."

"Nice."

I lift the lid off the serving tray closest to me. "My herb-baked chicken. I wanted to go with fried, but Raynell insisted on baked."

"It smells really good."

"Then we have my salmon cakes, mashed potatoes and gravy, macaroni and cheese, and green beans with ham hock."

"I'm glad I came hungry."

"Wait until you see the dessert spread—chocolate marshmallow cake and sour cream coconut cake."

"I guess I should have worn pants with an elastic waist," Gregory jokes.

"Please. You look like you can more than afford an indulgence or two." I try not to let my eyes linger on his body as I say this.

"It's a balance," he says. "Some indulgences amass calories." His eyes give me a quick once over. "And I guess certain other indulgences burn them."

I let out a quick laugh and feel my face get hot. I'm not used to flirting, and I'm certainly not good at it. I'm at a loss for anything to say in response to his suggestive comment when Raynell intrudes on our banter.

"Everything ready to go?"

"Yep."

Raynell gives a signal to the deejay, and he announces that the buffet is open.

As Gregory, Raynell, and I watch people line up and start moving through the serving stations, Wavonne appears with a fresh cocktail in her hand. "I told you to tell me before you opened the buffet to everyone, so I could get a good place in line."

"Sorry, I forgot."

"You know I can't move fast in these heels. Now I'm gonna be stuck behind this herd of cows . . . there'll probably only be scraps left by the time I get up there."

"There's plenty of food, Wavonne. Let's all go get in line."

As we move to take our place behind my old classmates, I notice Raynell's a little unsteady on her feet. She stumbles on her heels and, at one point, grabs hold of me to keep from falling over.

"Girl's drunk as a skunk," Wavonne says.

"I am not. I'm just a little dizzy. I need to eat something."

"I think that's a good idea," I say. "Wavonne, why don't you help Raynell to a table, and Gregory and I will fix plates for all of us?"

"Why I gotta take that mess to a table?"

"Because I asked you to."

Wavonne is about to protest further, but then she shifts her eyes from me to Gregory and then back to me again. "Oh. Okay. I got you, Halia." She leans in and whispers, "I'll let you have this one. You go on . . . get you some."

She grabs Raynell by the elbow. "Come on. Let's sit your drunk ass down."

I vaguely hear Raynell insist, once again, that's she's not intoxicated as Wavonne leads her to a table.

While we wait for our turn at the buffet, Gregory and I get a chance to catch up. I tell him about Sweet Tea, and how it sucks up most of my time. He gives me the lowdown on how he started South Beach Burgers and leveraged it into a regional chain. Conversation between us flows naturally, and I find myself glad we are at the end of the line—it gives us more time to talk.

We eventually make it to the table with four loaded plates and sit down with Wavonne and Raynell. Alvetta is seated at the table as well with a few of Raynell's other former high school minions. As I unwrap my silverware I notice that Raynell and her comrades have on colored neon necklaces. Alvetta's is pink and Raynell's, just like in high school, is green.

"You didn't have those on earlier, did you? Where did you get them?" I ask Alvetta, pointing to her necklace.

"I brought them," Janelle Sanders says before Alvetta can respond. "I got them online. A little nostalgia for the evening."

"How fun," I say before I catch sight of yet another cocktail in Raynell's hand. "How'd she get that?" I ask Wavonne.

"She said she pay for my drink if I got one for her, too."

I groan. "The last thing Raynell needed was another drink, and it wouldn't be the worst idea in the world for you to slow down with the booze, either," I suggest. But despite my displeasure with Wavonne contributing to Raynell's further intoxication, I must say, drunk Raynell is way more pleasant than sober Raynell. The booze seems to have mellowed her out—she even compliments my food. "Halia, this macaroni and cheese is *so* good!" She takes another bite. "You were right." The slight slur in her speech that I detected earlier in the evening has progressed, and her words are starting to become garbled. "This baked chicken . . . chicken . . . it's nice chicken . . . but, like you said, we should have gone with the fried . . . yeah . . . the fried."

"You can come by Sweet Tea for fried chicken anytime."

"I can?" she asks. "Thank you, Halia. You're so nice." *Boy, is she drunk.*

Raynell spends the remainder of the meal saying things that only half make sense while the rest of us at the table chat about high school and flashback to the eighties. As we begin to finish up dinner, the deejay cranks up the volume on the music, and the lights above the dance floor come alive.

"That's my jam!" Raynell yells when Pebbles's "Mercedes Boy" starts blaring from the speakers. She hops up from her seat and hurriedly staggers to the dance floor. She's the only one out there, but that doesn't stop her from busting a move . . . or, quite frankly, stop her from making a fool of herself. She more fumbles than dances as everyone looks on. She twirls around and lifts her hands over her head, swinging them from left to right. Then she starts doing a clumsy move that resembles the funky chicken. Finally, when she starts lifting her dress and swinging it back and forth like a cancan girl, I see Christy and Alvetta get up from the table and approach her. Raynell is not ready to call it quits and protests their attempts to remove her from the dance floor, but she eventually concedes and lets the two of them help her across the room.

When they come back to the table to get Raynell's things, Alvetta suggests that Christy retrieve Raynell's car and bring it around.

"I'm not ready to go home. I'm having fun. I haven't even danced with Gregory yet," Raynell slurs while putting her hands on Gregory's shoulders.

"No more dancing, Raynell," Alvetta says. "We need to get you home. Come with me."

Gregory and I stand up to say our good-byes and offer any help that might be necessary to safely get Raynell to her car.

"At least let me say good night," Raynell insists, and gives Gregory a hug—a hug that's tighter and lasts longer than it should considering it's between a married woman and a man who is not her husband. She even takes a moment to move her arms up and down his sides, feeling his back muscles. "I'll see *you* later," she says. "Good night, ladies . . . and Wavonne." She starts laughing hysterically. "Did you hear that? Ladies . . . *and Wavonne.*"

"Yes, I heard it," Alvetta replies disinterestedly. As she starts to lead Raynell out of the ballroom I catch sight of Raynell's neon green necklace, which, thanks to her antics on the dance floor, is hanging down her back rather than her chest. Raynell and Alvetta are about to clear the exit when it suddenly occurs to me what was amiss about Kimberly's painting.

"Excuse me," I say, and get up from the table. I quickly by-pass Raynell and Alvetta and stride toward the auction room.

"Kimberly, you little devil, you," I say under my breath once I'm in the room standing in front of her canvass. I can't help but laugh as I take in the painting a second time. I get a good look at the green pasture, the barn, the horse, the chickens . . . but it's when my eyes zero in on the pig that my hunch about what was odd about the painting is confirmed—the pig is wearing a collar. That's what must have struck me as unusual earlier. I'm no country girl, but I don't think farm pigs gener-ally wear collars. Oh, and did I mention the collar is neon green?

I'm still laughing as I pick up a pen and place a bid on the painting.

CHAPTER 18

After placing my bid on Kimberly's painting I return to the main ballroom. By this time, without Raynell scaring everyone off by gyrating like a crazy woman, the dance floor has started to fill.

"Shall we?" Gregory asks when I reach the table and Billy Ocean's "Get Outta My Dreams, Get Into My Car" begins to play.

"Sure."

"I'm comin', too," Wavonne says, and the three of us hit the dance floor. I haven't been dancing in years, but boy, is it fun. When you own a restaurant your nights out are few and far between, so an evening of cocktails and dancing is a real treat. The deejay plays a mix of Top 40 and R & B hits from the late eighties. We get down to Janet Jackson, and Bobby Brown, and Madonna, and Morris Day, and Whitney Houston . . . and, yes, even Tony! Toni! Toné! and J. J. Fad. We're all having a good time until Roxette's "She's Got the Look" hits the speakers. While not quite as intoxicated as Raynell, Wavonne, too, has been a frequent visitor to the bar and, let's be honest, she's not exactly the most inhibited person sober. The longer we stay on the dance floor the more, shall we say "ill-mannered," her moves become—she jiggles her breasts back and forth, waves her hands in the air, and shakes her booty like a go-go dancer in a rap video.

"Look at me doin' the Stanky Leg to white people music," Wavonne says as she brings her knee in and pushes it out to the music of a white Swedish rock band. I definitely know it's time to go home when I hear her call to Gregory, "Come on, let's do the ghetto booty freak." Wavonne maneuvers herself in front of him, and, I swear it couldn't have been timed any better in a *Saturday Night Live* sketch—right when "She's Got the Look" hits its pause . . . you know, when the music completely cuts out between "And I go la la la la la" and picks up again with "Na na na na na," Wavonne bends over in front of Gregory—she bends over in front of Gregory, and all of us within earshot are treated to the tearing sound of nineteen dollars worth of multicolored zigzagging fabric.

My mouth drops as I see her dress literally split right along the middle of her behind. Gregory looks on, bemused, as Wavonne straightens herself up.

"Oh, Halia, please tell me what I think just happened didn't just happen."

I don't answer. I just wince in response to her question.

"Those bitches at Gussini are gonna get a piece of my mind tomorrow," she says before directing her attention to the people next to us on the dance floor. "What are you lookin' at?!"

I refrain from saying, "It's not Gussini's fault you were trying to shove a size-sixteen woman into a size-fourteen dress." Instead, I turn to Gregory. "I think it's time to take Wavonne home," I say to him as I watch Wavonne reach behind and try to pull the fabric back together, but the dress is too tight for her efforts to be productive. "Come on," I say to her. "I'll walk behind you."

"Can I reach you at Sweet Tea? I would love to connect again before I go back to Miami."

"Sure. Of course."

Right then, for the first time all night, the deejay plays a ballad—Exposé's "Seasons Change." I hate to admit it, but I'm silently cursing Wavonne. It's bad enough that she imposed herself on us for the upbeat songs, but now she's wrecked my chance to get a slow dance in with Gregory.

"I'll call you."

"Great." I lean in, give him a quick hug, and begin to try to discreetly remove Wavonne and her torn dress from the premises.

"All those times . . . those *many, many* times I've told you to stop 'showin' your ass' . . ." I say to her as we approach the exit. "And this time I get to really mean it."

CHAPTER 19

"Well, look what the cat dragged in," I say to Wavonne. We're at home the morning after the reunion, and I'm sitting at the kitchen table.

"Shhh," she says, rubbing her temples. She's still in the oversized T-shirt she slept in.

"I told you to slow down with the liquor last night."

She directs a hungover stare at me before making her way to the coffee pot.

I'm not sure most people who know her would recognize Wavonne when she first gets up—before she paints on the heavy makeup, plunks a wig on her head, and accessorizes herself to high heaven with flashy costume jewelry. She's getting close to thirty, but, at the moment, without all of her trademark razzle-dazzle, she still looks like a teenager.

"Why'd you get me up so early?" She sits down across from me with a cup of coffee.

"It's seven thirty, Wavonne. Not five a.m. I want to go by Christy's this morning and pick up the check for the reunion catering before we head to Sweet Tea. It's out of the way, and I'd like to be at the restaurant by nine thirty to help set up for brunch. We need to get moving shortly. Laura covered for us last night, so she's taking the morning off today."

I get up from the table and set my mug in the sink. "You better get in the shower. I want to be on the road by eight thirty."

Wavonne yawns, slowly gets up from her chair, tops off her coffee, and heads out of the kitchen with her cup.

While she's getting showered I get up to reach for my phone, lean against the counter, and start swiping through last night's photos. Looking at the images, I recall that I had originally planned not to go to the reunion, but now I'm certainly glad I did. It turned out to be a fun evening. I liked having a night off from the restaurant, catching up with some old friends, and especially enjoyed reconnecting with Gregory. I feel like he was flirting with me, but I'm so out of practice in that arena I may be completely off base. I'm also not sure if he has something going with Raynell. I know she's married, but married women cheat all the time. And I don't think she would get as territorial about Gregory as she seemed to last night if he were just a casual friend or real estate client—and the way she hugged him before she left was pretty intense for platonic friends. But, who knows—Raynell was highly intoxicated, so her behavior may have been a result of the alcohol.

I'm about to brush off the whole evening and let go of any expectations where Gregory is concerned when my phone buzzes with a text from him.

gregory here . . . got your cell number from christy . . . good to see you last night . . .
still up for getting together to trade restaurant stories?

I have to say I can feel my pulse quicken when I read his words. As Wavonne and Momma love to point out, I don't date much, and once you've crossed the line over to the less desirable side of forty without landing a man, your hopes for a relationship aren't exactly lofty. In my twenties I was optimistic about getting married and very picky about who I dated. During my thirties the pessimism started to set in, and I began giving guys who weren't "attractive enough" or "smart enough" . . . or "ambitious enough" a few years earlier a second look, but nothing ever panned out. By the time I hit forty, and after one too many dates with men who still lived with their mommas or thought I was supposed to be their nursemaid, I pretty much gave up on romance and decided a single life focused on family, friends, and a thriving restaurant career wasn't so bad.

I text back.

Sure

The moment I hit send, I wonder if I responded too soon. *Do I seem too eager? Maybe I should have let some time pass before I replied.* Like I said, I'm not good at this.

I wait for him to text me back, but when I don't get a response after a few seconds, I drop my phone on the table and walk down the hall to hurry up Wavonne. With a little cajoling from me, I manage to get her ready to roll just shy of eight thirty.

"So, are you going to see him while he's still in town?" Wavonne asks as I throw a few things in my purse.

"Who?"

"What you mean, *who?* Gregory."

I refrain from telling her about his text. "I don't know, Wavonne. I think he's only here for a few days, and I've already taken one night off from the restaurant."

We're about to head out the door when I hear some quick scurrying coming from the hallway.

"Gregory? Who's Gregory?" Momma asks, hurriedly turning the corner. We had a dachshund growing up who I swear could hear you unwrap a piece of cheese from the other side of the house and show up at your feet in a nanosecond wanting his share. Momma's ears have a similar talent when any mention of a possible man in my life materializes.

"Nobody," I say. "We're late, Momma. We have to run."

Momma maneuvers herself between me and the front door. "*Who* is Gregory?"

"He's one of Halia's old classmates who was puttin' the moves on her last night."

"Really? What's he look like? Employed? Father material? Is he a Christian?"

"We were just friends in high school, Momma."

"She went to prom with him."

"That lanky fellow with the big ears?"

"He's not so lanky anymore," Wavonne says. "Brotha is fine these days."

"And he's interested in *Halia?*"

I glare at Momma. "Don't act so surprised!"

"Single? Divorced? Never married?"

"We didn't talk about that, Momma, but he was not wearing a wedding band, and I'm sure Nicole would have told me if he were married."

"Are you going to see him again? What's he do?"

"I don't know. And he owns a chain of restaurants."

"He's in the restaurant business as well. He sounds perfect for you."

"He lives in Florida, Momma. He's only in town for a few days."

"Well, you better jump on board that train before it leaves the station then. This is no time to dawdle." She says this as if Gregory is the last helicopter out of Saigon.

"I agree with Aunt Celia. He was into you, Halia. I could tell. Some brothas dig the full-figured matronly types . . . go figure," Wavonne says with an evil grin.

As I scowl back at her, my phone buzzes again. I grab it from my purse, take a look at the screen, and see another text from Gregory suggesting a date tomorrow evening.

"If you must know, he just asked me out, so I guess we are getting together after all."

I see the excitement in Momma's face. "Fantastic! You'll need to get your hair done, and Wavonne and I will help you with your makeup."

"Whatever, Momma. We're late."

Hopeful that her only daughter may not be an old maid after all, Momma steps out of our way and let's Wavonne and me pass. We walk out to the van and finally hit the road. Sunday traffic is light, so it doesn't take us too long to get to Christy's building.

Her apartment is in an older garden community of three-story buildings in Temple Hills. There are no elevators, so Wavonne and I walk up three flights of stairs to her unit on the top floor. When I knock on the door, there's no response, so Wavonne knocks a second time. A few moments later we hear some stumbling on the other side of the door and see the knob turn.

"Halia," Christy says after opening the door. She appears groggy, like she's just gotten out of bed. There are even sleep lines from her pillow on her face. She clearly was not expecting us.

"I'm sorry. Did we wake you? Raynell said to come by this morning to get a check for the catering."

She narrows her brow. "No. Raynell didn't say anything to me about it."

"So you don't have our money?" Wavonne asks.

I turn to Wavonne. "*Our* money?"

"No, I'm afraid I don't. I'll see Raynell on Monday. I can get a check from her then and drop it by the restaurant."

"Raynell's house isn't too far from here. Why don't Wavonne and I just drop by on our way to the restaurant?"

"Okay. I'll call her and let her know you're on your way. But I must warn you, she's not really a morning person, and I'm sure she's hurting from last night."

"Thanks. I'm sorry we woke you."

"It's okay. I have a lot to do today, and it's time to get moving."

"Why don't you just let Christy bring you the check on Monday?" Wavonne asks after Christy closes her door. "You really wanna wake up the dragon lady so early on a Sunday? She might breathe fire at us."

"I've been in this business for a long time, Wavonne. And if I've learned nothing else, it's that people have a short memory where owed-money is concerned. First it's 'I'll pay you on Monday.' Then it's 'I have appointments all week. Can I pay you on Friday?' Then they stop answering the phone when you call altogether. For all we know, Raynell has dipped into the reunion fund to cover a new pair of shoes or one of her fancy designer outfits you're so infatuated with."

"Fine, but you know Medusa's gonna be in a mood."

We get in the van and buckle up. Before I start the ignition and back out of the parking space, I say to Wavonne, "She can be mad as a wet hen for all I care as long as she can sign her name on a check made out to Mahalia's Sweet Tea."

CHAPTER 20

"This is where Raynell lives?" Wavonne asks as we pull up in front of her house, and I park on the street. "Fancy!"

"It is quite nice, isn't it?"

We step out of the van and walk up the driveway.

"How much you think this house is worth? A million bucks?"

"I have no idea, Wavonne."

When we reach the front door, I press the bell and hear it chime on the other side. We wait a few moments. When there is no response, we press the button again. We linger a tad longer, and when there is still no answer, I start to get a little suspicious. First Raynell tells me to pick up a nonexistent check from Christy, and then she conveniently doesn't answer the door when I come by to get it from her directly.

While we stand outside waiting for someone to answer the door, I notice that the window next to the door is open . . . actually all the windows along the front of the house are open.

"Raynell?" I call through the open window closest to us. "It's Halia. I'm here to settle the bill for the catering."

"Want me to pull up Rihanna's 'Bitch Better Have My

Money' on my phone and blast it at full volume? That should get her moving."

"I don't think we're quite to that point yet, Wavonne, but I'll let you know."

"Have it your way." Wavonne steps away and peeks into the garage. "Her Escalade's in there."

I look through the window next to the door and see Raynell's gold Michael Kors keychain on a console in the foyer. "I see her keys on the table. Her car's here . . . and she wouldn't leave the house without her keys. I think she's just ignoring us."

"Maybe she really did dip her greedy hooves into the reunion fund. I bet that's why she ain't answerin' the door. She don't have your money."

I knock forcefully on the door rather than hitting the bell for a third time. "Raynell!" I yell through the window again. When my voice is, once again, met with silence, I instinctively try the doorknob and find it unlocked. I give it a full turn and open the door just enough to poke my head in.

"Raynell, it's Halia and Wavonne. Christy said she'd call you to let you know to expect us." I open the door wider. "I see your keys on the table. You must be here."

I hate to think the worst about people, but I'm now convinced that Raynell is indeed trying to put one over on me, and get out of paying the bill for my catering services. She was a conniving little monster in high school, and clearly she's no different today.

"All right . . . enough." I throw the door open and step inside. "Raynell!" I call up the steps. "We know you're here. I need to collect payment for services rendered."

"Yeah! Fool!" Wavonne says.

"Shut up, Wavonne," I say as we stand in the foyer waiting for Raynell to show herself.

"If she's not comin' down, then we're goin' up," Wavonne

says. "If we happen upon her closet and stop to check out some of her clothes, then so be it."

"You stay out of her closet," I command, and follow Wavonne up the steps. "Raynell!" I call again, and begin to wonder if maybe she isn't hiding from us . . . maybe she isn't well from all her drinking last night and is still passed out.

"Yo! Raynell! Show your tired ass."

"Wavonne!"

"What?"

"Take it down a notch. You're not helping," I scold. "Let's look down there."

We walk down a long hall past a large bathroom and what appear to be a few guest rooms. When we reach the doorway at the end of the hall, we see what is obviously the master bedroom. It's a cavernous space with a long row of picture windows that frame a seating area in front of a fire place. A large flat-screen TV hangs on the wall across from a king-size canopy bed.

I look at the disheveled linens on the bed. "Where is she?"

"I don't know, but I bet that's the closet." Wavonne points to a pair of double doors on the other side of the bed. Her eyes are fixed straight ahead like a fox at the entrance to a hen house.

"I think I'd better call Christy, and see if she reached Raynell earlier." I pull out my phone as Wavonne creeps toward the closet. "You stay out of there," I say, but before I have a chance to make my call, Wavonne has already opened the doors to the Holy Land.

"This must be what heaven's like," I hear Wavonne say as she steps inside the closet.

Curiosity gets the best of me, and I can't help but follow behind her into the expansive space, which is literally bigger than my living room. More clothes than any one person should own hang from two sets of rods on both sides of us—one close to the ceiling and one about midway down the wall. In front of us is a complex shelving system adorned with a selection of shoes that could easily rival the footwear department at Macy's. There's even a ladder that runs along a track surrounding the entire room to reach the purses displayed on the highest shelves. In the middle of the room is a large dresser with cabinets and drawers on both sides.

"Leave it alone," I call to Wavonne as she looks at the dresser.

I watch as she slowly walks alongside the clothes, looking closely at certain pieces and trying to read the labels if there's enough space between garments to see them. I wonder if she's aware that her mouth is hanging open. I'm not a fashionista by any means, but even I'm awestruck by the sheer volume of meticulously organized high-priced clothing. I hate to admit it, but for a moment, I think we both forget that we were even looking for Raynell.

"I bet there's a few hundred thousand bucks worth of clothes and shoes in here." Wavonne approaches the dozens of shoes stored along the back wall. "Prada, Louboutin, Fendi, Valentino," she calls out as she peruses the designer footwear. "Oh my God, Halia! I saw these Manolos on the Neiman Marcus Web site for more than two thousand dollars!"

"Okay, Wavonne. I think we've had enough. I'm not sure where Raynell is, but we don't have any business poking around her closet. Come on."

I start to walk out of the closet, and Wavonne reluctantly follows. "So now what?"

"I guess we go. I'll give Christy a call on the way to Sweet Tea and set up a time to get the check, assuming they're still some funds in the reunion committee's account."

We're about to make our way out of the bedroom when Wavonne spies another door on the other side of the room.

"You think that's Terrence's closet?" she asks as she steps toward the door.

"I don't know. It doesn't matter. No more closet snooping, Wavonne. Let's go," I say, but Wavonne, being Wavonne, grasps the doorknob anyway.

"Oh hail no!" I hear her shriek when she opens the door.

"What?" I scurry in her direction and look over her shoulder while she stands frozen in place. The door doesn't lead to Terrence's closet. It leads to the bathroom—there's a long deep tub, a pristine glass-enclosed shower, two gleaming white pedestal sinks presiding over a polished marble tile floor—a polished marble tile floor that would be lovely . . . just lovely, if it wasn't for the fact that Raynell is laying facedown on it with a pool of blood around her head.

CHAPTER 21

"Oh *hail* no!"

"You said that already," I retort, slightly dazed as my eyes take in the sight before us: Raynell, in nothing but a nightshirt, flat on the floor. A shallow puddle of red surrounds her head and, at some point, streamed into the grout lines between the marble tiles.

"And I'll say it again. Oh *HAIL* NO!!!"

I try to remain calm while I bypass Wavonne. I carefully step around the blood, and lower myself to pick up Raynell's hand. I feel her wrist. "There's no pulse. She's dead."

I gently lay her hand back on the floor and stand up.

"Not again." The words involuntarily come from my lips as I try to make sense of what lays before us. This is not the first dead body Wavonne and I have stumbled upon. Last year, when we came across the deceased body of one of my restaurant investors (a bit of a shady fellow) in the kitchen of Sweet Tea after closing, I made the big . . . HUGE mistake of not calling the police for fear of the effect such awful publicity would have on my restaurant. Wavonne and I dragged his body out of Sweet Tea in hopes of keeping my restaurant out of the news surrounding a murder investigation. The whole thing turned into a huge disaster with Wavonne almost going to jail. I'm *not* making that blunder again.

I grab my phone and dial 911. "I need the police. I've found a dead body."

The operator asks a few questions and connects me with the police. I provide the few details that I can, and the officer on the line advises us to stay put and not touch anything until the authorities arrive.

When I disconnect from the call, I maneuver myself around Raynell's body and cautiously step out of the bathroom. I stand next to Wavonne just outside the door. We both can't do anything but stare. As we take in the dastardly scene I oddly begin to notice the sound of birds chirping outside. It's already pretty hot even though it's still morning, but there is a light breeze coming through the open window in the bathroom, and the morning sunshine is cascading through a skylight in the ceiling. I can't help but notice how Raynell, lying lifeless on the floor, is such a sharp contrast to the beautiful day outside.

"Standing here staring at her is not going to bring her back to life." I lightly pull Wavonne by the shoulders a few steps back from the bathroom door.

"What do you think happened?" Wavonne asks.

"I don't know. Maybe she fell. She was really drunk when she left the reunion."

"Or maybe someone pushed her."

"Maybe."

"So what are we supposed to do now?"

"I don't know," I reply. "The officer on the phone said not to touch anything, so I guess we should just stay put."

Wavonne and I do just that for about five minutes. We are hovering next to the bathroom door when we hear a loud knock on the door downstairs.

"Prince George's County Police," I hear a male voice call up the steps.

"We're up here."

Wavonne and I hurry out of the bedroom and down the hall. We meet the officer at the top of the steps.

"She's in the master bedroom . . . the bathroom, actually."

"And you are?" the policeman asks.

"Halia. I'm Halia Watkins, and this is my cousin, Wavonne Hix. We came by to pick up a check from Raynell. When she didn't answer the door we became concerned."

"How did you get in?" he asks as the three of us quickly walk down the hall.

"The door was unlocked. We let ourselves in."

"You're friends of the deceased?"

"Yes . . . well, no . . . sort of. I went to high school with her. We planned our reunion together. It was last night. I catered the event, and Raynell was supposed to have a check for me this morning."

"Fine, fine," the officer says as we reach the bathroom.

He looks at Raynell and back at Wavonne and me. "Have you touched anything?"

"Aren't you going to confirm she's dead?"

"Don't need to. See how her feet are sort of a bluish brown color? That's blood pooling. She's dead." He says this like it's just another day at the office. I guess for him, maybe it is.

"Did you touch anything?" he asks again.

"No . . . well, the door handle to let ourselves in. Maybe the banister on the stairway."

"I opened the bathroom door," Wavonne says.

"And we opened the closet door over there when we were looking for Raynell . . . and I felt her wrist to check for a pulse. I think that's it."

"Have you seen anything suspicious or out of the ordinary since you arrived?"

I look at Raynell's dead body and then narrow my eyebrows at him.

"Other than the deceased, that is."

"No. Nothing that I can think of."

"You think she fell? Or did someone whack her?" Wavonne asks. "Girlfriend was not the most popular sista in PG County."

"I have no idea, but a crime scene team is on the way. For now, I think it's best if you ladies step outside until we get a formal statement from you."

He starts talking into his walkie-talkie, and Wavonne and I do as we are told and leave the bedroom. But before we make it out of the house, the homicide team arrives, and a small group of people walk past us on the stairs. They have their hands full with cameras and cases and plastic bags . . . and pay us zero attention.

"You!?" I hear from a male voice as Wavonne and I step outside the front door.

"Detective Hutchins. We meet again."

Detective Hutchins and I have a wee bit of a history. He was the homicide detective on the case that involved the first dead body Wavonne and I had the pleasure of stumbling upon. He mostly regarded me as a pest during that investigation . . . at least until I ultimately solved the case and identified the murderer.

"What are you doing here?"

"Wavonne and I found Raynell's body. We came by to collect payment for a catering job. When she didn't answer, we let ourselves in and found her in the bathroom. I—"

He cuts me off. "I'll have an officer collect a statement from you. Please wait out here."

With that he enters the house and leaves Wavonne and me to stand outside until someone sees fit to speak to us. I call Laura while we wait and, without giving any details, I tell her that Wavonne and I are delayed and ask if she can go into the restaurant and cover for me. She agrees even though I had promised her the morning off, which is fortunate considering nearly an hour and a half passes before the same officer who first came to the house comes outside and officially interviews us. By this time, Wavonne and I are misty from the heat, which has probably gone up ten degrees or so from when we first got here.

We go over our story again, give him details about last night including Raynell's condition when we last saw her alive at the hotel. I tell him that it's my understanding that her husband is at a church retreat in Williamsburg, so she was likely home alone last night. He asks a few more questions about the reunion and requests Christy's contact information as we told him that she drove Raynell home.

"Thank you for your cooperation. You're free to leave," he says when he's done questioning us.

I feel like saying, "What if I don't want to leave?" but I refrain. Instead I nod and motion for Wavonne to follow me as I walk toward the van.

"We're leaving?" she asks.

"Of course not," I say. "Has he gone back inside yet?"

Wavonne looks over her shoulder. "Uh-huh."

"Good." I stop walking. "We'll wait here until Detective Hutchins comes out."

"Can we wait in the van with the air conditioning on?" Wavonne wipes her brow with the top of her hand. "Much longer in this heat, and this wig's comin' off . . . and don't nobody need to see that."

"Fine." I hand her the keys. "Go wait in the van."

While Wavonne heads off to sit in the air conditioning, it occurs to me that perhaps I should call Terrence or maybe Alvetta, and she can break the news of Raynell's death to him.

I fumble for my phone in my pocket and tap the screen a

few times. "Hey, Alvetta. It's Halia," I say after lifting the phone to my ear.

"Hi, Halia. How are you? Fun night last night. The food was just—"

"Alvetta," I interrupt her. "Sweetie, I have some bad news."

There's silence on the other end of the phone.

"It's about Raynell."

"What? What is it?"

"Gosh. Now I'm thinking I shouldn't have called you. I should deliver the news in person."

"News? What news? Just tell me."

"Alvetta." I take a deep breath. "Raynell . . . Raynell appears to have had a fall or something. It looks like she hit her head on the bathroom sink or the side of the tub . . . and . . . well . . . well, she didn't survive the fall."

"She's dead?"

I pause before responding. "Yes."

"Oh my God!"

"I'm so sorry."

I go into the whole story about why we came over, how we found her, and explain that the police are currently in the house, but I'm not sure she's really hearing any of it.

"Alvetta, are you at home?"

"Yes."

"I'll be leaving here shortly. Why don't you give me your address, and Wavonne and I will stop by and check on you. Do you want me to call Terrence, or would you rather do that? Or we could let the police make the call."

"No, no. He shouldn't hear it from the police. I will tell him."

Wishing I had just gone to see Alvetta in person to begin with, I try to wrap up the call as delicately as I can and remind her that we'll be over shortly.

I'm about to end the waiting game for Detective Hutchins

and drive over to Alvetta's when he finally emerges from the house.

"What are you still doing here? Officer Taylor told me he asked you to leave."

"No. He said we were 'free to leave.'"

Detective Hutchins sighs.

"What did you find out? Do you think it was just an accident?"

"I'm sorry. I should be sharing details of a crime scene investigation with you *because?*"

"Because you know I won't leave until you do. Look, she was a friend," I lie. "And I'm the one who found her. Can't you just give me an idea of your initial thoughts?"

Another sigh. "It appears that she fell. You and your cousin both indicated that she was extremely inebriated last night. In fact," he says, opening a folder in his hand and looking at a piece of paper, "according to the statement by your cousin, and I quote, 'She was straight-up crunked out her mind when she left the party.' There are no signs of forced entry or that she struggled with an attacker. We'll need her husband to confirm nothing is missing, but we didn't find any indication of robbery, either. It's logical to deduce that she slipped in the bathroom and hit her head on the edge of the tub. If she did survive the fall, she probably was unable to get up or call for help. She likely either died from the impact or blood loss."

"Well, an autopsy certainly needs to be done to confirm the cause of death."

"*Really?* Thanks for the tip, Ms. Watkins. We never would have thought of that."

I roll my eyes.

"Of course there will be an autopsy, but it may be awhile. The OCME is backed up and cases way more suspicious than this will take precedence."

"OCME?"

"Have I stumped the all-knowing Detective Halia Watkins?" he asks with a snarky look on his face. "Office of the Chief Medical Examiner."

"Oh. Good to know," I say. "I assumed her husband has not been notified. I've asked a good friend of both Raynell and her husband to break the news to him."

"That's fine."

"Okay. Thank you, Detective Hutchins. I guess I'll be on my way."

I turn away from the house and join Wavonne in the car. The cool air emitting from the vents in the dashboard is a welcome relief from the heat. I'm about to put the van in drive when we catch sight of Raynell's body concealed in a gray plastic bag being wheeled out toward a white van.

"Guess that's the last we'll see of Raynell Rollins," Wavonne says.

"I guess so."

"Can't say I liked her much, but I will say this: the sista did have some good hair."

"Well, I'm glad you thought of something positive to say about her," I reply as I put the car in drive and head to Alvetta's home.

CHAPTER 22

"I can't believe she's dead," I say to Wavonne as we veer off the highway toward National Harbor, a haughty waterfront development on the Potomac River.

"I guess the phrase 'too mean to die' don't apply in her case."

"Detective Hutchins seems to think it was just an accident—that she fell over drunk."

"Detective Hutchins didn't know her, and how salty she was . . . and how many people hated her."

"The woman is dead, Wavonne. No need for name-calling."

"Just speakin' the truth, Halia."

"Maybe so . . . maybe so," I say. "Now, what's the building number again?" I ask as I maneuver the van down Waterfront Street and take in all the hotels, glitzy shops, and restaurants.

"Turn here. It's on American Way."

I make a left, and we head up a hill.

"There it is." Wavonne points to a swanky building about twelve stories tall. The awning over the main entrance reads "The Echelon."

Alvetta mentioned that we could park in the garage and

get a visitors' pass from the front desk, but I see an open spot on the street and decide to grab it instead. I pay the meter and Wavonne and I walk toward the building. When we reach the entrance, I punch in a code that Alvetta gave us and hear a buzzing sound as the door unlocks.

"This looks more like a Ritz Carlton than an apartment building," I say to Wavonne as we step into the cool air and breathe in the scent of a mammoth display of fresh flowers on an elegant round table in front of the doorway. We step across the lightly hued bamboo floors and find that not only is there a front desk with a clerk clicking away on his computer, but, on the other side of the lobby, is a sharply dressed young lady sitting behind a wraparound counter with the word "Concierge" adorned across the front panel in gold letters.

"Classy." Wavonne takes note of the sleek furnishings and modern light fixtures on our way to the elevators.

"We in the wrong bidness, Halia. You should have opened a church instead of a restaurant."

I laugh. "It quite possibly would have been more profitable . . . and maybe less work."

We step into the elevator and Wavonne presses the PH button.

"I was thinkin' I needed to land me a pro football playa, but maybe what I really need is a minister."

I'm considering, once again, reminding her that she could actually try to earn her own money as we ride to the top floor of the building, but decide not to bother.

When the elevator doors open, Wavonne and I make our way to Alvetta's unit, and knock on the door.

"Hello," I say when she opens the door. "I'm so sorry."

"Thank you." She motions for us to come in.

For a moment the three of us just stand there in her softly lit foyer. I'm unsure of what else to say, and Alvetta doesn't seem to quite have it together. She's in a robe, and, while her eyes are looking at Wavonne and me, I can tell that her thoughts are elsewhere.

"I'm sorry," she eventually says. "Please. Let's go into the living room."

We follow her into an expansive living room decorated with contemporary furnishings, and Alvetta sits down on a long sofa.

"Talk about a 'deluxe apartment in the sky,' " Wavonne says under her breath as we lower ourselves into a pair of lounge chairs with polished stainless steel frames.

"That's a lovely view." I look past the sofa through the glass doors that lead to a terrace overlooking the Potomac River.

"It is. I was sitting out there having my coffee when you called . . . enjoying a rare Sunday morning at home with Michael out of town." Alvetta pauses for a moment. "It's really true? Raynell is really . . ."

"I'm afraid so. It looks like she slipped in the bathroom and hit her head."

"I just can't even wrap my head around it." Alvetta's looking at her lap. I can see her mouth begin to quiver as she tries to keep from crying. "She was just . . . last night . . . I just saw her last night. . . ."

Her attempt at holding back tears is unsuccessful.

"I know. I know. We are all shocked." I join her on the sofa and put my arm around her.

"I don't know what I'll do without her. We've been best friends for more than twenty years."

I keep a hold on her and just let her cry while Wavonne grabs a box of tissues from an end table and brings it to Alvetta.

"I wish I knew what to say, but . . ." I struggle to find words. "Have you reached Terrence?"

"Yes. Well . . . no . . . I talked to Michael, actually. He said he would break the news to Terrence. They should both be home shortly." She wipes her eyes with a tissue and tries to pull herself together. "Are the police sure it was an accident?"

"They seemed pretty sure. There was no sign of forced entry or struggle . . . or anything like that."

Alvetta wipes her eyes a second time and blows her nose. "I don't know . . . I wonder. I love . . . *loved* Raynell like a sister, but even I can admit that she had a mean streak. There's no shortage of people who might want her dead. Raynell probably had some sort of high school run-in with half the people at that reunion. Remember she was supposed to share a locker with Gina Holmes and threw her books all over the hallway. And how she thought it was funny to steal other girls' towels when they were in the shower so they had nothing to dry off with. And what she did to Kimberly Butler with the Nair. God bless Raynell, but she really could be horrible. And, back then, I guess I wasn't much better. I stood right along side her malicious reign. I think half the reason I stayed friends with her was because I feared the alternative."

"I don't dispute that she could be really awful. But do you really think anyone would still hold that much of a grudge? That they would kill her?"

"If you axe me," Wavonne says, "from what I've heard, she makes the chicks in that white teen movie about the 'mean girls' seem like Girl Scouts."

"She was rough in high school."

"She wasn't exactly Mary Freakin' Poppins as an adult, either."

"Wavonne, the woman is dead. Show some respect," I reprimand.

"She's right," Alvetta says. "Maybe she wasn't as mean as she was in high school, but girlfriend was still a little rough around the edges."

"A *little?*"

I give Wavonne a look.

"I'm just callin 'em like I see 'em, Halia. Like Alvetta said, there are probably people out there who wouldn't mind seein' her dead."

"It seems there're almost too many people to count," I say. "Gina Holmes, Kimberly Butler . . . every girl she ever stole a towel from."

"Even Gregory Simms might have a motive," Alvetta says.

"Gregory?" I ask. "What do you mean? Wasn't he just working with Raynell to find a local property for his restaurant?"

"Yes, but him seeking out Raynell to work as his real estate agent always seemed odd to me . . . you know . . . given their history."

"What history?"

"Come to think of it, I guess few people knew, but Raynell and Gregory dated senior year."

"No way."

"Yes. Of course, in true Raynell-fashion, the whole thing was quite nefarious. Raynell was only using him."

"For what?"

"Haters can say what they want about Raynell, but she was a smart cookie with enough ambition for two people, which is why she was such a good real estate agent. She was very organized, detail oriented, and could market a house just shy of being condemned as 'a quaint fixer-upper with loads of potential.' But one thing she never could master was math . . . numbers, figures—she had absolutely no aptitude for them."

"And Gregory led the math team to a state championship," I say.

"Exactly. Raynell had the extracurriculars and the grades in everything but her math classes to get into the best colleges . . . and she could achieve a tidy score on the verbal portion of the

SATs, but her math score was dismal. That's where Gregory came in."

"I don't remember them being a thing."

"No. You wouldn't. Raynell put the moves on him, and they started dating, but Raynell insisted they keep it on the down low. There was no way she was going to let the entire school know she was dating a math geek. At first she only got him to tutor her, but eventually she convinced him to let her cheat off him in calculus. And I don't know how, but somehow Raynell managed to engineer a swap when they took the SATs and Gregory completed her test, sacrificing his own score."

"Seriously?"

"Yep. Leave it to Raynell. Like I said, she was no dummy and could come up with schemes that would make a professional con artist jealous. She strung poor Gregory along for several months, but after he tutored her, let her cheat off him, and took the SATs for her, he was of no use to her anymore. By the spring, she'd gotten her college acceptance letters, and there was no way she was going to the high school social event of the year with a nerd. She dumped him a few weeks before prom, forbade him to tell anyone about their relationship, and managed to snag Trey Lotti as her prom date."

"I can't believe he never told me. Gregory and I were friends. We were on the debate team together. I never knew he had a thing going with Raynell. I actually ended up going to prom with him. I had no idea I was a rebound date."

"He was probably afraid to tell anyone," Alvetta says. "After the way Raynell treated him, it's odd that he reached out to her for help with his real estate aspirations. Although, maybe she reached out to him if she got word he was looking for space in the area and convinced him to come on board with her. Raynell is . . . was a master manipulator. She was able to cast a spell over him in high school. Maybe she did it again."

"Maybe," I say. "Who knows what Gregory's motives were, but I knew him pretty well in high school, and I just can't imagine he could kill someone—even Raynell."

"What about that Kimberly chick?" Wavonne asks. "We saw her eyes shootin' daggers at Raynell all night."

"Really?" Alvetta asks.

"Yes," I confirm. "She was visibly jarred when she caught sight of Raynell at the reunion. And rightfully so, given how terrible Raynell was to her. But I suspect Kimberly got her revenge by just showing up and looking fabulous."

Alvetta takes a breath. "All this speculation is probably silly. It sounds like it was an accident. We all saw how drunk she was when Christy drove her home."

At the mention of her name, I'm about to ask Alvetta if she is aware of any motive Christy would have for killing Raynell when we hear some clatter at the front door and see Michael walk into the apartment.

Alvetta gets up from the sofa to greet him, and he gives her a hug. "I'm so sorry," he says. "I still can't believe it."

"I know. I know," Alvetta responds. "How is Terrence doing?"

"I think he's mostly in shock. I was already on my way home when you called, so I had to tell him over the phone. It should have been done in person, but I wanted to tell him before the police did."

"Is he back in town? Should we go over and stay with him?"

"No. He drove on to Roanoke to tell Raynell's parents in person. He may stay there tonight or come back later this evening," Michael says, and just now seems to take note of Wavonne and me. "Hello."

"Hi, Michael," I say. "We just stopped by to check on Alvetta. We'll get going now that you're here."

"Thank you. I'm sorry you had to . . . to find her . . . well, you know."

"Yes. I'm sorry, too." I offer a polite smile. "Come on, Wavonne. Let's go and give them some privacy."

We hug both of them and then head toward the door.

"So sad," I say to Wavonne once we're out in the hall. "I'm glad Michael is there with her."

Wavonne pushes the button for the elevator. "So what do you think, Sherlock? You think Raynell buyin' the farm was an accident?"

"I don't know. It seems like it probably was, but if she were a nicer person, I'd be more confident that no foul play was involved. I know better than to not call the police immediately after finding a dead body, but I wish I had taken some time to look around the Rollinses' house before they got there, and see if anything seemed out of sorts. I had been to the house once before. I may have been able to tell if anything was out of place. Although I guess Terrence can do that when he gets home."

"Terrence? Terrence is a *man*, Halia. Men don't notice anything unless it involves a football or a pair of titties."

I snicker. "That's not too far from the truth, Wavonne. Maybe we could swing by the house before going back to Sweet Tea. The cops may still be there. Maybe we can just say we stopped by to see if they needed anymore information from us, and then I can try to poke around a bit." I look at my watch. "Actually, by the time we get back over there they will have probably gone. They were wheeling Raynell's body out of the house when we left earlier. I'm guessing they were probably about finished and locked the house. We won't be able to get in."

We step into the elevator.

"Promise you won't get mad?" Wavonne asks as the doors close.

"Mad about what?"

Wavonne raises her eyebrows at me.

"*What?* What did you do, *Wavonne?* Why do you look like a puppy that's just chewed up a pair of designer shoes?"

"If the cops are gone I might be able to help with the house being locked thing."

"How so?"

"You won't get mad?"

I take a deep breath. "No, Wavonne, I won't get mad."

"Well . . . I kinda helped myself to this on the way out." She reaches into the side pocket of her purse.

"Wavonne!" I say as she pulls out a gaudy Michael Kors keychain.

CHAPTER 23

"You took her keys?!"

"You said you wouldn't get mad."

I close my eyes for a second and take a deep breath. "Why . . . *why* did you take her keys, Wavonne?"

"I thought . . . I thought maybe I could go back at some point . . . I mean, she's got no use for all those fancy shoes and handbags."

"You were going to break into her house and steal her shoes and purses?!"

"I don't know if I would have actually done it, Halia. I guess I just wanted the option. And, we've had this discussion before. She's *dead*. It ain't stealin' if she's dead. She's got no use for any of that stuff."

"Unbelievable!"

"She just had such nice things, Halia. I'm so *over* cheap stuff—dresses that rip when I bend over. I'm tired of Gussini and Plato's Closet and Ross Dress for Freakin' Less . . . and being the only black girl shoppin' at Latina Fashion."

"Then I suggest you save up some money so you can *buy,* rather than *steal,* some nice clothes."

"I wasn't goin to take any *clothes* . . . I couldn't fit all *this* into those outfits made for her short weeble-wobble body. But what's the harm in helping myself to a pair of Ferragamo shoes . . . or maybe a Michael Kors bag?"

"I *know* . . . let's just show up with a moving van and help ourselves to the whole lot . . . the shoes, the purses, the belts, her jewelry . . . hell, let's take the furniture . . . maybe the food from the kitchen, too. She's dead. What does she need with any of it?"

"All right, all right . . . pump your brakes, Halia. I was just talkin' about an item or two, and I probably wasn't goin' to do it anyway."

"Just give me those." I grab the keys from Wavonne.

"What are you goin' to do with them?"

"I don't know." I hesitate for a moment. "I guess we should take them back . . . put them back where you found them. And if we take a moment to look around while we're there, then so be it. Michael said Terrence wouldn't be back anytime soon, so if we're going to do it, we better do it now."

We step out of the elevator, and I call Laura at Sweet Tea to see how things are going and let her know that Wavonne and I will be further delayed. Laura assures me that she has things under control, so Wavonne and I return to my van and head back over to Raynell's.

"Here." I hand Wavonne the keychain and continue to drive while digging through my purse with one hand for a Wet-Nap and a tissue. I eventually find both and hand them to Wavonne. "Hold them with the tissue and wipe them down to get any fingerprints off of them."

I'm hoping that, just maybe, the police are still there when we reach the house, so we can walk in without having to use the key, make up some excuse as to why we came back, and discreetly place the keys back on the console. Maybe we can just say we came back to tell them that we have seen Alvetta and Michael and wanted to let them know that Terrence was en route to inform Raynell's parents of her death.

Regrettably, we see no sign of the police when we arrive.

"What are you goin' to do?" Wavonne asks as we sit in the van in front of Raynell's house.

"I don't know. I thought the cops might still be here. I can't believe the place isn't even sealed off with police tape or something. Looking at the house, you wouldn't know anything out of the ordinary had just happened there."

"So we go home? Back to the restaurant?"

I grasp the steering wheel tightly while I think for a moment. "I'd really like to get in there for just a few minutes to look around. Detective Hutchins seemed to have all but determined that Raynell's death was an accident. If the police were convinced that there was nothing dubious about her death, they may not have conducted a thorough search."

"So we're goin' in?"

I take my hands off the wheel and clasp them together tightly while I consider our options. Then I look around through the van windows and see if anyone is watching us. There is no one in sight. "Yes. I suppose we are."

"Fun!" Wavonne says.

I step on the gas pedal. "Let's park away from the house, so no one will see the van in case someone comes while we're still in there."

We drive a few blocks down from Raynell's house and park the van.

I've got a few boxes of latex gloves leftover from the catering job last night, so I grab one and pull out two pairs. "Put these on. We don't need to be leaving fingerprints."

We slip on the gloves, exit the van, and scurry up the sidewalk back to the Rollinses' home.

I take a last look around to make sure no one is watching. "Go ahead," I say to Wavonne. She slips a key into the dead bolt, and we hurriedly let ourselves in.

"Let's check upstairs first."

Wavonne shoves Raynell's keys in her pocket, and we climb the curved staircase to the second floor and walk down the hall to the master bedroom.

"You need to return those keys when we come back downstairs," I say as we reach the top of the steps. "Now, you stay out of that closet!"

"Yeah, yeah."

"It's all cleaned up," I say when we reach the doorway to the bathroom. "As if nothing ever happened."

"Sista-girl had no shortage of beauty supplies." Wavonne steps ahead of me into the bathroom and begins thumbing though Raynell's collection of creams and balms. "You'd think girlfriend would've looked a little less like a hedgehog with all these potions."

"Don't you stuff any of those cosmetics in your pocket!"

We continue to poke around the bathroom for a few minutes. Then we comb through the bedroom, looking through the dresser drawers and under the bed. We don't come across anything particularly suspicious, so we take a quick look in the guest bedrooms and bathrooms. I'm not sure what we are looking for, but whatever it is, we don't seem to be finding it upstairs.

"Let's check downstairs."

We descend the stairs and start our search of the lower level in a messy office off the foyer. The wraparound desk is piled high with mail and papers and various promotional materials for Raynell's real estate business. I'm about to start rifling through all the papers when we hear a knock at the front door.

"Shhh," I say to Wavonne. "Just stay here."

There's another knock and, when we still don't respond, whoever is at the door decides to let him- or herself in. We hear the doorknob turn, and then the sound of feet walking across the foyer and up the stairs.

"Let's get out of here while whoever just barged in is upstairs," I whisper to Wavonne.

I put a finger to my lips and tiptoe out of the office. Wavonne follows, and we both step lightly toward the front door. We're about halfway across the foyer when Wavonne stubs her toe on a chair along the wall. It makes a screeching sound as it scoots an inch or so across the floor. We immediately hear footsteps scurrying in the hall upstairs. Instinctively, I grab Wavonne's hand and lead her toward a side door. I quickly open it, and we dash into the garage.

"In here." I open the door of Raynell's SUV.

Wavonne follows my lead, and we climb into the Escalade and squat down out of sight.

"Who you think it is?"

"I don't know." I lift my head just enough to peer out through the side window. "But they're coming in here, whoever they are," I say as I see the knob on the door into the garage turn.

"What!?!" Wavonne says. "Suppose whoever it is killed Raynell?" She reaches up and pushes the garage opener, and then presses the ignition button.

Thanks to Raynell's key fob still being in Wavonne's pocket, the Escalade comes to life, and I watch as Wavonne uses the rear view cam to back the vehicle out of the driveway.

"What are you doing!?"

"Whoever it is pokin' around this house may have offed Raynell. They ain't killing us, too."

When we reach the end of the driveway and pull out onto the street, Wavonne sits upright in the seat and puts the car in drive. Just before she steps on the gas, I peek out through the window and see a woman hastily stick her head through the side door leading into the garage. It was very quick, but from the end of the driveway there's no mistaking who it is.

What is Kimberly Butler doing nosing around Raynell's house the very day Raynell was found dead? I think to myself as Wavonne stomps on the accelerator, and we hightail it out of Raynell's neighborhood toward the main road.

CHAPTER 24

"Have you lost your mind?!" I yell at Wavonne as she turns Raynell's Escalade onto the main road.

"Were we supposed to stay there and end up worm food like Raynell?"

I inhale deeply and try to collect myself. "I don't know" is the best response I can come up with.

I turn and look out the back window to make sure no one is following us. "It's bad enough we let ourselves into Raynell's house, but now we've taken her car. A judge may label such things 'breaking and entering' and 'grand theft auto.' "

"We had a key to the house, and we're only *borrowin'* the car. What choice did we have, Halia? God knows who was in the house and what weapon they had on them," Wavonne shoots back. "Who do you think it was?"

"I *know* who it was. I saw her stick her head out the door to get a peek at us."

"Who?"

"Kimberly Butler."

"Really? What do you think she was up to?"

"I don't know, but it's very suspicious."

"Sure is. Ain't no reason she should be snoopin' around a dead woman's house." Wavonne adjusts herself into a more comfortable position in the driver's seat. "Damn, this thing handles like a dream . . . rides so smooth. We need to ditch that raggedy-ass van of yours and get one of these babies, Halia."

"The car we need to ditch, Wavonne, is this one."

"Aw, let me drive it a bit longer. I ain't never driven a Cadde-lac before. I feel like one of those hookers on the *Real Housewives of Atlanta*. I wish it was winter so I could try out these heated seats." Wavonne looks at all the buttons on the control panel. "Oh hell, let's turn them on anyway . . . heat up my bootie."

As soon as Wavonne flicks the seat warmer switch the Escalade starts to sputter.

"What did you do?!"

"Nothin'. I just turned the tushie warmer on. What's all that noise?"

The sputter turns into more of a clanking sound. Then there's a loud bang before the SUV loses power and abruptly cuts off.

Wavonne looks at the dashboard. "You got to be freakin kiddin' me! It's outta gas!"

Wavonne pulls the coasting vehicle over to the shoulder.

I lean over and see that the gas gauge is, in fact, on empty.

"Get out!" I holler. "Let's get out now before someone offers to help us."

"Where do you think we are?" Wavonne asks. "Freakin' Disneyland or somethin'? What's makes you think any one of these fools whizzin' by is gonna stop and help us . . . unless I get out and show some cleavage."

"Just get out before someone sees us, and we're charged with stealing Raynell's car."

Wavonne and I hurriedly exit the Escalade and begin walking along the side of the road. I take a quick look back, and I'm glad to be reminded that the windows are heavily tinted, so while we saw Kimberly, she didn't see us.

"Hurry up," I say to Wavonne. "Let's go to that shopping center up ahead. We'll blend in with the customers there and call Momma to come get us."

"What are the two of you up to?" Momma asks as we get in her car.

"Nothing, Momma. We met up with Nicole to go shopping, and she had an emergency and had to leave. She didn't have time to take us back to the van."

"You, who hates to shop and has barely ever left the restaurant during the brunch rush, randomly decided to go shopping on a Sunday afternoon?" Momma looks up through the windshield at the signs on the façade of the "well past its prime" shopping center. "And at which one of these *destination* stores did you and Nicole specifically get together to go shopping? The Walgreens? The YMCA? The Afghan kebab place?"

Damn, I really should have thought through this whole shopping-with-Nicole thing a bit more.

"We were just makin' a pit stop, Aunt Celia," Wavonne calls from the backseat. "We were on our way to Pentagon City."

Momma turns and looks at Wavonne and then at me. She holds her gaze on me just long enough to let me know she doesn't believe that story, either. "I'll ask again. What are you girls up to?"

"Honestly, Momma, it's just better if you don't know," I say, hoping she will let it go.

"Make a left." I direct Momma out of the parking lot. "The van's in Raynell's . . . I mean Nicole's neighborhood. It's about a mile up the road."

"You girls have me worried. Now, tell me what's going on."

I really don't want to get into Raynell's death with Momma,

and I certainly don't want to tell her that Wavonne and I had to abandon an Escalade we just stole out of her garage, so I do the one thing that I know will refocus her attention and distract her from wanting to know why Wavonne and I need a ride back to my van.

"Was that my phone?" I ask and pull it from my purse. "Another text from Gregory," I lie.

"Gregory?!" Momma turns toward me with excited eyes. "What did he say?"

"He's just wondering when's a good time for us to get together."

"Did you say 'about twenty years ago?'" Wavonne calls from the backseat.

Momma laughs.

"No. I need to look at the schedule at Sweet Tea and confirm I can sneak away tomorrow night."

"Well, for Christ's sake, get back to him soon. You said he's only in town for a little while."

"Yes, Momma," I say. "Make a left up there."

Mom turns into Raynell's neighborhood, and I direct her to the van.

"Thanks, Momma."

Wavonne and I quickly step out of the car before she has a chance to ask anymore questions about our misadventures.

"Why don't you drive?" I say to Wavonne. "I want to look through the mail I grabbed from Raynell's office."

We hop in the van, and on the way to Sweet Tea I start sorting through the stack of envelopes.

"What do you think you're gonna find in there?" Wavonne asks.

"Who knows? Maybe a phone bill that notes some incriminating conversations or something like that."

"Like late-night phone calls between Raynell and Gregory?" Wavonne takes her eyes off the road for a moment and looks at me. "Are you tryin' to find a motive for Raynell's murder or just tryin' to figure out if Raynell had a thing goin' with your new man?"

"Gregory is hardly my new man."

I continue to riffle through Raynell's papers—there's an electric bill, a Bed Bath & Beyond coupon, some credit card promotions, another Bed Bath & Beyond coupon, some political advertisement, another Bed Bath & Beyond coupon, some grocery store circulars . . . junk mail, junk mail, junk mail. There doesn't appear to be anything in the pile that's going to yield any clues until I come across a plain white envelope. It's not sealed, so I open it easily and pull out a handwritten note.

"Get this." I start reading aloud. " 'Hey, good-lookin'. Anxiously awaiting our next encounter when I get to wrap my arms around you and kiss your sweet lips.' It's signed *M*."

"Ooh . . . Raynell's husband's name don't begin with no *M*," Wavonne says. "That bougie ho was gettin' some bump and grind on the side."

"Sure seems like it."

"It's not signed *G*. So at least you know it ain't Gregory."

"I guess."

As we pull into the parking lot in front of Sweet Tea, I take a closer look at the note and read it again. "Something about it is familiar to me," I say to Wavonne as I continue to study it.

"The note? What?"

"I'm not sure . . . it's like I've seen it before."

"Where?"

I look at the ceiling and think for a moment. "You know, I'm not sure." I fold up the paper and put it back in the envelope. "But I intend to find out."

RECIPE FROM HALIA'S KITCHEN

Halia's Double-Crust Chicken Potpie

Crust Ingredients

1½ sticks salted butter (¾ cup)
⅓ stick butter flavored vegetable shortening (⅓ cup)
½ cup water
3 cups all-purpose flour
½ teaspoon salt
2 teaspoons sugar
Pinch of baking powder

Filling Ingredients

¾ cup sliced carrots
1 cup diced red potatoes (skin on)
⅓ cup butter
1 garlic clove, minced
⅓ cup finely chopped scallions
½ teaspoon salt
½ teaspoons pepper
⅛ teaspoon ground Cayenne/red pepper
⅓ cup flour
1¾ cups chicken stock
⅔ cup whole milk
3 cups torn, cooked chicken
¾ cup frozen peas

- Preheat oven to 375 degrees Fahrenheit.

- Place butter, shortening, and water in freezer for 20 minutes prior to use.

- Cut cold butter and shortening into 1/4-inch slices.

- In food processor, pulse together flour, salt, sugar, and baking powder. Add butter and shortening. Pulse until mixture clumps into size of small peas. While continuing to pulse, slowly add water until dough begins to form a ball. Remove dough from food processor and form into two balls. Insert balls in separate plastic bags, seal, and refrigerate for 30 minutes.

- On floured work surface, roll out one ball of dough into a circle (1/8-inch thickness/11 inches in diameter). If dough sticks to surface, work a small amount of flour (a tablespoon at time) into dough and re-roll.

- Lightly flour top side of crust prior to delicately folding it in half to transfer to 9-inch pie pan. Gently unfold in pan, pressing against edges. Trim excess crust and flatten evenly on rim of pie plate. Hold a fork at a slight angle and lightly press the tines into pastry to create a "fork edge" around the rim of the crust.

- Poke holes in bottom of crust with fork, line with parchment paper, and fill with pie weights. Bake for 20 minutes. Remove parchment paper and weights and bake for another five minutes or until golden brown. Remove crust from oven and cool.

- Boil carrots and potatoes in large saucepan for 8 to 10 minutes, until crisp tender. Drain.

- In large sauce pan, heat butter over medium–high heat. Add garlic and scallions. Stir constantly until garlic and scallions are fragrant (about 1 minute). Add salt, pepper, and red pepper. Slowly add flour. Continue to stir until sauce bubbles. Add chicken stock and milk, continuing to stir until sauce thickens. Stir in chicken, peas, carrots, and potatoes. Pour mixture into cooked pie crust.

- Roll out remaining dough and place over filling. Trim edges and create a "fork edge" around rim of top crust. Cut four slits/vents into top crust. Bake for 35 minutes or until top crust is golden brown.

Eight Servings

CHAPTER 25

This morning's antics took up so much time that by the time Wavonne and I finally get to Sweet Tea the brunch rush is long over. We have only a few customers when we walk through the front door.

I see Jack Spruce, a local police officer and Sweet Tea regular, having a late lunch at a table in the corner. He has one of our summer specials on his plate—fresh corn on the cob. I buy it by the truckload from June through August. We steam it and let customers decide if they want one, some, or all of the following on it: salt, pepper, Old Bay seasoning, butter, lemon, shredded cheese, and/or spicy mayonnaise. It's hugely popular with the customers despite the price, which I set at a premium—not because the corn is expensive, but because shucking hundreds of corn cobs a day cost me a mint in labor expenses.

Wavonne and I smile and wave hello to Jack on our way to the kitchen.

"Aren't you gonna go chat with your boyfriend?" Wavonne jokes. She's convinced Jack has a crush on me, and, I'll admit, she's probably right. I'm sure he really does love the food here, and we offer free soda and coffee to all the local police officers if they feel like stopping in when they're making their rounds. But Jack comes in the most of any of them and has asked me out a time or two. I've always declined as politely as I can. I do like him as a person. He's very nice, but I guess we all know "very nice" is the kiss of death when you're talking about someone with a romantic attraction to you. He's about my age with a dark brown complexion, closely cropped black hair, and a bit more of a belly than a police officer should probably be carrying—if he ever had to chase down a reasonably fit criminal, I'm afraid I'd have to bet on the criminal. But his being overweight isn't a problem for me. It's not like I'm not carrying around my share of extra pounds as well. There's just something a little *too* nice . . . or simple . . . or easy . . . or *something* about him. Much as I'd like to be attracted to him, I'm just not. I hate to admit it, but I need a man with a bit more of an edge.

"I'm so sorry you had to come in and deal with the Sunday-morning crowd after I left you here alone last night," I say to Laura after stepping inside the kitchen.

"No worries. We were busy and short a server with Wavonne being out, but we muddled through."

"Thank you, Laura. Why don't you take the rest of the day off? I'll be here until closing."

Laura gladly agrees to leave Sweet Tea to me, and Wavonne and I go to the break room to drop off our purses. When we return to the dining room I see Tacy at a booth along the wall rolling silverware into linen napkins for the dinner service. Tacy's official title is prep cook, but he's sort of a jack-of-all-trades and just helps out with whatever requires some attention.

"Why don't you help Tacy with the silverware while it's slow?" I say to Wavonne.

Wavonne groans.

"What's with the groaning? Good Lord. I'm not asking you to mine coal in West Virginia. Come on. I'll help, too."

"What up, Tace-Man," Wavonne says when we reach the table.

"Nothing much. Trying to get the silverware done, so I can finish up the prep work in the kitchen for tonight's special."

"What's the special this evenin'?"

"Shrimp and grits."

"Ooooo, I'm gonna have me some of that," Wavonne says.

"It looked like we're almost ready with the special when I was in the kitchen with Laura a few minutes ago," I say to Tacy.

"There's still some chopping to do . . . parsley, scallions—"

"Bacon?" Wavonne asks. "I didn't hear you say nothin' about no bacon."

"The bacon has been chopped, Ms. Hix."

"Good. That's what makes it so delish."

Wavonne is at least partially right. We fry up the bacon first and then use the bacon fat to sauté the shrimp with some cream, lemon juice, fresh corn, parsley, scallions, garlic, just a touch of dry sherry, and, of course, chopped bacon. We serve the shrimp and sauce over two homemade triangle-shaped grit cakes. All the ingredients play a role in making the special so popular, but, like Wavonne said, the bacon, which I get from a local pig farmer just south of Frederick, is key—it gives the dish a different kind of richness than we would get from butter or olive oil.

"Tacy, why don't you go on back to the kitchen and finish your prep work, and Wavonne and I will take care of the flatware."

"Sure thing, Ms. Watkins."

"Why'd you send him away? Now we're gonna have to do all this ourselves." Wavonne gestures toward the basket of forks and knives on the table.

"It's not that much. And he's got work to do in the kitchen if we're going to have the shrimp and grits ready to go by dinner."

Wavonne grabs two forks and a knife and starts to wrap them in a napkin before shifting the conversation back to Raynell. "So, what do you think Kimberly was doin' at Raynell's house?"

"I wish I knew, but she must have been up to no good. Assuming Raynell was, in fact, murdered, the only reason I can come up with is that Kimberly killed her, and must have come back to try and cover her tracks."

"Too late for that considerin' the popo have already been there and canvassed the place."

"True, but she may not have known that Raynell's body had already been discovered until she got there. She could have thought she still had some time to go back and alter the crime scene. Suppose she killed Raynell in a heated moment and fled last night. Once she regained her senses this morning, she might have decided to come back and try to get rid of her fingerprints in the house . . . or maybe she was going to try and hide Raynell's body to buy some time. Who knows. Whatever the reason, the police should really know she was snooping around."

"You ain't thinkin' of tellin' them?"

"No. Of course not. We can't tell the police about Kimberly breaking into Raynell's house without telling them about *us* breaking into Raynell's house. Maybe I'll just give Kimberly a call, and see what I can find out. I'll be right back."

I get up from the table and make a run to the break room to retrieve my purse.

"What do you need your purse for?" Wavonne asks when I return to the table and sit back down.

"Kimberly gave me her contact info last night. It should be in here somewhere."

My purse tends to be packed with stuff, and I really have to dig to find Kimberly's business card. While I'm looking around in my bag past makeup and tissues and ChapStick and notepads, I come across the church bulletin from Rebirth. I thoughtlessly stuffed it in my bag after I attended the service there last weekend. Putting my hand on it sparks a memory.

"You know what?" I pull the bulletin from my purse. "I think I remember where I've seen the handwriting on the note we found in Raynell's office."

"Where?"

I unfold the bulletin and hold it up for Wavonne to see. " 'The Word,' by Pastor Michael Marshall," I say, as I once again search through my black hole of a purse to find the note I took from Raynell's desk.

"Look." I lay the letter on the table next to the church bulletin featuring Michael's handwritten weekly column. "The handwriting is an exact match."

Wavonne walks over, sits next to me, and looks at the two papers. "Ba-bam!" she says. "That ho-bag was doin' the nasty with Michael. A *minister!*"

"Not to mention her best friend's husband."

"Damn, that Raynell was gettin' busy all over PG County."

"No kidding. If she was having an affair with Michael, that opens up a whole series of motives for killing her. The affair could have gone south, and Michael wanted her dead. Alvetta may have found out that her supposed best friend was sleeping with her husband and lost it. Or Terrence could have found out and flipped out as well. The possibilities are endless."

"Yeah, but, unlike Kimberly, none of them were slinkin' around Raynell's house today."

"Good point."

Wavonne's words remind me of why I was digging through

my bag in the first place, and I continue my search for Kimberly's business card. Just as I'm pulling it out of my purse, Jack appears at the table.

"Hey, Jack. How are you today?" I ask. "Working on a Sunday?"

"Hello, ladies," he says to Wavonne and me. "Yes. I'm just finishing up lunch. Then I've got to get back out there and make my rounds. I thought I'd say hi and let you know that the fried pork chop I had for lunch was delicious as always. And that fresh corn on the cob hit the spot."

"Glad to hear it. I only use really thin chops so they fry up nice and quick and don't get too greasy."

"Is that why they come out perfect every time?"

I smile. "I guess so."

"Well, it was good to see you. I hope you have a good day."

"It can't get no worse," Wavonne says.

"Oh?"

"Let's just say it's been a long day already."

"Why?"

"One of Halia's old classmates croaked, and we were the sad suckers who found her body."

"Oh wow. I'm sorry to hear that," Jack says. "Wait. Your classmate wasn't that Rollins woman I heard some chatter about over the radio this morning, was she? The woman who was severely inebriated, slipped in the bathroom, and hit her head?"

"I'm afraid so. Although I'm not entirely sure she slipped. She had a lot of enemies, so her being *pushed* rather than *slipping* is not out of the realm of possibilities."

"Hmm," Jack says. "I know Detective Hutchins was at the scene. I'm sure he'll check out all the angles."

"I hope so."

"Well, I've got to run. Again, I'm sorry about your classmate, and what you had to go through this morning."

Jack's about to be on his way when he notices Kimberly's business card sitting on the table. "Who's that?" he asks.

"Another one of my high school classmates, Kimberly Butler."

"No kidding?" Jack picks up the card and looks at it closely. "I had an encounter with her late last night . . . early this morning really . . . about two a.m."

"Really?"

"Yes. I came across her sound asleep in her car at the Herald Shopping Center."

"The Herald Shopping Center? That's over by Raynell's neighborhood."

"I tapped on the window to see if she was okay and tell her the shopping center does not allow overnight parking or sleeping in your car on the property. It took a few hard taps to rouse her. She didn't look good. She said she wasn't feeling well and needed to pull over for a bit."

"Was she drunk?" Wavonne asks.

"No. She didn't appear well, but I wouldn't let her drive without a sobriety check. She passed a breathalyzer test and insisted that she was okay to drive home."

"That's very interesting," I say.

"How so?"

"Let's just say high school cruelties are not easily forgotten, and Raynell committed many of them against Kimberly. Isn't it a little suspicious that Kimberly was found asleep and out of sorts so close to Raynell's house the same night she died?"

"Hmmm . . . maybe."

"You'll pass this information on to Detective Hutchins?" I ask.

"Sure, sure. I'll tell him, but from what I heard coming across the radio today, all indications lead to an accidental fall that resulted in Ms. Rollins's death." Jack sets Kimberly's card back down on the table. "I really do have to run. I hope your evening is better than your morning."

"Thanks Jack."

"This is startin' to get interestin'," Wavonne says as Jack steps away from the table.

"It is." I grab my phone and start typing in Kimberly's number. "It certainly is."

CHAPTER 26

I try to sweep thoughts of Raynell from my brain as I walk into an Italian restaurant in Camp Springs. It's the day after Wavonne and I found Raynell's body, and I'm having a hard time letting go of her death and my feelings about whether it was an accident or the result of foul play.

I'm anxious to talk with Kimberly and find out what on earth she was doing prowling around at Raynell's house, so I invited her to come to Sweet Tea for lunch today, but she had already made plans. She did, however, agree to swing by the restaurant tomorrow. Until then, I'm in sort of a holding pattern with the whole thing. Given the events of late, I'm not really in the mood to go on a date, but I agreed to meet Gregory tonight nonetheless—he's in town for only a week or two, and some conversation with an old friend will do me good.

The smell of wood-fired pizza pleasantly wafts in the air as the door closes behind me. When I eat in restaurants other than my own I tend to favor ethnic establishments that offer food that's completely different from what I cook and serve all day. Now, don't get me wrong—I make some of the best food around, but sometimes a girl gets a hankering for something other than soul food. My tastes run the gamut—Italian, Greek, Chinese, Thai, Middle Eastern . . . I enjoy virtually any cuisine but Indian (not a fan of curry . . . the taste or the smell) or Ethiopian (never had it, but it looks disgusting).

The host is about to greet me when I see Gregory at a table behind him. I smile at the host and point to Gregory in an "I'm with him" fashion and make my way into the dining room.

"Hello." Gregory stands and greets me.

"Hi. Sorry I'm late. Trying to drive anywhere around D.C. this time of day is an exercise in frustration. Traffic is terrible."

"No worries. I was just answering e-mails on my phone."

"E-mails?" I inquire with a grin, eyeing his phone, which is currently lying on the table displaying an animated dragon and some colorful medieval scenery.

"Ah . . . you caught me." Gregory laughs. "Once a video game nerd. Always a video game nerd."

"Were you into video games in high school? I don't remember that."

"Into them? That's pretty much all I did outside of schoolwork. I didn't have much of a social life in those days. I spent many a Saturday night in front of Nintendo playing *The Legend of Zelda* and *Super Mario Bros.*"

"Really? I knew nothing about video games in high school . . . and I guess I know nothing about them now."

"I'll admit I still enjoy them. They help me relax."

"Hmm . . . maybe I should take up video games then. I could use some de-stressing here and there myself." I take a seat at the table, and Gregory does the same. "So, I'm guessing you've heard about Raynell?" I ask.

"I did. Word gets around fast these days. Such horrible news."

"It really is. I feel so bad for her husband and her family."

"It's just awful for her to die so young. I didn't really get the details, though. From what I know, someone found her at home . . . she'd had a bad fall or something."

"That's about all I know as well." I refrain from telling him that Wavonne and I were actually the ones who found Raynell's dead body. He doesn't appear to know, and I just don't feel like getting into all those details.

I find myself thankful when the waiter arrives at our table, giving us an excuse to cease conversation about Raynell.

"Hello. My name is Sam, and I'll be your server this evening. Can I start you off with a beverage?"

"Up for sharing a bottle of Chianti?" Gregory asks.

"Sure," I reply. "And some water as well, please," I say to the waiter.

"So, there must be something more pleasant to talk about than Raynell," Gregory says.

"Yes. There must be." Part of me would like to linger on the subject a bit longer, so I can ask him about his secret high school relationship with her and why he chose her, of all people, to help with his local real estate ambitions. But I can't begin to imagine that Gregory had anything to do with her death, so I don't really see any reason to bring it up and make him uncomfortable. Besides, Raynell has been on my mind for almost two days straight, and, quite honestly, I need a break. "So, tell me more about South Beach Burgers."

"Some people have spouses . . . children . . . pets. I have a restaurant chain. It's pretty much my entire world at the moment. It doesn't leave time for much else."

"I hear that. I only have one restaurant, and it's my world as well. But I'd be lying if I said I didn't enjoy it."

Gregory laughs. "Me too. Every day is different. I love the variety and the challenges . . . of which there are *many*."

"That's for sure. I could do without the irrational customers who want a free meal because a server messed up their drink order or brought them the wrong salad dressing . . . or the ones with substance abuse issues who pitch a fit when we cut them off at the bar . . . or the parents who think I'm supposed to magically make squash appear in my kitchen, so my already overloaded staff can stop everything to make custom zucchini fries for little Malik or Jayla instead of French fries."

"I'm sure we could trade all sorts of horror stories—the customers who use the bathroom for sexual trysts, employees showing up to work high as a kite reeking of marijuana—"

"Kitchen staff purposely messing up orders because they don't like the server who put the order in, employees with fake social security numbers, water leaks, broken equipment . . . we could go on for days."

"I'm sure we could, but overall it's a rewarding career, and it beats sitting in an office in front of a computer all day."

I agree with Gregory, and we spend the next hour trading stories over ravioli Florentina and pesto primavera. I had planned to stick with only one glass of Chianti, but I don't protest when Gregory refills my glass. I'm not much of a drinker, so two glasses of wine is enough to give me a little buzz.

By the time Sam sets down a large serving of tiramisu in the middle of us the conversation turns more personal.

"How is it you're still single?" Gregory asks as we both dip our forks into the dessert.

"I might ask you the same question."

"There have been a few relationships here and there. I had more time for that sort of thing before I opened South Beach Burgers. Now I mostly work and spend what little free time I have with good friends."

"No woman in your life? I find that hard to believe, Gregory. The girls in Florida must be all over you. Every woman at the reunion was practically tripping over each other to talk to you—like you were the last Cabbage Patch Kid at Toys 'R' Us on Christmas Eve."

Gregory laughs. "That's not true."

"Please. You had to have noticed all the attention."

"Maybe." Gregory takes another bite of the tiramisu. "But, you have to understand, Halia. All this attention from women— it's new to me. I haven't looked like this for that long. I'm sure you remember me in high school. I was definitely *not* a looker."

"Nonsense. I always thought you were handsome," I cajole, even though "handsome" isn't exactly the right word. In high school, I found Gregory "cute" in more of an endearing sort of way. He was gangly with big ears, but he was nice, and smart, and quite witty when he wasn't being shy.

"That's sweet of you to say, Halia, but we both know the truth. It wasn't until I started making some real money that I began to grow into myself. I think my success in business boosted my confidence, and women can sense that sort of thing. The financial rewards of my work also allowed for a personal trainer and a nutritionist . . . and better clothes . . ." Gregory lifts his hands behind his ears and pushes them forward. "And surgery to get these babies pinned back where they belong."

I chuckle as Gregory lets his ears fall back into place. "So you're just a different kind of handsome now."

"You sound like a politician, Halia. *You*," Gregory says, putting his fork down on the table and leaving the last bit of the dessert for me, "on the other hand, were lovely in high school and have barely changed at all."

"Now who's the politician?" I ask even though I guess I don't think I've changed that much since high school. I was a thick girl back then, and I'm still one now. And if there is one advantage of being a full-figured sister, it's that it adds some plumpness to your face and keeps away the wrinkles.

"No. I mean it." Gregory smiles and gives me a long stare, and I'm not sure if it's the wine, or fatigue after a long day, or just the fine-looking man across the table from me giving me the eye, but I'm starting to feel light-headed.

When the check arrives I grab my purse and begin to pull out my credit card, but Gregory insists on paying. I thank him for dinner, and he walks with me to my van.

"I'm really glad we had this chance to reconnect," Gregory says as I reach for my keys and hover next to the car door.

"Me too."

Gregory lingers in front of me and, suddenly, we are like two awkward teenagers trying to navigate a good-night kiss. It's actually amusing to see traces of a clumsy adolescent emanating from such a polished man. "Sorry. I'm really bad at this," he says, and we both laugh. "So what now? A kiss, a hug . . . a handshake?"

"I think I'd feel a little slighted if all I got was a handshake," I joke, and a lumbering moment or two passes before Gregory leans in and kisses me. It's not an especially long kiss, but it is a nice one. I feel myself getting light-headed again as our lips part, and I place my hand on the car to steady myself.

"I hope I can call you again before I head back to Florida."

"Sure."

"Great. I'll be in touch then. Drive safe."

"I will. See you soon."

I step inside my van and watch Gregory walk to his car. As I start the ignition I hear my phone chirp. I pull it from my purse and see a text from Wavonne.

aunt celia wants know how your date's going . . .
thinks it must be going well since you're out so late . . .

I text back.

it was okay . . . we had dinner . . . mostly talked about the restaurant business . . .
on my way home now . . .

The evening definitely went better than "okay," but if Wavonne tells Momma that Gregory and I had a great evening topped off with a good-night kiss, Momma will have me in David's Bridal first thing in the morning trying on wedding dresses and talking baby names. *No,* I think to myself. *It's much better to play it cool and not let Momma get too excited.* But as I pull out of the restaurant parking lot it occurs to me that maybe it's not Momma who I'm worried about getting too excited after a promising first date with a handsome, single, gainfully employed man. Maybe it's *me* I'm worried about getting too excited. I haven't been on a good date in a long time, but I have been on some, and, needless to say, they have not led to anything significant.

What's it matter, I think to myself. *If nothing else it was a nice evening with an old friend over some good Italian food. If it doesn't lead to anything more, that's fine.* Yep, that's what I told myself . . . now if I could just believe it, too.

CHAPTER 27

I have got to stop letting it bother me, I think to myself as I look up from some invoices I'm reviewing at the bar and see yet another customer eating my food while looking at his phone. He's by himself, shoveling my chicken croquettes in his mouth with a fork via one hand and using his other hand to scroll and intermittently type. Occasionally he grins or even chuckles as if something on the screen is amusing him.

I see this behavior all the time, and I have to fight the urge to walk over and ask him why he doesn't just down a protein shake or stop into Wendy's for some rubber chicken on a bun if he's not going to pay any attention to what he's eating anyway. Yes, I know, I make money whether customers consciously eat my food or not, but my team and I put so much thought and work into every dish that comes out of the Sweet Tea kitchen that it just pains me to see people eating our food as if it were no better than a bowl of oatmeal.

I learned many of the recipes we use at Sweet Tea through years of helping my grandmother prepare Sunday dinners, and some of them were tweaked and refined over generations. Grandmommy developed the recipe for those chicken croquettes my customer is currently shoving in his mouth with

no appreciation for the perfectly crisp coating that Grandmommy initially made with bread crumbs, but later crafted
with corn flake crumbs to improve the taste and texture. I further updated the recipe with panko breadcrumbs (I *LOVE*
panko breadcrumbs) to give them the ultimate crispness. I've
tried using a full egg yolk and egg white wash as well as an egg
white wash alone to see which one holds the coating better.
The chicken stock we use in the recipe is made in house here
at Sweet Tea. We chop fresh parsley and add a touch of lemon
juice from freshly squeezed lemons to the chicken mix before
we skillfully shape them into a traditional cone shape, affording
not only a taste that's out of this world but visual appeal as
well. Before bringing them to the table we top them with a
piping-hot stewed potato gravy, fresh black pepper, and a
sprinkle of paprika. All of this!—And, for the attention this
young man is paying to them, I might as well have thrown a
few Chicken McNuggets on a plate and slapped them down in
front of him.

Truth be told, that's not the only one reason smartphones
get under my skin. Of course, they've become a necessity of
everyday life, and even I admit I can't imagine life without
mine. But, let me tell you, they have been one of the worst
things to hit the restaurant industry in decades. It has never
been my desire to run a "turn and burn" establishment—I sin-
cerely want my customers to have a relaxed outing where they
enjoy my food and each other's company without feeling
rushed, but smartphones have redefined what constitutes a
"relaxed" evening. In the days before iPhones and Androids
we would seat customers, they would order shortly after, enjoy
some conversation and their courses . . . and then skedaddle,
allowing us to seat new customers.

Now, after customers are seated, they might spend several
minutes on their phone before even opening the menu, then
take photos of themselves and their companions, and of course

take photos of their food, which they then take the time to post to Facebook and Instagram. And when they're finished eating, these days, patrons tend to linger for inappropriate amounts of time just surfing on their phones, taking up valuable restaurant real estate, and costing me money. Over the years, we've learned to manage these customers and, if they linger for an extra lengthy spell following payment of their check, we'll generally approach the table and ask if there is anything else we can get for them. Fortunately, they typically take the polite hint and head on their way.

I remind myself once again to not let the man on his phone bother me. I'm about to return my attention to the invoices when I see Kimberly speaking with Saundra at the hostess stand. When we chatted on Sunday I asked if she would consider swinging by Sweet Tea to discuss commissioning some artwork for the restaurant. I only occasionally change up the artwork I have displayed in Sweet Tea as I'd never part with the family picnic mural I had painted along one wall when we first opened, and I've gotten attached to the old photos of church ladies preparing Sunday buffets we have hanging throughout the space. But I do switch out a piece or two here and there, and interest in her art was as good an excuse as any to meet with Kimberly and pump her for information.

I hop off the stool and walk over to greet her.

"Kimberly. So good to see you again."

"Yes. You too. I'm glad to have a chance to finally check out your restaurant. I don't come back to the area very often, so I've never had the opportunity before."

I wait to see if she's going to mention anything about Raynell's death. When she doesn't, I decide not to broach the subject just yet. "Well, I hope Sweet Tea doesn't pale in comparison to those fabulous New York restaurants you must be used to."

Kimberly smiles. "I'm sure it won't. My parents are still close by . . . in the same house I grew up in, in Clinton. They dine here often and love it. I'm staying with them while I'm in town. If I go back there without some of your fried chicken, I'll have hell to pay."

"We can't let that happen. I'll wrap some for you to take," I offer. "So, why don't I show you around a bit and let you know what I'm thinking in terms of artwork for the restaurant, and then we'll have lunch?"

"Sure."

"I looked at your Web site—your paintings are stunning. It's no wonder you've made such a name for yourself. I see you have a showing at a gallery in Greenwich Village next month." We step toward the back of the restaurant. "Over here"—I point to the wall behind the bar—"is my collection of antique photos and paintings. As you can see they're mostly of women preparing meals, family gatherings, church picnics . . ." I lead her farther toward the back of the restaurant. "And there's more along the back wall. That's my grandmother." I point to a large black-and-white photo of Grandmommy pouring waffle batter onto an iron. I had it enlarged when I opened the restaurant and made it the focal point of the rear wall. "Mrs. Mahalia Hix. I was named after her. People think Mahalia's Sweet Tea is named for me, but it's really in honor of her— such a special lady. I adore her smile in the picture. She loved preparing Sunday dinners, and her joy really shows in the photo."

"It really is charming," Kimberly says.

"I was wondering if you might be willing to create a painting from it." I had planned to ask her to create something original that we could add to the collection on the wall, but as I was looking at the painting of Grandmommy, the idea of a painting based on my favorite photograph of her came to mind. And it's something I might actually be interested in purchasing from Kimberly—maybe I didn't bring her here under false pretenses after all.

"Really? Hmm," Kimberly says. "That's not something I really do. I've never tried to create a painting from a photo before."

I'm about to respond that I understand, but she speaks again before I'm able to.

"But for you, a former classmate, and one of the nice ones, I'd give it a shot."

"That would be great. I can get you a copy of the photo to take back to New York. However long you need is fine."

"Yes, please send me a copy, but I'll just snap a photo of it with my phone for now," Kimberly says. "I have a few other projects I need to wrap up, but I could probably complete it in a few weeks."

"That would be great. So, what are you thinking in terms of price?"

Kimberly thinks for a moment, which makes me nervous. I saw on her Web site that some of her paintings have gone for tens of thousands of dollars.

"For you, I'll do it for a thousand dollars . . . oh, and that takeout fried chicken you promised for my parents."

"I think you've got yourself a deal." This is way more than I'd generally pay for artwork, but I'm genuinely excited about the idea of a custom painting of Grandmommy. "Why don't you have a seat?" I gesture toward the table next to us. "I'll get you a glass of the lemon blueberry iced tea we're serving today, and you can look over the menu and decide what you'd like for lunch. We have some chicken croquettes on special today."

A few minutes later I return with two glasses, a pitcher of iced tea dotted with blueberries and lemon slices, and a menu.

I offer the menu to Kimberly and fill the glasses.

"You know, I don't think I need to look at the menu. I haven't had chicken croquettes since I was a girl. I'll go with those."

"Good choice." I wave for Wavonne to come over to the table, and we watch her leisurely approach. "Sorry. Wavonne has three speeds: slow, slow, and slow. Unless there's only one pair of discount heels left on the shelf at DSW—then all of a sudden, she's Flo-Jo."

Kimberly laughs. "Aren't we all Flo-Jo when a discount pair of heels is at stake?"

"What are you two ol' hens cluckin' about?" Wavonne asks.

"Nothing. Just discussing shoes."

"Shoes? My favorite topic."

"It's good to see you again, Wavonne," Kimberly says.

"Yeah. You too," Wavonne replies, and turns toward me. "She tell you why Jack found her all loopy doopy in a parking lot by Raynell's house Saturday night?"

"Wavonne!" I say.

"Yeah. I figured you hadn't gotten to that point yet." Wavonne plops herself down next to Kimberly. "I personally wouldn't blame you if you did the bitch in. She had it comin'. Sista mess with *my* tresses and leave *me* bald, I'd take her down, too."

"What is she talking about?" Kimberly asks me.

"What she's talking about in her complete lack-of-tact way"—I glare at Wavonne before turning my attention back to Kimberly—"is that a local police officer happened to stop in for lunch yesterday when I had your business card out on the table. He recognized your photo and said he had an incident with you at the Herald Shopping Center in Fort Washington. He said he found you in your car in a peculiar state very late Saturday night . . . Sunday morning, really. I guess Wavonne and I just thought it was . . . well . . ." I'm trying to find a less offensive word than "suspicious" to use here. "*Curious* that you were found sleeping in your car so close to Raynell's house the night she died."

Kimberly's mouth drops. "Are you guys accusing me of something?" she asks. "Did you really ask me here to discuss a painting or to talk about Raynell's death?"

"Maybe a little of both, Kimberly." I reach for the pitcher on the table. "More tea?" I ask—a little gesture of goodwill before I begin pummeling her with questions.

CHAPTER 28

Kimberly quickly goes on the defense. "For your information, the Herald Shopping Center is on the way from the hotel to my parents' house. I didn't think I had drunk *that* much at the reunion, but once I got on Indian Head Highway, I really started to feel the liquor from earlier in the evening affect me. I didn't feel drunk as much as I just got a really bad . . . *terrible* headache. I didn't think I should be driving, so I pulled off the road to let it pass."

"I'm sorry, Kimberly. I didn't mean to upset you."

"Well, I hope I've explained myself. I only stopped at the shopping center because I was in no condition to drive. I've never gotten a headache like that from alcohol before—it was really intense." She starts to get up from the table. "I think I will pass on lunch. I don't have much of an appetite anymore."

"So, you explained why you were asleep in your car late Saturday night," Wavonne says just before Kimberly walks off. "Care to explain what you were doin' traipsin' around Raynell's house Sunday afternoon?"

Kimberly's eyes dart from Wavonne to me and then back to Wavonne.

"Yeah. We know *all* the good stuff," Wavonne says.

"How do you know that? That I was at Raynell's?"

"Does it really matter?" I ask before Wavonne has a chance to speak. "And come to think of it, when you came in, you said you were staying at your parents' house in Clinton. The reunion was in Greenbelt, Kimberly. Fort Washington is in no way on the way from Greenbelt to Clinton."

Kimberly gives me a long stare. "Okay. So I was at Raynell's yesterday . . . and, fine, Saturday night, too. But I swear I have no idea how Raynell died. I had nothing to do with whatever caused her death. All I wanted was a little payback."

"What do you mean?"

"You know what a wicked demon she was to me in high school. I was bald for most of junior year thanks to her. I still have post-traumatic stress from the *Nair incident*—I've spent thousands on therapy to get over my days of being bullied, and that hussy was so callous she didn't even remember what she did to me when we reconnected at the reunion. And on top of it, she wanted a favor from me. A *favor?* Are you freakin' kidding me?!" Kimberly takes a moment to collect herself and sits back down at the table. "I'm not sure I'd throw her a life raft if she was drowning, and she had the nerve to ask me to appraise a painting for her—so ridiculous! But at least her request gave me an excuse to show up at her house."

"Which you did? On Saturday night?"

Kimberly nods. "I wasn't crazy drunk by the time I left the reunion, but I had had a few drinks, or at least enough to get up enough gumption to even the score with Raynell. With a nice buzz from the liquor, I left the hotel, stopped by an all-night drugstore, and picked up a bottle of Nair. I had planned to go to Raynell's under the pretense of evaluating her painting, sneak into her bathroom, and put the hair removal cream in her shampoo bottle just like she had done to me."

"Ooh," Wavonne says. "I should be writin' this down, so I can sell it to BET."

"You were going to show up at Raynell's in the middle of the night to look at a painting? That wouldn't seem a little odd?"

"Yes, it would seem a little . . . *very* odd for me to come to her house at midnight to appraise some artwork, but I was tipsy and just seeing that awful woman got me going. I wasn't thinking straight. I figured I could tell her I had a change of plans and was leaving town early the next day. If she wanted me to look at the portrait, it would have to be then. I was afraid I'd lose my nerve if I waited any longer. When I got there, she didn't answer the door, but it was unlocked, so I snuck in and found her passed out on her bed. I simply tiptoed past her to the master bath, switched out the contents of her shampoo bottle, and left. I swear!

"I thought I was starting to sober up by the time I got to Raynell's, but on the way back to my parents' house, the drinking really caught up with me. My head hurt, and I felt more woozy and light-headed than liquor has ever made me feel before. But, somehow, I had the sense to get off the road and sleep off the booze before going back to my parents'. I still had a terrible headache when the police officer found me, but I blew a clean breathalyzer, so he let me drive home. Honestly, I still have a lingering headache, and it's been two days. I don't know what they put in the drinks at the reunion, but it was strong."

"So, why did you go back on Sunday?"

"Because, once my head cleared, I felt silly and juvenile about the whole thing, and, honestly, I was a little afraid of what Raynell would do when she likely figured out it was me who switched out her shampoo. It's been more than two decades since high school, but I got the sense that Raynell was as nasty as ever, and who knows what she would have done when she connected me to her bald head. I didn't even know she was dead when I went back. I was just going to knock on the door, feign interest in her painting, and make an excuse to use her master bath. I had planned to just drop the shampoo bottle in my purse and be on my way before she had a chance to use it. Most sisters only wash our hair once or twice a week, so I figure there was a good chance she hadn't used it."

"So, when you went back to her house on Sunday, you didn't know she was dead?"

"No. I heard about it yesterday evening when the news starting showing up on Facebook. Nothing seemed out of order when I was there until I heard someone downstairs . . ." Kimberly pauses for a moment. "Wait. It was you . . . it was the two of you who were downstairs when I was there . . . and the two of you who drove off in Raynell's Escalade."

"Don't be silly." I try to feign innocence, but I can feel the guilt showing in my face, and the quick looks Wavonne and I exchange erase any doubt that we were the culprits.

"How else would you have known I was there?"

"Fine," I admit. "I'm not convinced Raynell's death was an accident, and we were there Sunday looking for clues as to who might have killed her."

"Do you really think she was killed? So far everything I've heard indicates she fell."

"I don't know what to think. Believe me, you are not the only one who wanted revenge on Raynell. The woman racked up enemies faster than frequent-flier miles."

"Well, I assure you I had nothing to do with her death." Kimberly looks up and off to the right as if something just occurred to her. "But you know who might?"

"Who?"

"Gregory. Gregory Simms. Saturday night, just after I got back in my car, after switching out Raynell's shampoo with Nair, I saw a car pull up in front of her house."

"Gregory?" I'm hoping I misheard. Not only do I hate the idea of him possibly having something to do with Raynell's death, but I don't want to stomach him having a late-night rendezvous with her after he spent the evening flirting with me.

"Yep. It was dark, but I recognized him. Brother is looking fine these days."

"You got that right," Wavonne says.

Kimberly's demeanor has softened now that she's explained her actions to us. Her tone is friendlier and much less defensive. "Before I drove off, I saw him get out of the car and walk toward the front door. I figure if he and Raynell had a thing going, it was none of my business. But maybe his intentions were more sinister than an affair with a married woman. Not sure what his motive to kill her would have been, though."

"I guess he had as much motive as you did," I say. "Raynell did him dirty in high school just like you. And, oddly, he recently connected with her to help him find potential Maryland locations for his restaurant, which doesn't really make much sense. There must be a few thousand real estate agents he could have sought help from. Why did he decide to partner with the one who used and abused him so many years ago?"

"What did she do to him?" Kimberly asks.

"It's a long story," I say as Darius walks by with a tray holding two plates of our special for the day on his way to another table. I note Kimberly's eyes light up as she sees the chicken croquettes and takes in the faint scent they leave behind. "Has your appetite returned? Would you like to hear the Raynell/Gregory story over some lunch?"

Kimberly smiles. "Now that you mention it."

"And shouldn't you get back to work?" I ask Wavonne. "Go put in a croquette order for Kimberly, would you?"

"All right, all right," Wavonne says, and gets up from the table.

Kimberly and I watch her leisurely meander toward one of the POS stations to put the order in, and I can tell we are both thinking the same thing: *slow, slow, and slow.*

CHAPTER 29

So, here I am back at Rebirth Christian Church, but, as it's a weekday, the parking lots are mostly empty. After nabbing a space close to the entrance and walking into the massive building, I follow the instructions Alvetta gave me for finding her office. We spoke on the phone earlier, and I told her I had an errand to run in the neighborhood and wanted to check in with her and see how she's doing following the loss of Raynell.

I make a left down a wide hall to an elevator, which promptly deposits me on the third floor. I stride past a large office with "Pastor Michael Marshall" displayed on the open door. I take a quick peek inside and see a spacious executive suite fit for the CEO of a *Fortune* 500 company . . . and given the amount of revenue this place brings in, I guess it shouldn't be surprising.

When I reach Alvetta's office I find her on the phone. She smiles and waves me in. While it's not quite as grandiose as Michael's space, I'd still be surprised if Michelle Obama had a more lavish office in the White House. I step onto the thick cream-colored carpet and sit down in a beige leather chair across from Alvetta. She's seated behind an imposing wrap-around wooden desk that sits in front of a bank of floor-to-ceiling windows that overlook the church grounds and some of the few remaining acres of farmland in Prince George's County.

"Hello, Halia," she says to me after hanging up the phone. "The work of a minister's wife is never done. I'm trying to make final arrangements for Raynell's service, and my phone won't stop ringing. Three couples want the chapel for their weddings the first week in October, and they are all trying to sidestep the process and get me to work it out for them."

"Chapel?"

"Yes, it's on the other side of the building. It's a smaller space than the main sanctuary . . . only holds five hundred people. Parishioners often prefer to have their ceremonies in a more intimate setting. And some like that the chapel has the feel of a traditional church with wooden pews and stained glass windows."

"I love that a space that seats five hundred people is considered an *intimate* setting."

Alvetta laughs. "It's all relative I guess. Welcome to the megachurch world. Very little is done on a small scale here."

"Hey . . . whatever works." I take a slow look at her face. "So, are you okay? You and Raynell were so close. How are you coping?"

"How I always cope—by staying busy. Raynell and I talked almost every day. I would fill her in on church gossip, and she would tell me I looked tired and needed a new moisturizer, or that my hair was going limp, and she'd heard about a new balm that would help."

I smile. "God bless her. She was no stranger to offering criticism."

"That was just her way. Somehow it made her feel better about herself. I never took it to heart." I notice Alvetta's eyes start to well up. "She was really the sister I never had. Yes, she was bossy and sometimes . . . well, much of the time she built herself up by tearing other people down, but she always looked out for me."

She pauses for a moment to keep the lonely tear lingering just outside her right eye from erupting into a full-fledged sob and grabs a tissue to delicately wipe it away. "She even introduced me to my husband."

Your husband, whom she was having an affair with, I think to myself.

Her affection for Raynell and angst over her death does *seem* sincere. If she knows about Raynell's affair with Michael or had anything to do with her untimely demise, she's hiding it well.

"Sorry." She lifts her shoulders and raises her head, determined to fight off further tears. "I'm still grieving I guess, but I don't like to get emotional in front of other people."

"There's no shame in crying over a loved one who's passed."

"I know, but as First Lady of this church, I've gotten used to not letting my emotions take over. I've been to more funerals than you can count, and it's my job to be strong and keep it together so I can comfort others. I guess it's just habit." She gives her eyes one more dab with the tissue. "And speaking of funerals, I've got a meeting with the choir director to go over the music for Raynell's service in a few minutes, so I do need to run shortly, but it really was nice of you to drop by, Halia."

"Sure. I'll let you get back to work, but before I go, do you mind if I ask you a few questions?"

"Not at all."

"When we talked the other day you said Gregory and Raynell had a secret romance in high school and had recently reconnected. Did you ever find out who reached out to whom to start working together? Do you know if he initially contacted Raynell, or if she reached out to him about her real estate services?"

"I asked Christy about it, and she said Gregory originally called Raynell. He claimed he had heard she was the best and wanted her help in scouting restaurant locations and a home in the area."

"A home? He was looking to move here as well?"

"I guess . . . or at least spend enough time here to warrant owning a house."

"Interesting."

"What do you mean?"

"I just can't get past the idea of Gregory reaching out for help from someone who wronged him so badly. Raynell probably stood to make a lot of money off any sales she facilitated for him. Why would he want to reward someone who did nothing but use him—even if it was a long time ago?"

"You're not back to that whole murder thing? The police met with Terrence yesterday and assured him it was an accident. Besides, you don't really think a successful restaurant entrepreneur like Gregory would risk everything and kill someone over some petty high school shenanigans, do you?"

"I normally wouldn't, but I have it on good authority that Gregory was at Raynell's house the night she died."

"How do you know that?"

"I really can't say, but someone saw him approach her house late Saturday night."

Alvetta hesitates for a moment. "Well . . ." She takes a breath and looks down at her desk. "That's really not surprising. Terrence was out of town, and Raynell and Gregory . . . well . . ."

"They had a thing going?"

"I shouldn't be sharing this. Wow . . . I feel like I'm violating Raynell's confidence, but, yes, Gregory and Raynell shared more than just a business relationship."

"Wow" just falls from my lips as I try to make sense of him flirting with me at the reunion and my date with him on Monday night. *Why is he showing a romantic interest in me if he had a relationship with Raynell?*

"Yes. I loved Raynell, but, like all of us, she was imperfect and didn't always make the best choices. Apparently they started working together and . . . you know . . . one thing led to another."

"Did Terrence know?"

"No. At least I don't think so. Raynell's work involved all sorts of odd hours, so I doubt Terrence would have gotten suspicious if she wasn't home some evenings. And she and Gregory had the perfect excuse to spend time together. I think she worked it out so Christy handled many of the business outings with Gregory—that way Raynell's time with him could be more . . . shall we say *social*."

"Really?"

"Yes. It was mostly Christy who showed Gregory commercial properties and multimillion-dollar homes. She scheduled the appointments and did the research . . . and answered his calls."

"Multimillion-dollar homes? Gregory's restaurant chain must really be doing well."

"It would appear that it is. And what you said earlier about Raynell standing to make a lot of money is very true. Commissions on commercial leasing are steep, and whoever sells him a home now will probably net tens of thousands of dollars from that commission alone, and—"

Alvetta's interrupted by a buzzing sound. She looks at the screen on the phone. "That's the choir director. I really do need to meet with her."

"Sure, sure."

"Thanks again for stopping by."

"Of course. I hope you and Michael will come by the restaurant some time soon."

I get up from the chair and try to give Alvetta a hug, but

the desk is too wide. Instead, I take her hand in mine. "Please call me if I can do anything for you. I'm sure this a rough time."

I exit Alvetta's office with my mind aflutter. She has given me so much to think about. Despite her apparent grief, I still wonder if she knows about Raynell's affair with Michael. Your supposed best friend sleeping with your husband is certainly motive for murder. I also wonder if Terrence knew about Raynell's affairs with Michael . . . and/or Gregory. (Sister *got around*. That's for sure.) Another motive for murder. Then I consider whether or not an old high school wound is enough motive for Gregory—or Kimberly—to kill Raynell. And, as I make my way to my van, I can't help but think about what Alvetta said . . . how, with Raynell out of the picture, whoever helps Gregory close some real estate deals stands to make out like a bandit. If Christy has been Gregory's go-to girl all along, wouldn't she be his logical choice to assist him now that Raynell is dead? Is being positioned as the next in line to a hefty real estate commission enough reason for Christy to kill Raynell?

Alvetta, Terrence, Gregory, Kimberly, Christy—they all had reasons to do away with Raynell. I guess it's now up to me to figure out if any of them actually acted upon those reasons.

CHAPTER 30

When the elevator opens on the main level of the church I quickly scurry down the hall toward the exit. I'm in a rush to get back to Sweet Tea so, as I hasten toward the door, I almost miss her. But, as I pass the reception counter, my eyes take note of a familiar petite figure talking to the security guard. She's holding a large cardboard box with both hands.

"Christy?"

"Halia. What are you doing here?" Christy asks and steps toward me.

"I just came to check on Alvetta. What brings you this way?"

"Alvetta asked me to pick up some photo albums from Raynell's house and bring them over. She's working on a tribute for Raynell's service. I e-mailed her a bunch of electronic ones, but she wanted some of the older prints as well."

"Why didn't she ask Terrence?"

"Because Terrence probably wouldn't have known where to find them."

"But you did?"

"Please. I know where everything is in that house. When you work . . . *worked* for Raynell, you have a very loosely defined job description. I did much more than just assist her with her real estate business. When you pick up and put away someone's dry cleaning, organize her closets, and oversee the installation of her new hardwood floors, you learn where things are."

"I guess so. Sounds like Raynell kept you very busy. Alvetta was just telling me that you were the one who did most of the work to help Gregory scout locations for his restaurant and find a home in the area."

"I guess that's true, but he's a nice person . . . easy to work with."

"So will you continue to work with him now that Raynell has passed?" I'm hoping it doesn't sound too obvious that I'm fishing for information. "Sounds like you deserved whatever commissions were to come from the deal anyway."

"Maybe so, but unfortunately I'm not a licensed agent, so I'm not eligible for commissions. Technically, I shouldn't have even been showing Gregory properties without a license, but Raynell wasn't exactly one for always following rules."

Well, that blows my theory that Christy offed Raynell to get her hands on some real estate commissions. "I guess Gregory will have to find a new agent." I almost add "and another mistress," but keep those words to myself as I have no idea if Christy is aware of Raynell's proclivity for extramarital affairs. No wonder she needed Christy to do all of her work. She was too busy swinging from the chandeliers with Gregory and her best friend's husband, and God knows who else, to sell real estate.

"Terrence has asked me to stay on for a few weeks to help field Raynell's phone calls and settle some affairs, so I'm a little swamped, but I'll give Gregory a call this week and set him up with another agent in Raynell's office."

"That's nice that you're helping Terrence. I'm sure it's a difficult time for him . . . and for you. How are you doing?"

"I'm okay. Raynell was a hard ass and not the most respectful person in the world, but . . . I don't know . . . I sort of miss her. She was like one of those yippy little dogs that growls and tries to nip everyone, but you sort of get used to having them around . . . and they leave a void when they're no longer there."

"So you miss her like you might miss a mean Chihuahua? I hope you're not writing the eulogy," I say with a smile.

Christy laughs. "No. I'm not sure who is . . . probably Alvetta or Terrence."

"How is Terrence?"

"He's hanging in there. I haven't seen him in a few days."

"He wasn't at the house when you went to pick up the albums?"

"No. I think he had some errands to run."

I want to ask her how she got in the house if Terrence wasn't there, but I think I've asked enough nosy questions for the time being. And, besides, it's probably safe to assume she has a key to the Rollinses' house given all the personal work she did for Raynell.

"Well, give him my best next time you see him."

"Sure. I'll probably be helping him out for another week or two, and then I need to start searching for a new job."

"I'm sure you won't have any trouble on that front. What's it they say about New York? 'If you can make it there you can make it anywhere.' I think the same thing goes for working with Raynell. If you can work for her, you can work for anyone."

"I hope you're right," Christy says. "I guess I had better get these albums to Alvetta."

"Okay. It was nice to run into you. Best of luck on your job search."

Christy and I part company, and, on my way to the parking lot, I visualize my suspect list in my head. I'm about to draw a line through Christy's name—if she's not eligible to receive any real estate commissions, that strips her of a key motive for killing Raynell. In fact, if she didn't stand to make any financial gain from Raynell's death, it's unlikely she'd kill the person who signs her paychecks and makes it possible for her to earn a living. I picture a line going through her name, but I'm not quite ready to cross her off the list entirely. Maybe she didn't get rich off Raynell's demise and is facing unemployment as a result of her death. But, much like everyone else Raynell came into contact with, she treated Christy pretty badly. From what I saw she mostly just barked orders at her all day. And that's how Raynell treated her in public—who knows how bad it was in private. Maybe Christy had enough, was going to quit anyway, but, before she did, figured she'd kill Raynell for no other reason than Raynell being an insufferable witch.

RECIPE FROM HALIA'S KITCHEN

Halia's All-Natural Margaritas

Ingredients

¾ cup tequila
¼ cup triple sec
⅓ cup honey
1 large orange, peeled and de-seeded
1 lime, peeled and de-seeded
1 lemon, peeled and de-seeded
6 cups ice

Combine all ingredients in blender. Blend on high until smooth. Salt rims of glasses if desired.

Four Servings

Note: If blender is not large enough to add 6 cups of ice at once, start with 4 cups, blend until smooth, then add remaining cups, and blend again.

CHAPTER 31

"Why don't you run home and change clothes before you meet him?" Wavonne asks. It's three o'clock. The last lunch customers have just left, and we're starting our midday closure. Gregory called this morning and asked if I'd give him my opinion on a property he's looking at, and I'm about to leave to meet him. "Khakis and a knit shirt ain't exactly date clothes."

"Forgive me, Wavonne, but I can't very well run a restaurant in stilettos and a miniskirt. Besides, there's no point. I told you. I'm not sure what Gregory is up to—why he was flirting with me at the reunion and kissed me the other night when he'd been having an affair with Raynell up until the night she died. Maybe he's just playing me for some free advice about the local restaurant scene. I don't think he's really interested in me."

"Halia, you say that like a brotha can't be interested in two women at the same time. That ain't true. If Raynell was doin' the freaky deeky with him and Michael . . . and, God forbid, maybe her actual *husband,* too, then surely Gregory could be interested in you even if he had somethin' brewin' with

Raynell. And let me assure you, you got the leg up over Raynell in this situation—considerin' you still have a pulse."

"Whatever. I'm not really interested in getting involved with someone who was fooling around with a married woman anyway."

"Oh blah blah whatevah. Who says you have to get *involved* with him anyway. For once in your life just have some fun, Halia. Ride the wave."

"Did you *just* meet me? I'm not exactly a 'ride the wave' type of person. The only reason I'm meeting him at all is to ask him some questions and nose around a bit . . . see if he might have had a hand in Raynell ending up in a pool of blood on her bathroom floor." I pull my keys from my purse and sling it over my shoulder. "I've got to get going. I should be back before we reopen at five."

"Fine. Go lookin' like that. Oh well . . . who knows . . . maybe Gregory's into the 'high school gym teacher' look. Stranger stuff has happened."

I ignore Wavonne's final comments before heading for the door. Evening rush hour is already starting, so traffic is heavy as I drive over to the Boulevard at the Capital Centre, an expansive shopping complex in Largo. It was built on the site that once housed the Capital Centre, an arena that, before it was torn down about fifteen years ago, was home to the Washington Bullets (now the Wizards), the Washington Capitols, and hosted all the big name concerts that came to the D.C. metro area back in the day. I think half of my high school went to see Lionel Richie there back in the eighties.

The Boulevard started off with a bang when it opened in 2003 and brought some much needed retail outlets and restaurants to the area. Unfortunately, it all quickly went downhill thanks to several of its major tenants going out of business (anyone remember Circuit City, Linens 'n Things, Borders?), rowdy teens causing mayhem . . . and . . . well . . . three men being gunned down at the Uno Chicago Grill back in 2008 didn't exactly help an already damaged image.

Gregory mentioned via text that he wanted my opinion on a location he was scouting by the Magic Johnson theater, so I find a space on the east end of the parking lot and head toward a vacant storefront a few doors down from the theater.

"Hey there," Gregory says when I find him standing outside the property. When he leans in and gives me a hug I feel the firm contours of his chest. Suddenly, I wish I had taken Wavonne's advice and spruced myself up a bit before meeting him.

"Hi." *Do I really look like a high school gym teacher?* "Sorry, I'm a mess. It was a busy day. But I guess I don't need to tell you about life running a restaurant. How many do you run now? Seven?"

"Twelve. Six in Florida, three in Georgia, one in South Carolina, and two in North Carolina. And hopefully my first location in Maryland very soon." The proud smile on his face and jovial demeanor seem out of place for a man who just lost his mistress. Come to think of it, he didn't seem terribly bothered or distracted by Raynell's death when we had our date earlier in the week, either.

"Impressive. I can barely keep up with one restaurant."

"From what I hear, you are keeping up just fine." Gregory opens the door to the vacant space and gestures for me to follow him.

I look around me at the concrete floors and unpainted drywall. "It's a good-sized space."

"Yes. I've already got the floor plan mapped out, found a local contractor, and I've been doing some research on the shopping center."

"Research on the shopping center? So you're aware it has a precarious history?"

Gregory smiles. "Yes, but the landlord has really started to turn things around and is eager to attract new tenants."

"That's nice to hear. I noticed when I drove in that a lot of the empty retail spaces have been filled."

"They've lured several new shops and restaurants and really improved security. I think now is a good time to get in. The owners are offering a rent abatement while I do the build out and will even chip in on some of the construction costs."

"That's great. I didn't get any such concessions when I opened Sweet Tea so many years ago. But, at the time, I didn't really know to ask for them. Live and learn."

"That's for sure. I learn so many new things with every restaurant I open. For instance, I really appreciate the big lots here. I made the mistake of opening a location just outside Atlanta with only street parking. I think the lack of convenient parking is the reason sales at that location have been soft."

"Yes. Easily accessible parking was a must when I opened Sweet Tea . . . and lots of street lights for safety . . . that was important, too. There's good lighting in the lot here—that's definitely a plus."

"I also love that this space is right next to the movie theater. I can really take advantage of people going to and from the movies with an appetite."

I turn around and give the space another look. "If the price is right, and the square footage meets your needs, maybe you really did find a great site for the next South Beach Burgers. Shall I plan to be the first in line for a Miami Deluxe in a few months?"

"How do you know about the Miami Deluxe?"

"A third pound of Certified Angus Beef on a brioche bun with Muenster cheese, avocado, crispy onion rings, and Russian dressing," I say. "I gave your Web site a quick look before I came. It's very nicely done."

"Thanks. I have a great designer. If you have any advice

about the Web site . . . or about anything really, I'd love to hear it."

"I'm sure you've got general restaurant management down to a science at this point, but I bet I can give you pointers on all the local regs you'll need to deal with—the permits and licenses, the signage restrictions, the building codes . . . all that jazz. I would have loved for someone with my current experience to walk me through all those hoops when I got Sweet Tea up and running. So many ridiculous rules and fees—it almost made me wonder if the county wanted any new businesses to open at all."

"I hear you. I think it's all designed to make lawyers money. I have to hire a local attorney for each area that I expand into."

"And their services are expensive. At least it sounds like you're getting a good deal on this place."

"I think I am. Raynell . . . well, Christy mostly, showed me several properties and this one really seemed to be the best of the bunch."

"Speaking of Raynell . . ." I'm assuming this is the best opportunity I'll have to move the conversation toward the topic of her demise. "Are you holding up okay following her passing?"

Gregory looks at me as if I've just asked him an odd question. "Sure. I'm fine. It's very sad for her family and friends, though."

"Sad for her family and friends? No one else?"

"What do you mean?"

"It's not sad for you?"

"Of course it's sad for me, but we were not exactly close. I guess we had been working together for several weeks scouting restaurant locations, but it was really just a business arrangement."

I narrow my eyebrows at Gregory. "Is that what the kids are calling it these days? A *business arrangement?*"

"What are you getting at, Halia?" He's trying not to show it, but I can sense that my questions have unearthed some anxiety.

I don't say anything for a moment or two, but when it's clear that he is not going to come clean I speak. "Alvetta told me about your affair with Raynell."

Gregory's jaw drops. "How did Alvetta know?"

"Those two told each other everything. They've been a pair of cackling hens for almost thirty years."

Gregory stares at me, clearly embarrassed that I know about his indiscretion. Then he looks down at the ground and then back at me again. "There wasn't anything between us."

"Oh?"

"Really. I didn't feel anything for Raynell . . ." He seems to stumble for words. "The whole thing with her was just . . . just complicated. I didn't even like her. You, Halia . . . *you,* I like."

"Apparently, you liked her enough to show up on her doorstep after the reunion Saturday night."

I see that familiar jaw drop again, and with it, Gregory knows he's already shown his guilt. There is no point in denying that he was there.

"Yes. I know you were at her house the night she died."

"Okay . . . you've got me . . . I was there, but I didn't even see her."

"What do you mean?"

"Terrence was out of town, so we made plans to get together after the party, but by the time I got there, she must have been out cold. She didn't answer the door. And, honestly, I was relieved." Gregory steps closer to me. "We . . . you and me had spent such a nice evening together. You were on my mind. Not Raynell."

"Then why the late-night rendezvous with her?"

"Like I said, it was complicated. I had my reasons, but none of them involved any affection for Raynell Rollins."

"I think you'd better share those reasons with me, Gregory. Not everyone is convinced that Raynell's death was an accident. And, honestly, you being seen late at night at her house hours before she's found dead might sound very suspicious to some people."

Gregory cocks his head at me and laughs nervously. "You don't seriously think I had something to do with Raynell's death?"

I actually take a moment to really ponder the thought before responding. "You know, I guess I don't. At least I don't think the Gregory I knew in high school was a killer. But unless you can shed some light on what was going on with you and Raynell, I'm going to have to tell the police about your whereabouts the night she died."

Gregory takes a long slow breath and lets it out. "I'm not sure where to begin."

"I suspect it all started sometime in the eighties."

Gregory laughs nervously again. "You would suspect right." He pauses and then looks me in the eye. "That woman . . . Raynell . . . she really hurt me. Yeah, it was more than twenty years ago, but some scars never heal."

"That woman . . . Raynell . . . hurt a lot of people."

"Maybe so, but she led me to believe she cared about me. You remember me in high school—I was skinny and gawky . . . and shy. When Raynell took an interest in me I started to feel like I was *somebody*. I trusted her and even agreed to keep our relationship quiet. From the outside I'm sure it seems like I should have known she was only using me for help with her studies, but . . . I don't know . . . sometimes we believe what we want to believe. It nearly killed me when she dumped me after I took the freaking SATs for her. She had been so nice to me, and I thought we really had a good time together. But when she turned on me, boy did she *turn* on me. The last words I remember her saying to me before we reconnected this year . . . the last words I remember the girl I was in love with saying to me were: 'If you tell anyone about us, I'll make your life a living hell.' "

"And anyone who knew Raynell was well aware that she could and would make that happen."

"I was dumbstruck by her behavior . . . and man, was I hurt, but I was smart enough not to cross her. She could be as mean as a rattlesnake, and I knew better than to end up on the other end of a strike attack."

It's been decades, but as Gregory talks about her, I can see the pain in his eyes that Raynell inflicted on him. It makes me sad for him.

"So life went on. I slowly got over it I guess . . . and let it go. At least, I thought I had, but then . . ."

"Then what?"

"Facebook. That's what."

"What do you mean?"

"I was late to the Facebook party, but when my team started putting together a Facebook page for South Beach Burgers I decided to go ahead and put up a personal page as well. I had barely had a profile up there for a day when friend requests from old classmates started coming in like crazy. I just accepted them without much thought. Then one day, I clicked on that little "you have a friend request" icon, and a photo of Raynell popped up. I tell you, my heart sank to the floor all over again just from seeing her face. I accepted her request and, stupid me, thought she might actually send me an apology for how she behaved in high school."

"I take it she didn't do that?"

"Of course not, but she did e-mail me . . . multiple times. She told me how 'fine' I looked now, and how she wished she wasn't married so she could get 'all up in that.' From there her e-mails got even more suggestive. I'll admit I enjoyed the attention I was receiving from her, but getting back in touch with her also showed me that she hadn't changed. She would e-mail with hateful gossip about classmates, and I'd see condescending comments she'd write on other people's posts. Chatting with her via Facebook and seeing how she was still the same old Raynell stirred something in me. That feeling of inadequacy began to rear its head all over again. I'd dealt with her using me and then dumping me once I'd served my purpose so many years ago. I think I let *that* go. But the fact that she threatened to ruin me if I told anyone about our relationship was too much to ever let go. It made me feel like I was such a nothing—less than a nothing—that I was so awful Raynell didn't want anyone to know we'd had a relationship."

Gregory goes quiet as his head hangs with his face toward the floor. Then he inhales slowly and looks at me. "I'm a success now. I'm rich. I look good. I should have been above revenge. . . ." He lets his voice trail off.

"But?"

"Word of the reunion was all over Facebook. I thought it would be fun to attend, and I really am looking to expand South Beach Burgers into Maryland. I figured if I was going to make the trip anyway I may as well give Raynell a taste of her own medicine."

"You're starting to scare me a little bit," I say. "Your taste for revenge didn't end up with Raynell dead on her bathroom floor, did it?"

"Of course not. I would never kill anyone. But all I could think about after getting back in touch with her was how, back in high school, she said she would ruin me if I told anyone about us. So, you know what?" Gregory is silent for a second or two as he rolls his shoulders back and lifts his head. "I decided I would ruin her."

"Ruin her? How?"

"She made it clear in our online chats that she was attracted to me and had no problem being unfaithful to her husband. That gave me an idea. What if . . . what if I took advantage of her loose morals and lured her into an affair, made her fall in love with me the way I fell for her . . . and then . . . and then made sure her husband caught us. After Terrence found out and threatened divorce, I planned to agree to be there for her when she left him . . . and then . . ." There's a wicked twinkle in Gregory's eye. "Ditch her the same way she ditched me in high school. I was all set to make sure she was left without me, without Terrence . . . and without any money when Terrence divorced her ass for cheating on him."

I can't help but look at Gregory with startled eyes as I take all of this in. "So, did Terrence ever find out about your affair with Raynell?"

"I don't know. I left a monogrammed men's T-shirt just under his side of the bed when I was there last, and I always made sure to wear heavy cologne when I met her at their house, so the scent would linger on the sheets when Terrence got home. If she had let me in after the reunion I was going to leave this ring. . . ." Gregory holds up his hand. "This *man's* ring behind . . . make it look like it had fallen between the bed and the nightstand."

As I continue to listen to him speak I try not to let my facial expression show what I'm feeling, but he can read me anyway.

"You think I'm pathetic, don't you? Hell, *I* think I'm pathetic. That *woman* just had such an effect on me."

"I don't think you're pathetic, Gregory," I say, even though I guess I sort of do. "But why was it so important to get back at her? You got yours—like you said, you're successful, you look great, you're rich . . ."

"I don't know, but so many years after high school, she was still able to get under my skin. But I assure you, Halia, I never would have killed her and I—" Gregory gasps as if he's just been hit with a revelation. "Oh my God! What if I did play a role in her death?"

"What are you talking about?"

Gregory leans against the wall and puts his hands on his forehead. "My goal was to have Terrence find out about us and kick Raynell to the curb, but what if . . . *what if* he found out she was cheating on him and went to a much further extreme?"

I think about what Gregory has just said and consider telling him that he was not the only one Hottie McHot Pants was cheating on her husband with, but I don't think telling Gregory about Raynell's affair with Michael Marshall would serve any purpose, so I keep it to myself.

"But you don't know if Terrence found out about your affair with Raynell?"

"No, I can't say for sure. But what I can say for sure is that I did *not* kill Raynell Rollins. If you have to tell the police about me being at her house the night she died, then so be it. But I wish you wouldn't." He steps in closer to me and lightly grasps my hand. "It's just an intrusion in my life I really don't need at the moment. I'm busy . . . really busy expanding my restaurant, and, honestly, I'd love to find some time to reconnect with you, Halia."

I look at his big brown eyes staring down on me, and I can see what a handsome man he is, but he just isn't attractive to me anymore. The bizarre revenge game he was playing with Raynell . . . his unhealthy obsession with settling the score over something that happened decades ago . . . that he would be intimate with a woman he hated . . . it's all just too creepy.

"I'm really busy, too, Gregory, and I imagine you'll have to be getting back to Florida soon."

He looks away from me. "I'm assuming that's a nice way of saying you're not interested."

I don't respond. I just look at him, try to smile, and clumsily remove my hand from his grasp. It seems nicer than verbally confirming his assumption, but it doesn't make the situation any less uncomfortable.

"I've really got to get back to Sweet Tea." I can hear the awkward tone in my voice as the words come out. "We re-open for dinner soon."

"Okay," he responds, a defeated look on his face. "Thanks for coming by."

"You're welcome." I turn to leave. "This really is a nice space. I think you'll have a lot of success with it."

"I hope so."

As I walk toward the door I wonder if Gregory is worth keeping on my suspect list. I wonder if Terrence killed Raynell over one or more of her affairs. I wonder about Alvetta and Christy. But mostly, when I see Gregory's reflection in the glass door on my way out—his attractive face, his full lips, his solid stature—I wonder if I just made a huge mistake by turning down his romantic advance.

CHAPTER 32

"Wouldn't it be easier to just chop all this meat with a knife?" Wavonne asks me as we stand next to the counter hand-tearing chicken breasts.

"I suppose, but hand-torn chicken just tastes better than chopped chicken. I don't know why. It just does."

And I really don't know why hand-shredded chicken tastes better than chopped, but we only use shredded chicken in our chicken salad, our chicken and dumplings, and the chicken potpies we are preparing now. We always start with roasted bone-in skin-on chicken breasts. The bone adds flavor to the chicken, and the skin left intact adds a little fat and moisture to the meat as it cooks.

Farther down the counter, Tacy is rolling out the crusts for the potpies. We've already prepared the batter based on Grandmommy's simple recipe—flour, sugar, salt, butter, butter-flavored shortening, ice water, and a pinch of baking powder. But I must confess, unlike Grandmommy, we no longer mix the recipe by hand. We use my commercial food processor to save time and labor and, fortunately, it produces a pie crust just as light and flaky as the one Grandmommy made. Once she perfected the recipe Grandmommy used the same one for all her pies whether she was preparing a savory pie like the chicken potpies we are making now or sweet creations like apple or peach tarts.

"So, do I get to wait on them when they get here?"

"Who?"

"Alvetta and Michael."

"No. I asked Darius to take care of them."

"Why does he always get all the good tables?"

"Because I can count on him to consistently provide a high level of service."

"*I* provide a high level of service."

"Of course you do . . . when the mood strikes you."

"Well, the mood is strikin' me tonight," Wavonne says. "I know they ain't comin' here for a leisurely dinner. You've got an angle for invitin' them, and I wanna know what it is."

"I don't have an *angle*, Wavonne. I just thought having them as my guests would give me a chance to talk to Michael."

"Michael?"

"Yes. He was with Terrence at the retreat in Williamsburg. If Terrence knew about Raynell's affair . . . *affairs*, and decided he wanted her dead . . . well, Williamsburg is not that far from here . . . barely three hours if there's no traffic. He could have easily slipped out of his hotel room, driven up here, pulled Raynell from a drunken slumber, bashed her head against the porcelain tub, and been back at the hotel before daybreak."

"What do you think Michael's gonna be able to tell you?"

"All sorts of things. He can tell me how late it was when he last saw Terrence on Saturday night . . . and when he first saw him on Sunday morning. Terrence would have needed at least six hours to pull the whole thing off. Michael might also be able to tell me something about Terrence's demeanor Sunday morning. He was bound to have been edgy and unsettled if he'd just killed his wife hours earlier."

"Instead of Michael and Alvetta, I think you . . . *we* should talk to Terrence directly . . . get his side of the story. And if he happens to offer to hook a sista up with a wealthy Redskin, then so be it. I've been—"

Laura cuts Wavonne off when she pokes her head through the kitchen door. "Halia, your guests are here. Mr. and Mrs. Marshall. They're at table four by the window."

"Thank you, Laura." I put the chicken I was handling back on the counter and step over to the sink and wash my hands. "Wavonne, can you finish up the chicken, please? We need to get those pies in the oven." Fortunately, we just need to add the meat to the filling, which we've already prepared, and then pour the mixture into the pie crusts Tacy is about to wrap up. Everything in the pies is already cooked, so we only need to brown the crust and heat the contents. Then they will be ready to serve to the dinner rush that is beginning to gather outside the kitchen door.

"Hey!" I smile after I step outside the kitchen and greet Michael and Alvetta. "Welcome."

They stand up. Michael shakes my hand, and Alvetta gives me a hug. I've actually grown to like her during the last few days. Her close association with Raynell is not exactly a selling point, but aside from that, she's seems to have matured into an affable person.

"Please, please. Have a seat," I say as I take one myself next to Alvetta. "I'm so sorry I couldn't make Raynell's funeral this morning. I've been running my assistant manager ragged lately. She was scheduled to be off today, and I just couldn't ask her to cover for me again. I hope it went well . . . as well as can be expected, at least."

"It was a lovely service . . . very sad of course, but I think it helped to give her friends and family closure and say our good-byes," Alvetta says, trying to not get emotional as she speaks of the funeral, but I can see the grief in her eyes.

"Alvetta worked day and night to make it special. She put

together a very touching tribute," Michael says and directs his eyes from me to Alvetta. "You did a wonderful job, honey. You did Raynell proud," he adds as Darius appears at the table.

"Welcome to Sweet Tea. My name is Darius, and I'll be taking care of you this . . ." Darius lets his voice trail off as he notices that he may have interrupted a sensitive moment. "Should I come back?"

Alvetta adjusts herself in her seat. "No . . . no. We're fine. Thank you," she says, and takes in a long breath. "Actually, I would love a drink."

"I can certainly help with that. Just for the summer we are featuring crushed-ice margaritas. No syrups or mixers. We make them with fresh oranges, lemons, and limes."

"That sounds lovely," Alvetta says.

"Just a draft beer for me," comes from Michael. "Michelob Ultra if you have it."

"We only have that in the bottle."

"That's fine."

"One margarita and one Michelob Ultra," Darius confirms. He's about to step away from the table when he notes my raised eyebrows. He grins at me, pulls out his pad, and writes down their drink order. I'm not a fan of waiters failing to write down orders, even very simple ones. It's a pet peeve of mine. A good server like Darius can generally gauge when he needs to write an order on his pad rather than commit it to memory, but even he can get tripped up if something distracts him on the way to inputting the order into the computer system. Customers get testy enough if their order comes to the table without the sauce on the side as they requested or with the onions they asked to be left out when a server *has* written the order down. If we mess up (yes, it happens on occasion, even at Sweet Tea ☺), and their server didn't write the order down, people get *really* annoyed. Even if one of my servers had some sort of extraordinary memory skills and never forgot anything, I'd still require that he or she write orders down. Some customers might be impressed that a server can remember the most lengthy and complex of orders, but the mere act of a waiter not recording their order makes them anxious that their meal will not come to the table exactly as they requested. That's not how I want my customers to feel. I want a night out at Sweet Tea to be a relaxed, positive experience in every way.

"Are you having anything?" Alvetta asks as Darius departs from the table.

"I'm sure Darius will bring me an iced tea."

"Aw. Don't make a girl drink alone. Have a margarita with me."

"I wish I could. I have a long night ahead of me. The dinner rush is just starting. I need to keep a clear head. I thought I'd just sit with you for a bit and say hi and then let you two enjoy your evening. I'm sure you could use a relaxing night out after . . . well . . . you know . . . events of late."

"That's very thoughtful of you, Halia. It has been a challenging time."

"I don't know if a few drinks and some good food can even put a dent in the grief I'm sure you're feeling, but maybe it can help you take a little break from it for a few hours."

"Truthfully, it would be nice to not think of Raynell's death for a little while," Alvetta says. "Wow, that sounded really selfish, didn't it?"

Michael reaches for Alvetta's hand across the table. "Not at all," he says. "You were the best friend anyone could have been to Raynell. And let's be honest, Raynell was not the easiest person to love. But you did love her, and you were a good friend to her." He holds her hand for another moment or two before letting it go. "Now, let's talk about something else."

"Yes," I say. "How about the retreat last weekend, Michael? How was it?"

"It was very nice . . . until we got the news about Raynell." Michael pauses. "No. We said we would take a break from talking about Raynell." He straightens himself in his chair. "It was actually very productive. If our church is going to continue to thrive, we need a strong online presence. We developed a strategy during the conference that I think will be quite effective."

"That's great," I say. "Terrence was at the conference, too, wasn't he? Was he involved in the discussions? I guess I don't think of a former football player being a technical guru."

Michael laughs. "No. Terrence is not terribly computer savvy, but I always ask him to attend our conferences. If churchgoers know Terrence Rollins is attending an event, we always get a sizable turnout. Terrence is professional sports royalty, and people just like to be around him. Like Saturday night at the hotel, he held court in the lounge until after two a.m."

"Really?" I ask. "Two a.m.? That must make getting up for morning service a bit tricky."

"Not for Terrence. That man has a lot of energy. I passed him on the way to the gym at six a.m. when I was going to help set up the hospitality room."

"Raynell always complained about Terrence being a morning person," Alvetta says. "Raynell would sleep until noon every day if she could."

"I suppose I would, too, but that pesky need to earn a living is a bit of an obstacle," I respond, grateful that I didn't have to find a way to tactfully grill Michael about Terrence's whereabouts the night Raynell died. If Terrence was hanging out at the hotel bar until after two a.m. and was later seen at six a.m., then he couldn't have killed Raynell. There simply wasn't time for him to drive back to Maryland, do the deed, and get back to Williamsburg by six a.m.

"Why don't I go check on Darius and see what's keeping those drinks."

I mentally cross Terrence off my suspect list as I hop up from the table and head toward the bar.

"What's the holdup?" I ask Darius.

"Word has gotten out about our margaritas. Everyone is ordering them. The blenders are backed up."

"I guess I'll need to order another one to get us through the summer."

"I'll bring the drinks to the table as soon as they're ready if you want to get back to your guests."

"Thanks! I'll give them some time alone."

"Found out what you wanted to know already?" Darius asks, a sly smile on his face.

"What do you mean?" I feign innocence.

"He means did you find out from Michael if Terrence had time to get back from Williamsburg Saturday night and lay waste to his cheatin' ho-bag of a wife?" Wavonne says, seemingly appearing out of nowhere.

I sigh, annoyed that Wavonne has been discussing Raynell's death and my little informal investigation with Darius. "If you must know, yes, I did get the information I was after. According to Michael, Terrence was in the hotel lounge until after two a.m. and was seen again on the way to the gym at six a.m., so I guess he's in the clear."

"What makes you think Terrence would want to kill Raynell anyway?" Darius asks.

"Because she was cheating on him all over God's creation—not only with an old high school classmate, but also with Michael Rollins," I say, and direct my eyes toward Michael.

"Yeah," Wavonne says. "We found this note in Raynell's house. It's from Michael. It's signed *M*, and it's his handwriting." Wavonne pulls the infamous note from her pocket.

"What are you doing with that?" I ask as Darius reads the letter.

"I just thought it might come in handy . . . be useful sometime. A certain someone"—Wavonne diverts her eyes across the room toward Michael—"might be willing to pay a sista a little something to keep his wife from seein' it."

I shake my head in exasperation. "That's called *extortion,* Wavonne, and could land you in jail."

I grab the letter when Darius is done reading it to keep it from getting back in Wavonne's hands.

"You know," Darius says. "This letter isn't *necessarily* for Raynell."

"What do you mean?"

"Look"—Darius points to the top of the note—"It just says 'hey, good-lookin'.'"

"What are you getting at?"

"You found the note at the Rollinses' home, right? Raynell is not the only one who lives there."

"But the note was in her office." Wavonne says.

"Actually, we really don't know if it was *her* office where we found the note," I counter. "Yes, her real estate paraphernalia was scattered about, but she had that stuff stored all over the house."

"Did it ever occur to you that the note could have been for Terrence?" Darius asks.

"From Michael to Terrence? But that would mean—"

Wavonne cuts me off. "What are you sayin'? That Terrence likes his bread buttered on both sides?"

"He's been rumored to be one of 'my people' since he was an active player back in the nineties. I have friends that swear he was a regular at The Bachelor's Mill back in the day . . . before everyone had cameras on their phones to snap photos of a closeted football player."

"The Bachelor's Mill?"

"It's a gay bar in D.C. Before he married Raynell, whenever reporters asked him about a girlfriend he always said he was too busy to date, or just hadn't found the right girl. When his engagement was announced everyone 'in the know' assumed it was just an arrangement. Besides, from what I've heard, why else would anyone marry Raynell Rollins?"

"So what you're saying is that Michael may have been having an affair with Terrence? Not Raynell?"

"Word on the street has always been that Terrence's marriage to Raynell was just for convenience. She got access to his wealth and status, and he got a beard to have on his arm at the ESPYs."

"Wow. This just gets more and more complicated." I stop to think for a moment. "But Michael is married to Alvetta. I just can't believe it. They are so good together. If what you're saying is true, then Michael must also . . ."

"Get the hots for the brothas?" Wavonne says. "Well, I know how we can find out for sure. Look, Alvetta's goin' to the ladies room." We watch as Alvetta heads toward the back of the restaurant. "I'm gonna saunter over there with my girls on display." Wavonne looks down at her chest, loosens her tie, and unbuttons her blouse. "If he's straight, you know he's gonna wanna get down with all *this*."

Darius and I observe from the bar as Wavonne sashays toward the table where Michael is looking at his phone. I can tell she's asking about changing out the salt and pepper as she jiggles her bazoombas in front of his face while she reaches for the shakers. Michael barely looks up from his phone and can't be bothered to stare at all when Wavonne drops her pen and bends over right next to him to pick it up.

"Gay as a pink feather boa," Wavonne says once she's back at the bar.

"Maybe you're just not his type," I protest.

"Of course I'm not his type. I don't have a—"

I look at Darius and break in before Wavonne has a chance to finish her tirade. "Why don't you try it?"

"Me?" Darius asks.

"Yeah," Wavonne says. "Go over there and strut your stuff. See if he bites."

Darius lets out a quick laugh. "All right. I'll play along. Looks like their drinks are ready anyway." He places Alvetta's margarita and Michael's beer on a tray.

"Serve the drinks and then turn around, put your hands in your pockets on the way back, and pull your slacks forward," Wavonne instructs as Darius walks toward Michael. "Show off what your momma gave you."

Darius reaches the table and sets the drinks down. Wavonne and I discreetly observe as Michael looks up from his phone and steals a quick look at Darius's chest. When Darius *accidentally* drops the tray on way back to the bar and bends over to pick it up, Michael's eyes follow and linger on Darius's backside way longer than any straight man's should.

"So Michael is having an affair with *Terrence*," I say to Wavonne as we see the spectacle unfold in front of us. "This changes everything."

CHAPTER 33

"I think I've stepped foot in this building more than most tithing members during the last several days," I say to Wavonne as we walk down the main hall of Rebirth Christian Church. I didn't want to be away from the restaurant too long, so we timed our visit to coincide with the end of the eleven a.m. service.

"I don't know why you made me come," Wavonne says. "That fool never called me . . . never texted me . . . nothin'," she adds about Rick Stevens, the gentleman we chatted with two weeks ago at the retreat table who tried to recruit Wavonne for the event in Williamsburg. "Now you want me to try and wrangle some information out of him."

"Who knows why he didn't call you, Wavonne. It hasn't been that long. Maybe he still plans to."

"Fine. But I'm gonna play it cool with him this time. I think I came off too eager when we were here last. Maybe that's why he didn't call."

"Just do whatever seems to make him comfortable. Whether he's called you or not, I could tell he was attracted to you. I figure you're my best bet for getting his version of what happened at the hotel in Williamsburg the night Raynell died.

Surely, we can't trust Michael's version, knowing what we do now about his relationship with Terrence."

"Raynell was bangin' Gregory. Michael and Terrence are hookin' up. The rate these thots are goin' at it, I wonder if there was a retreat at all. Maybe it was just a big swinger's convention."

I snicker. "It doesn't seem to be a very righteous group, does it?" I comment as my eyes catch sight of Rick looking dapper as ever in a beige suit, light blue shirt, and a patterned silk tie. Once again he's staffing the Church Retreat Ministry table.

"Well, hello, so good to see you again. . . ." He's clearly struggling to remember our names.

"Halia," I say, coming to his rescue. "And this is—"

"Wavonne," he says before I have a chance to. I guess he at least remembered Wavonne's name. "I owe you a phone call."

"Do you?" Wavonne asks, acting as though she hasn't been checking her phone every hour on the hour for more than a week. "So what goods are you peddlin' this week, Rick?" she continues, feigning disinterest.

"We have another retreat scheduled for September . . . this one's in Baltimore. It's called 'Journey to Reinvention.' It will focus on transforming our lesser qualities into strengths through focused self-improvement."

"Hmm . . . wonder if a certain gay minister can reinvent himself as a straight man," Wavonne says under her breath to me.

"What was that?" Rick asks.

"Nothing." I turn to Wavonne. " 'Journey to Reinvention.' That sounds like something you might be interested in."

"Me? I ain't got no lesser qualities I want to change."

I give Wavonne a look that asks her to drop the attitude and play along. When you spend as much time together for as long as Wavonne and I have, sometimes a look is all you need.

She reluctantly changes her disposition. "Okay . . . well,

maybe a weekend in Baltimore wouldn't be such a bad thing. I could get me some crab cakes and some of them Berger Cookies . . . you know, those shortbread cookies with the chocolate frosting on top."

"Yes. We do like our retreats to be all about the available local food options," Rick jokes.

"I've heard good things about the retreat last weekend in Williamsburg. If the Baltimore retreat is half as good, maybe Wavonne should check it out." I take my best stab at turning the conversation in the direction I want it to go.

"Really?"

"Yes. Pastor Marshall was at my restaurant the other night. He said the sessions during the day were very effective, and everyone enjoyed the social time afterward. I think he even mentioned some attendees mingling in the hotel lounge until the wee hours."

"We probably did stay up a bit too late Saturday night."

"So you were part of the after-hours crowd?" Wavonne asks.

"Guilty as charged. The day was intense. So it was nice to relax with friends."

"How late did the evening go?"

"I packed it in about two a.m."

"So I guess you didn't outlast Michael and Terrence Rollins . . . you know Terrence, right? The football—"

"The football player. Of course. Everyone knows Terrence. He's one of our celebrity members. Great guy. And what a career! But no, I think I outlasted him and Michael. Terrence isn't much of a partier. Michael, either."

"So how late did they hang out with you and the others in the lounge?"

"They didn't. I think they both retired to their rooms early. I'm sure they were tired. It was a busy day for them."

"So they weren't in the lounge on Saturday night? At all?"

"No. Why?"

"No reason," I say. "When Michael mentioned people gathering until very late, I assumed he, and probably Terrence, were part of the group."

Wavonne and I exchange looks . . . looks that say the same thing: *so Michael was not only lying about Terrence's whereabouts the night of Raynell's demise, he was lying about his own.*

All three of us are quiet for a moment, before I take an obvious look at my watch. "Look at the time," I say. "Wavonne, we really need to get going. Why don't you take some of the promotional materials and give some thought to the retreat in September."

"Yeah . . . okay." Wavonne haphazardly grabs a brochure and a couple of flyers.

"Let me know if I can answer any other questions . . . and I still owe you a phone call," Rick says to Wavonne. "You were going to give me some ideas about the church's Web site."

"Sure . . . whateveh," Wavonne says.

"Thanks again for the information," I offer before Wavonne and I begin to walk away from the table.

"He was lying," I quietly say to Wavonne.

"I know he was. He ain't gonna call me."

"Not Rick! Michael. Michael was lying about him and Terrence partying in the lounge until two a.m. From the sound of it, they went missing after dinner. You know what that means?"

"You think I played it okay with Rick . . . you know . . . actin' all indifferent?"

"Are you listening to me at all!? Michael lied about his and Terrence's whereabouts. They were not seen after dinner on Saturday night, which would have given one or both of them plenty of time to drive back to Maryland, furnish Raynell with a one-way ticket to being facedown on her bathroom floor, and be back at the hotel in Williamsburg in time for break-fast."

"So you think they both could've had somethin' to do with Raynell buyin' the farm?"

"They are both wealthy men. If they really wanted to be together, they would need to get divorces—divorces that might cost them half or more of their fortunes." As I say this, my eyes catch sight of Alvetta several yards down the long hall in front of us. Earlier, I was hoping to avoid her and figured it wouldn't be hard given that a few thousand people are milling about, but now I'm glad to run into her. When her eyes meet mine, and she waves in our direction, it occurs to me that if Michael and Terrence want to be a real couple and avoid messy divorces, getting rid of Raynell only solved half the problem. As the other half of the problem is walking toward me in a smart gray pantsuit with a familiar smile on her face, all I can think is *ticktock . . . ticktock.*

CHAPTER 34

"So good to see you back here," Alvetta says after she gives both Wavonne and I a quick hug. "You should have told me you were coming. I could have arranged for you to sit with me in the Pastor's Circle. Did you enjoy the service?"

"Um . . . we didn't actually make it to the service."

"Oh . . . no worries. What brings you by then?"

"Well . . ." I try to come up with some words. How do you tell someone that not only is her husband cheating on her . . . he's cheating on her with a *man* . . . and not only is he cheating on her with a man, but he and said other man may be plotting to kill her? It's not the sort of thing you just blurt out in the middle of a crowded church hallway. "Do you think we could talk to you in private, Alvetta? Maybe in your office?"

"Sure," she says, a curious expression on her face. "I'm due at a choir meeting. Let me just text the director and let her know I'll be a few minutes late."

Alvetta sends the text and leads us toward the elevators, which whisk up to the third level. When we reach her office, she takes a seat on the long sofa by the window rather than behind her desk. Wavonne and I sit down next to her.

"Lawd." Wavonne takes in the office. "Cookie Lyon don't have an office this nice on *Empire*."

Alvetta laughs. "It is a nice space. Took me months to furnish and decorate it. I wanted everything 'just so.'" She looks around the room as if to remind her how lovely it is. "I'm very blessed."

I want to say, "I'm not so sure about that." Instead I remain quiet, and there is a lengthy and awkward silence among the three of us.

"So?" Alvetta eventually asks. "What can I help you with?"

I clear my throat. "Gosh. I'm trying to figure out how to say this . . ."

"Say what? You're starting to make me nervous. Is something wrong?"

"Possibly," I say. "Possibly *very* wrong. Your husband . . . Michael . . ." I struggle for words. "He . . . well, he and Terrence. How do I put this—"

"Vetta, girl," Wavonne says. "Michael and Terrence are doin' the nasty, and Halia here thinks they may have teamed up to ice Raynell. And your bougie ass might be next."

"Very *tactful*, Wavonne." I glare at her while Alvetta does the same. She seems to be letting Wavonne's words settle in. "What Wavonne was trying to say is—"

"I know what she was trying to say, Halia. I may be a minister's wife, but I don't live in a bunker. I'm aware of what 'doin the nasty' means. But that's silly. I mean . . . *really* . . . where did you ever get such an idea?"

Though she claims to think the idea of her husband having an affair with Terrence is ridiculous, the look in her eyes and slight tremor in her voice betray her. Clearly, we've unsettled her.

"We came upon this note at the Rollinses' residence." I

hand the incriminating love note to Alvetta. "I recognized Michael's handwriting from his column in the church bulletin. At first I thought it was from him to Raynell, but given some recent events, I'm quite certain it was from Michael to Terrence." I spare Alvetta the details about the little experiment we conducted at Sweet Tea that established that Michael was clearly more interested in the goods Darius was peddling than the ones Wavonne put on display in front of him.

Alvetta takes the note from my hand and begins to read it.

"And it's not just the note." I take a breath. "Wavonne and I did a little checking today with Rick Stevens at the retreat table in the main hall. That's really why we came by today—to see him. According to him, Michael was not being truthful about his and Terrence's whereabouts the night Raynell died. Rick said neither one of them socialized in the lounge that night. In fact, he didn't see them at all after dinner."

Alvetta puts the note down on the table in front of the sofa and stands up. "Wow. Not much gets past you, Halia, does it?" She walks toward her desk.

"I'm sorry we had to be the ones to tell you this, but if you're in danger you need to know."

"Know?" Her back is toward us, and her hands are lightly resting on her desk. "Know? Oh, Halia, I've *known* for years. I knew before I married Michael."

"Sista, say what?!" Wavonne asks.

Alvetta turns around and leans against the desk, more looking at the floor than at us. "As with most things nefarious, it all started with Raynell—that woman could scheme a fat kid out of cake." She lifts her head and looks at us. "I don't follow sports, so I knew nothing about Terrence, football player extraordinaire, back in the day. But apparently, in the nineties, when Terrence was at his height with the Redskins, rumors were swirling that he . . . that he . . ."

"Prefers hot dogs to taco shells?" Wavonne says.

Alvetta nods. "This was almost twenty years ago. Professional football isn't exactly welcoming to gay men now, but back then, it was absolutely unthinkable for the truth about Terrence's sexual orientation to get out. His career would have been over. The rumors had to be squelched, and Raynell signed on to do the squelching. In exchange for helping Terrence keep up appearances, Raynell gained the celebrity of being a star football player's wife and, more important, access to his millions."

"So what does this have to do with you and Michael?"

"It wasn't long after Terrence married Raynell that he met a deacon with a gift for public speaking at a small Baptist church in Camp Springs."

"Michael."

"Yes. I guess one thing led to another, and Terrence and Michael became an item—an item that had to be kept on the down low. As Michael became more and more successful and moved to progressively larger congregations, he found himself in the same position Terrence had years earlier—he was also a star in his career field. But, unfortunately, much like Terrence, he chose a career that, at the time . . . maybe even now, could have been ruined by gay rumors. Thankfully this was before TMZ and Perez Hilton, but apparently a tabloid photographer had begun snooping around and noticing the extensive amount of time Terrence and Michael were spending together with no women on their arms. The attention was not good for either of them. So, once again, it was Raynell to the rescue.

"I was trying to make it as a model at the time, but I was spending more time waiting tables than booking photo shoots. Raynell recruited me to silence the rumors about Michael just like she had for Terrence. I was broke, and my mother was sick . . . and my modeling career was going nowhere fast. It was the right offer at the right time. Rebirth was not in this mammoth building back then, but it had already become a force to be reckoned with, and Michael had amassed a tidy fortune. And I liked him . . . I *still* like him. We're good friends . . . we enjoy each other's company . . . I enjoy my work here . . . and, yes, I'd be lying if I said I didn't revel in the status of being the First Lady of one of the largest churches on the East Coast. It's a mutually beneficial relationship for both of us."

"I guess I'm a little relieved you already knew about Michael and Terrence. I wasn't thrilled about having to be the one to break the news to you. But isn't it still possible that maybe they've decided they wanted to be together in a more . . . I don't know . . . *official* or *open* manner and could have killed Raynell to avoid a costly divorce?"

"No," Alvetta says without hesitation. "Both Raynell and I signed airtight prenuptials. Under the terms of the agreement, Raynell wouldn't have ended up destitute in the event of the divorce, but Terrence would have held on to the bulk of his fortune. The same goes for me and Michael. I would get a little something if we divorced, but definitely nowhere near enough to keep me living in the manner to which I've become accustomed. And, in reality, the legal agreement between Raynell and Terrence is irrelevant at this point. Raynell kept it a closely guarded secret, but several years ago she and Terrence made a series of bad investments and lost the bulk of Terrence's fortune. Terrence does pretty well doing local television, but he's certainly not making millions. That's why Raynell got into selling real estate and was so rabid for new clients in the market for expensive homes. They needed to supplement Terrence's earnings if they were going to keep up the same lifestyle they had before they lost most of their savings."

"So, even if you take money out of the picture, do you think Terrence and Michael's relationship could have had something to do with Raynell's death?"

"No. I can assure you Terrence and Michael have no plans of going public with their relationship. I know things have changed over the years. But Terrence is involved in the world of professional sports, which can still be a rough place for gay men. And Michael . . . well, you can't exactly be an out gay man and also lead a church with an Out of the Darkness ministry."

"What's that?"

Alvetta rifles through some brochures on the table, picks one up, and begins reading. "Out of the Darkness provides healing for individuals suffering from same-sex attraction with the goal of releasing these men and women from the bondage of these feelings."

Alvetta continues reading for another moment or two while Wavonne and I sit there speechless. And, honestly, the deceit and manipulation . . . Raynell and Alvetta marrying gay men for the fringe benefits . . . Michael running a ministry to rid people of same-sex attraction when he's, as Wavonne would say, "gettin' some" on the side with Terrence. It's all making my stomach turn.

When Alvetta is done reading aloud she sets the brochure back on the table only to have Wavonne pick it up and shove it in her purse. "For Darius."

"I don't think Darius is interested in changing anything about himself."

"I know. I'm just trying to hook a brotha up. He's been complainin' about a dry spell—sounds like a good place for a gay man to get a date."

"Have at it. I've never been terribly comfortable with the ministry, and given the way the tide is turning, I suspect its days are numbered," Alvetta says, and looks at me. "So you see, Halia, you're chasing a dead end if you think Terrence and Michael killed Raynell. The four of us had a good thing going, and it worked for all parties. Michael and Terrence were free to pretty much do whatever they wanted. There was no reason to take Raynell out of the picture."

"So, if Michael and Terrence were free to do whatever they wanted, does that mean Raynell was free to do whatever—"

Wavonne interrupts. "And *whoever* she wanted?"

"Yes, she was. Raynell had no shortage of her own affairs and, believe me, Terrence couldn't have cared less."

I let out a sigh. "I can honestly say this is not what I expected to hear when we asked to talk with you."

"It is a tangled web. I know. But you do what you have to do."

"Of course your relationship with Michael . . . Raynell's relationship with Terrence—they are really none of my business. I really just wanted to make sure you were not in danger."

"Michael is my best friend. He would never hurt me." She pauses for a moment. "At least not in that way." The look in her eyes tells me that perhaps she is *his* best friend, but he is a bit more than that to her . . . and that maybe this arrangement doesn't work quite as well as she was trying to have us to believe . . . at least not for her.

CHAPTER 35

"So, what have you got for me?" I ask Momma after I walk into the kitchen at Sweet Tea. Yesterday, I asked her if she'd whip up something special for me to take to Terrence. I wanted something especially yummy—something so good he'll be distracted by the taste and let his guard down while I discreetly pump him for information.

I've talked at length with Alvetta, Michael, Gregory, and Kimberly—Terrence is really the only one on my suspect list who I haven't had a real conversation with. Given Alvetta's insistence that he wouldn't have been bothered by Raynell's affair with Gregory and had no interest in a divorce, maybe it's unlikely that he's to blame for Raynell's death. But if he doesn't offer any information to incriminate himself, maybe he can provide some new leads.

Momma turns to the counter and lifts the top from a cake caddie to reveal a decadent yellow cake with a sugar glaze trickling down the sides and thinly sliced candied lemon slices on top. "Ta da. My brown-butter lemon pound cake."

"Aunt Celia, please tell me you made two of those? I need to have me some of that," Wavonne calls. She was completely engrossed in whatever trashy magazine she was reading on the other side of the counter. But now that the lid is off Momma's creation, Wavonne is taking a break from the latest celebrity gossip to eye the pound cake.

"Stop looking at it that way, Wavonne," I say. "There is only one, and it's for Terrence."

"Why does Terrence get *my* cake?"

"Because I need an excuse to go over to his house. I figure dropping off some delicious baked goods is a nice gesture while he's mourning the loss of his wife."

"Halia, I wish you wouldn't get involved. If that Rollins girl died as the result of foul play, let the police deal with it," Momma says. "Besides, you should be spending time with that nice Gregory fellow. Why don't you take him a cake?"

"Seriously, Momma? I told you about his antics with Raynell. And he's not off my suspect list just yet. You really want me dating a possible murderer?"

"I don't think that nice boy killed anyone. And if he did kill that Rollins girl it's only because she made him mad. Just don't make him mad, Halia, and he won't kill you . . . and I'll get my grandbabies."

I shake my head and roll my eyes. "Just give me the cake, Momma."

Momma snaps the lid back on the caddie and hands it to me.

"I should be back before we open."

As I start to walk out of the kitchen, I hear the hurried clicking of heels on the tile floor behind me. If I didn't know better I'd think the sound was coming from Wavonne, who hasn't changed into her work shoes yet. But "hurried" and Wavonne don't exactly intermingle. I'm through to the dining room and almost at the front door when I turnaround to find it is, indeed, Wavonne tailing me. Apparently, I *don't* know better.

"I'm comin' with you," she says. "If you won't let me have some of that cake, maybe Terrence will."

"Wavonne, I need you to stay here and wait on customers."

"You said you'd be back before we open."

I sigh. She's got me there. "I guess I did. Do you promise you'll behave yourself and not go anywhere near Raynell's closet?"

"Promise."

"Fine. But let me do the talking."

When we arrive at the Rollins residence Terrence is outside watering some shrubs with a hose. He waves to us as I park the van on the street in front of the house. I phoned him this morning before I left the house, so he's expecting us.

"Hello," I call to him as Wavonne and I get out of the van, cake in hand.

"Hello, ladies," he says as we approach him. "What do you have there?"

"My mother makes all the desserts at Sweet Tea, and I asked her to bake a little something special for you. It's not much, but I enjoyed reconnecting with Raynell, and Wavonne and I just wanted to stop by and pay our respects since we couldn't make the funeral."

"Thank you. That's very nice."

Terrence accepts the cake from me with a perplexed look on his face, as if he's surprised anyone would enjoy reconnecting with Raynell. "Please, come in for a few minutes. I'm about done out here. It's been so dry this summer. The gardener isn't due until Friday, so I wanted to give the bushes a little water."

Terrence leads us into the house and down the hall to the kitchen where he sets the cake on the counter. "Please have a seat." He points toward the kitchen table. "What can I get you to drink? I still have some coffee on if you'd like a cup."

"Yes. That would be nice."

Terrence grabs a few mugs from one of the cabinets, fills them with coffee, and brings them over to the table with a

small carton of half-and-half. "There's some sugar right there."
He points to a ceramic bowl on the table.

"You know what would go really well with the coffee?"
Wavonne says. "Some of my Aunt Celia's lemon pound cake."

"Wavonne, the cake is for Terrence. He may want to save it
for later."

"No, no. Let's cut it up." Terrence walks back to the
counter and pulls a knife from a wooden block. "Wow," he says
when he lifts the lid. "It looks so good. I hate to slice into it."

"Then let me do it." Wavonne gets up from her chair and
takes the knife from Terrence. "You get us some plates."

Terrence does as he's instructed, and moments later the
three of us are seated at the table about to get fat and happy on
coffee and pound cake.

Terrence takes a bite. "This is some good cake."

"Yes. Momma is the Queen of Desserts." I help myself to a
forkful as well. "So, how are you holding up, Terrence?"

"I'm hanging in there. There's been so much to do since
Raynell passed. Keeping busy has helped me cope. I'll start
back to work on Monday. I think that will be good for me."

"You must really be going through a lot."

"I guess so, but I'm not sure it's registered that Raynell's really gone. It's so quiet around here without her shouting orders
all day," he says with a laugh.

"Girlfriend did like to tell people what to do," Wavonne
says.

"That she did," Terrence agrees. "She knew what she
wanted and wasn't afraid to ask for it . . . *demand* it. Actually, I
kind of liked that about her. She wasn't always the most pleasant person, but, let me tell you, life with Raynell Rollins was
never boring."

"I'm sure of that." I shift around in my chair. "Can I ask
you something, Terrence?"

"Sure."

"There's been some talk . . . some talk that maybe Raynell's death was not an accident. I guess I'm just wondering what you think about that."

"I think that's just gossip. I've talked with the police and, though we're waiting on the autopsy results, they are all but certain it was an accident. There was no sign of anyone breaking into the house, nothing was missing, and there was nothing to indicate that she struggled with anyone. Raynell liked her cocktails, and sometimes she indulged a bit too much . . . *way* too much. I've seen her unsteady on her feet before from too much vodka. It's not that surprising that she lost her footing and fell hard. I just wish I had been here when it happened. I could have gotten her help."

His eyes start to tear up, and I can tell he's trying to keep his composure and prevent some full-fledged waterworks from starting. "If I had been here instead of at that stupid conference, I could have helped her . . . if she didn't die immediately from the fall, I could have gotten help, and she might still be here." He takes a long breath and lifts a napkin to his eye to catch a stray tear. "I know she could be difficult, but I don't think she ever did anything so bad that someone would want to kill her. And Raynell had another side that most people didn't see—she raised huge amounts of money for her foundation. She really did care about helping those kids. She was always sending money to her family in Roanoke . . . she even foot the bill for some crazy expensive surgery her 'what do I need health insurance for?' brother required. There was a lot to like about Raynell—she was full of energy, smart as a whip, and she knew how to make things happen. Honestly, I'm going to be a bit lost without her."

He may be gay, and there may not have been a romantic connection between them, but I can tell from the tone in his voice that he did have a certain fondness for Raynell, which makes me think it's highly unlikely that he killed her. In fact,

I'm beginning to wonder if she was killed at all. Maybe she really did just slip in the bathroom and hit her head on the side of the tub.

"You'll be okay." I reach for his hand on the table and place mine over it. "In time, you'll be okay."

He smiles at me, and the three of us sit quietly until Wavonne breaks the silence. "Who's up for some more cake?"

"None for me," I say.

"Me either," Terrence adds.

"Guess it's just me then." Wavonne gets up from the table and starts to cut herself another slice.

"Can you take that to go, Wavonne? We really need to get back to Sweet Tea." I get up from the table.

"There's some foil and Cling Wrap in the drawer right in front of you," Terrence says.

As Wavonne shamelessly packs up a piece of cake for herself, I'm just about to let my little amateur investigation of Raynell's death go when I look past Wavonne into the family room that adjoins the kitchen. My eyes catch sight of the painting of Sarah Vaughan that I noticed when I was here to pick up the antique desk more than a week ago.

"That painting . . . the one of Sarah Vaughan. Raynell told me a little about it when I was here before the reunion. It's such a lovely piece. Do you mind if I take another look at it?"

"Of course not. Raynell sure was disappointed to find out it's not a real Keckley, but I think she took a bit of liking to it anyway. I can't say I was terribly fond of it, though. I wish she would have donated it to the silent auction at her reunion."

Something looked slightly off about the painting from the kitchen, and, as I get closer to it, the image appears faintly different from how I remembered it. The colors somehow seem richer . . . or more vibrant than I remember. It doesn't have the same worn look it did the last time I was here.

"Wavonne? Are you about ready with the cake?" I call to the kitchen.

"Yep," Wavonne says, and appears in the family room.

"Good. We need to let Terrence get back to his day."

"It was nice of you to stop by. I've been getting a lot of visitors. I'm sure there will be more, and they'll love the cake."

"What's left of it," I say, my eyes shifting toward Wavonne and her doggie bag before I look back at Terrence and lean in and give him a hug. "If there's anything we can do, please let us know."

Terrence hugs Wavonne as well, and as we start toward the door, I immediately reopen the investigation I was about to close. I could be wrong, but I'm pretty certain the painting I saw of Sarah Vaughan the day of the reunion is not the same one leaning against the wall in Terrence's family room now. What if the one I saw earlier really was an original Keckley? Could someone who knew it was an original have switched it out with a reproduction?

I stop and think before I open the van door and get inside. *Who would know enough about art to determine the authenticity of the painting and have the skill to make an imitation?*

Only one person comes to mind: Kimberly Butler.

CHAPTER 36

"I don't think it was the same painting. I think someone switched it out," I vent to Wavonne as we head to the restaurant in my van.

"What painting?"

"The one in the family room. The one I was asking Terrence about . . . of Sarah Vaughan."

"Who?"

"Sarah Vaughan. She was a jazz singer long before your time. Apparently there was an artist . . . what was his name?" I think for a moment. "Keckley. Arthur Keckley. He painted portraits of famous singers who performed at the Lincoln Theater on U Street back in its heyday. Raynell said she thought the painting might be one of his creations. She bought it from a real estate client. Supposedly, if it's genuine, it's worth thousands of dollars . . . maybe hundreds of thousands."

"Get out!?"

"But Raynell said she had the painting assessed, and the art appraiser told her it wasn't a genuine Keckley."

"So if it ain't real, then why would someone swap it out?"

"I don't know. Maybe it *is* real, and Raynell's appraiser was wrong. Maybe Raynell told Kimberly just enough about the painting at the reunion to pique Kimberly's interest."

"You think Kimberly may've killed Raynell? Over a painting?"

"Maybe I do." My mind starts running through some scenarios. "Perhaps Raynell was actually awake when Kimberly came by after the reunion. What if she showed Kimberly the painting, Kimberly figured out it was the real deal, decided to knock off Raynell, and nab the painting for herself? She would have had just enough time to make a sloppy reproduction and bring it back the next day. Perhaps her whole story about coming back to switch out the shampoo bottle the day after Raynell was killed was just a ruse. Maybe she was really there to replace the legitimate painting with her imitation."

"Terrence didn't seem to think the painting looked any different."

"Weren't you the one who said earlier that men don't notice anything unless it involves a basketball or a pair of titties?"

"A *football* or a pair of titties, but same difference. And knowin' what we now know about Terrence, I guess the 'pair of titties' don't apply no more."

"Either way, Terrence probably never paid enough attention to the painting to notice, and he even said he didn't particularly care for it. If I hadn't found it so striking when I first saw it, I probably wouldn't have noticed it was different, either."

"You *sure* it's not the same painting you saw the first time you were there?"

"Yes . . . well . . . I think so. It really did have a different . . . a different *look* . . . I think."

"I don't know, Halia. You're not soundin' so sure anymore."

"Now you've got me questioning whether it really did

look different." I'm frustrated with my lack of certainty. "I
need to see the painting again and give it a closer look."

"So we gonna turn around and go back to Terrence's house?"

"Possibly." I hand Wavonne my phone. "Look up Terrence
in my contacts, would you?"

Wavonne does as I ask and hands the phone to me. "He
said he wasn't a fan of the painting, so maybe he'd be willing to
sell it to me."

"You want to buy it?"

"I'm not against the idea, but if I pretend I want to buy it,
it gives me an excuse to take a second look at it and really give
it a good once over."

I hit the call button on my phone and wait for Terrence to
pick up.

"Hello."

"Terrence. It's Halia. I'm sorry to bother you. I know we
just left a few minutes ago, but we're on the way back to the
restaurant, and I got to thinking about that painting of Sarah
Vaughan in your family room."

"Really?"

"You mentioned you didn't exactly love it. And . . . well . . .
I actually do like it. I thought maybe I could take the painting
off your hands . . . for a fair price of course."

"Um . . . I guess . . . maybe."

"Can we set up a time for me to take a second look at it,
and then we can talk about payment? Or Wavonne and I
could come back now."

"I have to leave for a meeting shortly, so now is not good.
Maybe we can set it up another time," he says. "And as far as
payment goes, I really have no idea what the painting is worth.
I know Raynell had hoped it was some long lost painting from
the Lincoln Theater or something. It turned out not to be, but
I guess it's still worth a few hundred bucks or so . . . maybe
more."

"Yes. Raynell did mention to me that she had it appraised."
Suddenly, I have an idea. It's almost impossible for me to be
one hundred percent sure the painting was replaced with an
imitation. But if anyone could conclude if the painting I saw
today is different from the one I saw almost two weeks ago, it
would be the appraiser. "Why don't we ask the appraiser to
take a second look and find out what he or she thinks it's
worth?"

"I guess we could do that. I'd need to check with Christy.
She set that up for Raynell."

"I've got Christy's number. Why don't I give her a call?"

"Sure. She'll be over here later this afternoon sorting
through some of Raynell's things for me."

"Okay. I'll be in touch. Thanks, Terrence."

I hang up with Terrence and hand my phone to Wavonne,
so she can pull up Christy's info while I'm driving. As
Wavonne pecks on my phone with a lone red fingernail, I
begin to draft plans in my head for the next day or two. I'll
need to make arrangements with Christy to get the appraiser
to take another look at the portrait. If he confirms it's not the
same piece of artwork he examined for Raynell, then I need to
figure out how to prove that Kimberly is the guilty party—that
she killed Raynell . . . and not over some petty high school
vendetta, but for the reason people have been killing each other
for centuries—greed!

RECIPE FROM HALIA'S KITCHEN

Halia's Country Grits and Sausage Casserole

Layer 1 Ingredients

1⅓ cups water
1⅓ cups half-and-half
1 garlic clove, minced
2 tablespoons butter
1 teaspoon salt
½ teaspoon black pepper
⅔ cup quick-cooking grits
½ cup mixed Mexican shredded cheese (Monterey Jack,
    Cheddar, Queso Quesadilla, and Asadero)
3 eggs lightly beaten

• Preheat oven to 350 Fahrenheit.

• Bring water and half-and-half to a boil in large saucepan.
  Stir in garlic, butter, salt, pepper, and grits. Lower heat to
  simmer mixture and continue to stir for 6 minutes.
  Remove from heat, stir in cheese, and let set for 10
  minutes.

• Stir beaten eggs into grits mixture until well combined.
  Transfer to well-greased, 12-inch cast-iron skillet and
  spread evenly.

- Bake for 20 minutes. Remove from oven. Use a spatula to lightly flatten any bubbles. Set aside.

Layer 2 Ingredients

½ pound mild ground pork sausage
1 cup mixed Mexican shredded cheese
4½ tablespoons all purpose flour
7 eggs
1½ cups sour cream
1½ cups whole milk
1 teaspoon salt
½ teaspoon black pepper
⅛ teaspoon ground Cayenne/red pepper
1 tablespoon chopped fresh parsley
1 tablespoon chopped fresh sage

- Brown sausage in a large skillet until crumbled. Drain and blot with paper towels.

- Sprinkle sausage and cheese over grit cake.

- Mix eggs and flour on medium speed until mostly smooth (about 20 seconds). Some small lumps will remain. Add sour cream, milk, salt, black pepper, and red pepper. Continue to mix on medium speed until well combined. Strain mixture through a sieve to remove any lumps. Stir in parsley and sage before pouring over grit cake.

- Bake at 350 degrees Fahrenheit for 30–35 minutes until firm.

- Cool for 20 minutes prior to serving.

Eight Servings

CHAPTER 37

It's been officially two weeks since Wavonne and I stumbled upon Raynell's dead body. We've just opened for Sunday brunch and the kitchen at Sweet Tea is busier than a tree full of Keebler elves. My prep staff is chopping fruit and making batter for pancakes and waffles, and the deep fryers are fired up for those first batches of fried chicken. Laura has enough home fries going on the grill to feed a small country, and, just now, the first sausage, egg, and grits casseroles are coming out of the oven . . . and they do smell heavenly. We start off with a base of grits, garlic, and cheese and top the mixture with some freshly browned sausage, eggs, and, yes, more cheese. It's one of our brunch specials for the day along with Grandmommy's brown sugar banana pancakes.

"Mmmmm!" Wavonne eyes the casseroles as Tacy lays them on the counter. "Those babies sure look good."

"That they do."

We'll sell out of the ones coming out of the oven by noon, so, just as Tacy finishes removing the last of the cooked casseroles, I move behind him and put in the reinforcements.

"Wavonne, why are you standing here? We're starting to seat customers. Get to work."

"I was hoping to get me a slice of one of these casseroles before I start my shift."

I barely have a chance to give Wavonne one of my signature glares when Saundra sticks her head through the kitchen door. "Halia, there's a young lady here to see you. She said her name is Christy. She has a painting with her."

"Thanks, Saundra. I'll be right out."

I take my apron off, hang it on a hook, and head out to the hostess stand. I called Christy a few days ago and explained that I was interested in purchasing the Sarah Vaughan painting. I asked her if she would connect me with the person who appraised it to help Terrence and me settle on a fair price. She told me the appraiser's name was James Barnett and gave me his number. We originally agreed that I would come by the Rollinses' house while she was there doing some work for Terrence to take a second look at the portrait and meet with James. But while I was chatting with her she mentioned how much she enjoyed her lunch at Sweet Tea a few weeks ago, so I suggested we all meet here. It would give her a chance to enjoy a nice meal and saves me the trouble of having to duck out of the restaurant on a busy Sunday morning.

"Christy. Hi. Thanks so much for coming."

"Sure," she says, grasping the painting with both hands.

"Can I help you with that?"

The painting isn't exactly *huge*—maybe four feet long and about three feet wide—but it's a bit much for Christy's petite frame.

"Yes. Please."

"Let's take it in the back." I grab the painting from her, and she follows me to two tables in the rear of the restaurant. I lay the artwork on one of the tables and signal for her to sit at the other. I give the painting a quick once-over. I'm still fairly convinced it's not the same one I saw at the Rollins house before the reunion.

"What can I get you to drink? A mimosa? Bloody Mary?"

"Just coffee, please."

"Sure. And I'll fetch some menus," I say. "Should I keep an eye out for Mr. Barnett? What's he look like?"

"Actually, I'm not sure. I haven't met him in person. I found him for Raynell on the Internet, and he met with her at the house several weeks ago."

"Okay. I'm sure Saundra will bring him back when he checks in."

I return to the front of the restaurant and pick up a few menus. I'm just about to head to the drink station to get some coffee for Christy when a slight black man walks into the restaurant. He's only about five and a half feet tall and maybe a hundred and thirty pounds. He looks a little lost as he hovers near the door.

"James?" I ask. "James Barnett?"

"Yes."

"Hi. I'm Halia. I'm so glad you agreed to come by."

"No problem. Thank you for having me. I don't get too many offers for a complimentary brunch."

"You're quite welcome. Christy, Raynell's assistant . . . *former* assistant is here already. She brought the painting. Let me show you to the table."

I lead James through the restaurant to the table in the back where Christy is already seated. She stands up when she sees us approaching.

"You must be James," she says when we reach the table. "Christy. So nice to meet you in person."

"You too. I appreciate you connecting me with Ms. Rollins. I had hoped to do more work for her in the future. I was so sorry to hear that she passed. She was such a nice lady."

Christy and I exchange looks. Clearly we are biting our tongues over the "nice lady" comment.

"I understand you want me to take a second look at the Sarah Vaughan portrait."

"Yes. It's right over there." I point to the adjacent table. "But let me treat you to brunch first." I motion for Wavonne.

"What up, boss?"

"You remember Christy."

"Yeah," Wavonne says. "Hey, sista girl."

"Hi, Wavonne."

"Can you bring Christy and me some coffee?" I turn to James. "And what would you like to drink?"

"Coffee is good for me, too."

"I'll give you a few minutes to look over the menu, but keep in mind we have brown sugar banana pancakes and a sausage eggs and grits casserole on special. I highly recommend both of them."

"The casserole is delish!" Wavonne says. "It comes with a blueberry muffin and fresh fruit."

"Sounds good to me," Christy says. "Bring it on."

"Make it two," James says.

"Two sausage, egg, and grits casseroles comin' up."

"Should I look at the painting now while we wait?" James asks after Wavonne walks away to put the order in.

"Sure."

The three of us get up from the table and gather around the painting.

"While not a genuine Keckley, it is a nice portrait, and likely produced around the same time as the original." James leans in closely toward the portrait. "It's a striking piece of work and captures the essence of Ms. Vaughan. It definitely has what we call 'wall power' and, given its age and great condition, I'd say it could fetch anywhere from one to two thousand dollars . . . maybe a bit more if someone really took a liking to it."

"Oh my. That's probably a bit too much for me to spend on artwork. Terrence and I were thinking it was only worth a few hundred dollars. I guess I'll need to think about it," I say. "So, I'm just curious. How can you tell it's not an original Keckley?"

"Right here." James points to the artist's signature on the painting. "Arthur Keckley always signed his paintings A. Keckley at the bottom right-hand side. The signature on this painting is signed Arthur Keckley, and it's on the bottom left side."

I lean in close to the painting to take a look at the signature, and, as I do, I get a whiff of a familiar scent. I can't quite place it, but I know I have smelled it before.

"Well, I guess that's that. It *is* a very nice painting," I say, even though I don't mean it. It must be the same painting I saw before the reunion. If anyone would notice it's different, it would be James. But I just don't find it anywhere near as alluring as I did when Raynell first showed it to me. And I definitely don't care for it enough to spend a thousand dollars on it.

"So, Christy," I say after we've moved back over to the other table to have our coffee, which Wavonne just delivered. "Terrence mentioned you were helping him with some of Raynell's things. How is that going?"

"Yeah, how is that going?" Wavonne slides into the seat next to me. "What's Terrence doin' with all those fab purses and shoes?"

"You forgot the jewelry, Wavonne. And what about the belts? And maybe the furniture?" I chide. "Honestly, the woman's body is barely cold, and you're already making a play for her wardrobe."

Christy smiles. "That's okay. Raynell did have quite the designer collection. Actually, I'm working with Alvetta to set up an auction for many of her things at Rebirth. All the proceeds will go to Raynell's foundation."

"Auction? When?" Wavonne asks.

"We haven't set a date yet, but I'll be sure to keep you in the loop."

"Satisfied?" I ask Wavonne. "Now would you get back to work, and go see if Christy's and James's entreés are ready?"

Wavonne lets out a huff and gets up from the table only to return a few minutes later with two loaded plates for my guests. She puts their dishes down on the table, and they look at them eagerly.

"Thanks, Wavonne," I say. "Can you bring us some more coffee, please?"

"And some ketchup if you don't mind," Christy asks.

Wavonne looks at me to see if I'm keeping a poker face. She knows I have a pet peeve with ketchup, and she's checking to see if my expression shows it. To me, ketchup is for one thing and one thing only—French fries.

Wavonne grabs a bottle of Heinz from a nearby, recently vacated table, and, as she heads off to get us some more coffee, I try not to grimace while James squirts out a long ribbon of ketchup on to his slice of my casserole. I just hate to see food that was perfected to be eaten a certain way ruined. I know it shouldn't—my customers pay for the meals and should be able to eat them however they choose—but it just bugs me when customers sprinkle excessive amounts of salt on carefully seasoned meals, drown a tenderly aged steak with A.1. sauce, or in this case, drench my Grandmommy's casserole in freakin' ketchup.

"You're not having any breakfast?" Ketchup Man asks me.

"No. Just coffee for me this morning. How do you like the casserole?"

"It's *very* nice," Christy says.

"Yes, very," I hear from James.

We chat for a while longer, and Christy shares some preliminary details about the planned church auction with me, how she's almost done wrapping up Raynell's business dealings, and how she'll be in the market for a new job soon. James is not much of a talker, but he does comment a bit on the painting and suggests that Christy talk to Terrence about including it as part of the church auction.

"Even if it's not the real deal, it is an antique, and could raise a nice little sum for Ms. Rollins's foundation."

"I think that's a great idea. I'll talk to Terrence about it when I take the painting back," Christy says. "Speaking of which, I guess it's time for me to get back over to the Rollins house. I have to start cataloging items for the auction. Thanks so much for a lovely brunch. I hope to come back again soon."

"You're so welcome. I appreciate you saving me the trouble of having to leave Sweet Tea to give the portrait another look. I'm sorry I wasn't able to make an offer on it, but I think it's just too expensive for my blood. I hope Terrence agrees to add it to the auction."

"I'm sure he will." Christy gets up from her chair and walks over to the next table.

"Why don't I help you with that?" James says as she's about to reach for the painting. He walks over and lifts the painting from the table. "Thank you, Ms. Watkins. Breakfast was quite a treat."

I nod and smile, and he begins to walk ahead of us toward the door.

"Can I ask you something, Christy?" I inquire as we linger back.

"Of course."

"You spent a lot of time with Raynell. What do you think—do you think her death was really an accident?"

"I suppose I do. You know as well as me that Raynell was no saint, but I can't think of anything that she ever did to anyone that was so horrible they would want to kill her."

"You're probably right. I guess it's time for me to just let it go."

I continue to walk Christy out, and we find James waiting by her car with the painting.

"Thanks for carrying the painting out for me," Christy says, and presses a button on her keychain to pop the trunk open. She's already got the backseat folded down, so James slides the painting in the trunk.

I watch Christy get in her car, and James climb into a small pickup truck a few spaces away.

I guess it's about time for me to let it go, I think, recalling how I just said that to Christy as they drive off, but, in reality, I'm not quite ready to do that. Before I'll really be ready to move on, there is one more thing I'd like to do . . . one more visit I'd like to make.

I grab my phone from my pocket and hit the screen a few times. "Hey, Kimberly. It's Halia. I was just wondering . . . if you're still in town, mind if I come by for a quick visit?"

CHAPTER 38

"Hello. I'm Halia Watkins, and this is my cousin, Wavonne. We're here to see Kimberly. You must be Mrs. Butler."

"Yes. She said you'd be stopping by," comes from the elderly woman at the front door of a modest split-level house in Clinton. "You're one of her classmates from high school, right?"

"Yes."

"She's in the garage. It was her makeshift studio when she still lived at home, and we never changed it. I guess her father and I were afraid she may not come back to visit if she didn't have somewhere to paint while she was here."

She waves for me to follow her down the steps.

"Those weren't good days for Kim . . . her high school days I mean," Mrs. Butler says. "Kim told me that horrible girl who caused her to lose her hair died a couple of weeks ago. I supposed it's sad for her friends and family who lost her, but I can't say I'm sorry."

"It was an awful thing to do. Even by high school 'mean girl' standards," I agree.

We follow Mrs. Butler through a quaint family room to a side door. "I'm not sure my Kim ever fully recovered from the incident. But I guess some good came of it. Being so out of place in school left her a lot of time to focus on her art, and now she's doing so well. She's been trying to move Mr. Butler and me to some grand new house for years, but this is home . . . we don't really want to leave."

Mrs. Butler opens the door, and the three of us step into the garage, where we find Kimberly screwing a spray nozzle on a metal can.

"Kim, your guests are here."

Kimberly turns to us and lowers the mask she had covering her nose and mouth. "Hi, Halia. Wavonne."

"I'll leave you three alone. Can I get you anything? A glass of water or a soda?"

"I'd love a Diet Dr. Pepper and if—"

"No thank you, Mrs. Butler." I cut Wavonne off. "Nothing for us. We just want to chat with Kimberly for a bit."

"Okay. It was nice to meet you."

"So what can I do for you?" Kimberly asks me as the door shuts behind Mrs. Butler.

"You could start by telling me a little bit about this piece you are working on." I figure there's no need to dive right into questioning her, and I really am curious about her art.

"It's nothing. I've just started experimenting with spray art. I thought it might be an area I could get into, but I'm finding it's too messy, and the fumes from the paint are a bit much. I don't particularly like wearing a mask while I work. But since I started this project I figure I may as well finish it."

"You ever make T-shirts with the spray art? Like they do at the beach?" Wavonne asks.

Kimberly looks momentarily horrified by the question. "Umm . . . no."

I take a closer look at the piece she is working on. "It looks like you're off to a great start."

"Thank you, Halia, but somehow I doubt you came over here to discuss my art."

"Well . . . no . . . no, I didn't," is all I manage to get out. I can't quite figure out how to delve into the subject of the Sarah Vaughan painting, but, as I look around at the extensive studio Kimberly has set up in her parents' garage, it's clear she definitely had the means to quickly create a replica of the original painting and hurriedly switch it out with a copy the morning after Raynell's demise.

Kimberly looks at me quietly as I try to find some words. "What is it, Halia? I assume this has to do with Raynell's death?"

"Yes . . ."

"Did you follow up on the lead I gave you about Gregory being outside Raynell's house the night she died?"

"As a matter of fact, I did."

"And?"

"It's a long story." I think of Gregory's affair with Raynell, and how it was all a pointless ploy to eventually leave her with no husband and no money . . . laughable, actually, considering her husband wouldn't have really cared and the money was mostly Raynell's earnings these days . . . but I decide it's more detail than I want to share with Kimberly. "I mean a *really* long story. But the jist of it is I don't think Gregory killed her."

"What about me, Halia? Do you think I killed her? She was a wicked toad of a woman, and I can't say I'm shedding any tears over her death, but I *did not* kill her."

"I never said you did, Kimberly, but . . . well . . . if I were to . . . to imply that you played a role in her death, there are some things that would support that conclusion."

"Like?"

"Raynell mentioned a painting to you at the reunion—a painting she thought might be an original by Arthur Keckley. He painted—"

"I know who Arthur Keckley was, Halia. And, yes, I remember Raynell mentioning the painting to me. As I told you earlier, I was going to use the painting as an excuse to pay her a visit—I had planned to tell her I was there to take a look at it, and let her know what I thought of it."

"And what *did* you think of the painting?"

"Honestly, I never saw it. When I got there and found her asleep upstairs, I made the shampoo switch and was on my way. There was no need to bring the painting into it."

"You would understand, though, if someone might think you actually did see the painting and used your knowledge of art to determine it was, in fact, a genuine Keckley."

"Um . . . okay. And so what if I did?"

"Well, you must know Keckleys are worth huge amounts of money. It wouldn't be unreasonable to think that you decided to steal the original, quickly paint a facsimile to replace it, and kill the one person who would know the difference—a person you really couldn't stand anyway."

Kimberly laughs. "Wow. You have quite the imagination, Halia, but there's a flaw in your reasoning."

"Oh?"

"Yes. You seem to think I would have stolen Raynell's painting, and killed Raynell, to make a fast buck."

"People have killed for far less reasons."

"I'm sure they have, but did you see the Tesla in the driveway when you came in? It stands out like a sore thumb in this working-class neighborhood."

"Actually, I didn't notice it."

"Girl, I noticed it," Wavonne says. "That is a *nice* ride."

"Well, it cost me about a hundred thousand dollars. The dress I had on the night of the reunion, it was J. Mendel—it cost me over six thousand dollars. And if you must know, I rent a loft in Manhattan for twelve thousand dollars a month . . .

and I have another house in the Hamptons that even I'm embarrassed to say how much I paid for it. Do you get what I'm saying here?"

I just look at her as I try to wrap my brain around someone renting an apartment for twelve thousand dollars a month. *Twelve thousand dollars!*

"What I'm saying, Halia, is that I don't need to *steal* paintings that would sell for a few hundred thousand dollars—I *create* paintings that sell for almost that much. You're barking up the wrong tree if you're looking at me as someone who killed Raynell for money."

I look down at the floor, embarrassed that Kimberly has shot holes through my accusations. Then I lift my head and sigh. "I've got no one left on my suspect list. Maybe she really did just fall in the bathroom in a drunken stupor."

"She was pretty wrecked when she left the reunion."

"Yes, she was," I agree. "I'm sorry I came over here pointing fingers." I feel like a puppy with its tail between its legs.

"I appreciate the apology. It's fine, really. But I'd like to get back to my work here."

"Of course. We'll show ourselves out."

I turn to leave as Kimberly lifts the mask back over her face, turns a knob on her canister, and aims it at the canvas in front of her. I'm about to step away when the smell of the streaming paint reaches my nose—the fumes Kimberly mentioned earlier that caused her to wear a mask. They have the same smell that I noticed when I got close to the painting when it was laying on the table at Sweet Tea. This little piece of insight gets the gears in my brain spinning and prompts me to turn around and walk back over to Kimberly as she carefully applies paint to her canvas. She sees me hovering next to her and shuts off the sprayer.

"Was there something else?"

"Yes. Just one thing. Would you mind lowering your mask for me . . . just for a sec?"

Kimberly lowers the mask from her face as if she's willing to do anything if it will get rid of me and my prying questions. With the mask lowered, I study her face for a moment while she looks at me, bemused.

"Thank you," I say. "You've no idea how helpful you've just been."

"How so?"

"I think you've just helped me figure out who actually did kill Raynell."

"By spraying paint on a canvas?"

"Yes."

"So who . . . who did it?"

"Why don't you come with us, and I'll show you."

CHAPTER 39

"I'm a busy man, Ms. Watkins," Detective Hutchins says to me as Wavonne and I step out of my van with Kimberly following. He must have arrived a few minutes before us. "I've got a few men here as well." He points toward two patrol cars also parked in the lot of Christy's apartment building. "We're spending taxpayers' dollars. This had better not be some wild-goose chase."

I called Detective Hutchins after leaving Kimberly's parents' house and asked him to meet us at Christy's home. I assured him that I can prove that Raynell's death was not an accident and, after much prodding, he finally agreed.

I lead us toward Christy's apartment. On the way, we pass by Christy's car and see that the painting is still on the folded-down backseat. James Barnett's truck is parked next to it.

We walk up the steps to her unit, and, when I knock on the door, we hear some scurrying around inside. Sometime later, Christy opens the door just enough to poke her head through.

"Hi, Christy. Can we speak with you for a few minutes?" I ask.

"Now is really not a good time."

"That's okay. We'll just be a minute." Wavonne pushes the door open and walks into Christy's apartment, with the rest of us following. We've barely entered the living room when we hear a door close down the hall.

"You can come out, James," I call. "I know you're here. I saw your truck in the parking lot."

James opens a door down the hall from the living room and steps out. He tries to smile as if he has nothing to hide, but he's not a good actor.

"Christy invited me back after lunch at your lovely restaurant," he says. "To . . . um . . . to . . ."

"I thought you said you'd never met James before today?" I ask Christy, interrupting James's stammering. "Do you always invite men you've just met back to your place?" I do the air quotes thing with my fingers when I say "just met."

"I'm not sure that's really any of your business, Halia. Is there something I can help you with?"

"Yes. We'd just like to ask you some questions." I point to my left. "You remember Wavonne and Kimberly . . . and this is Detective Hutchins with the Prince George's County Police Department."

Christy and James were clearly unnerved by our intrusion, but even more worry comes across their faces when they hear the word "police."

"Like I said, Halia, my bringing a man I've just met back to my place is really not any of your business."

"Man you've just met? You'd never met James prior to this morning? Really?" I don't wait for an answer. "Then how, pray tell, did you know he liked ketchup on his eggs?"

Christy looks at me with an inquisitive expression.

"You asked for ketchup after your entrees arrived at brunch today. You never used it, but James was certainly a fan. My momma used to do that for Daddy. He'd always forget to ask for Tabasco sauce before the waiter left the table, so Momma got in the habit of asking for it for him. That's what people who've been together for a long time do. They think for the other person."

"That proves that I knew James before today? Because I asked for ketchup? You've got to be kidding me."

"That's not all. James agreed to carry the painting for you when you were leaving Sweet Tea. He walked ahead of us while you and I chatted. And, when we caught up with him, he was waiting by your car. Funny how he didn't need any instruction on which car was yours."

Clearly flustered, she responds. "That's just a coincidence. He was just . . . he was just waiting for us and happened to be near my car."

"Hmm. Maybe." I switch gears. "So, we saw Raynell's painting out in your car."

"So? I plan to take it back over to Terrence later. You aren't accusing me of stealing it, are you? You asked me to retrieve it for James to reassess it at your restaurant. We all know it doesn't have any major value anyway . . . at least not enough to make it worth stealing."

"No, the *one* in the car doesn't have any significant value, but I suspect *that* one does." I point to some edges of a frame sticking out from underneath the sofa. "When you rushed to hide it from us when we knocked on the door, you should have made sure it was entirely out of sight."

"Ooh . . . it's about to go *down!*" Wavonne steps over to the sofa and slides the painting out from underneath.

I take a quick look at it. "Yes, that's the one I remember seeing at Raynell's weeks ago. It definitely has a more weathered look than the poor imitation out in the car. You know what else I noticed when I leaned in close to examine the imitation on the table at Sweet Tea?"

"What did you notice, Halia?" James asks, irritation in his voice.

"It had a certain smell—a smell that I just figured out over at Kimberly's studio earlier today was the scent of fresh paint. You'll notice this one"—I point toward the painting on the floor—"doesn't have a smell, which is how I knew James was lying when he said the copy he viewed at Sweet Tea, the copy that's down in your car as we speak, was painted about the same time as the original. Portraits that are decades old don't smell of paint, but newly made reproductions do. Any real art appraiser would have noticed the smell and immediately concluded that the portrait viewed at Sweet Tea was painted recently. But James isn't a real art appraiser, is he?"

No one answers my question.

"You arranged for James, who I'm guessing is your boyfriend, to pretend to be an appraiser so he could tell Raynell that the painting was worthless. You—"

Christy interrupts me. "I have no idea what you're talking about."

"Oh, I think you know a lot . . . about a lot of things, Christy. Let's take art for instance. Who would have guessed that an assistant to a real estate agent would have a master's degree in art history?"

"How did you know that?"

"I had Wavonne do a little digging on her phone on the way over here. You shouldn't keep things on your LinkedIn profile that you don't want others to see." I pause for a moment. "My guess is there are not a lot of jobs out there these days for art history majors, so you had to settle for what you hoped would be a temporary gig with Raynell."

"Having an art degree is hardly a crime."

"No, but it does give you the credentials to determine the worth of art or at least have an idea if a piece might be worth something. My guess is you knew the value of the Keckley as soon as you saw it, and you immediately began scheming about how to keep Raynell in the dark about it. I guess that's where

James came in. You two conspired for James to pose as an art expert and tell Raynell her painting had no value, when you knew that it was worth hundreds of thousands of dollars. I'm thinking you even had him tell her that her antique desk was worth a few thousand bucks to throw her a bone and keep her from getting suspicious."

"Pure fiction," James says.

"Real life is always more interesting than fiction, James. I bet killing Raynell was not part of the original plan. You probably just planned to switch out the painting with a better reproduction at some later date, but suddenly you needed to act fast when you heard Raynell asking Kimberly to take a look at the painting at the reunion. You decided to kill Raynell before Kimberly could tell her how much the painting was really worth, which would have led Raynell to investigate the two of you. Then not only would you have lost your chance at making some serious cash, but you may very well have found yourself in jail on conspiracy charges."

"This is silly," James says. "Okay, so you caught us with the real painting. Maybe we did switch it out. But you can't prove we killed Raynell. Besides, from what I've heard, all indications lead to her death being an accident. Word is there was no sign of forced entry or struggle."

"Of course there was no forced entry. Christy has a key to her house and, even if she didn't, she was the last one to see Raynell alive when she put her to bed the night of the reunion. She could have left the door unlocked for reentry later."

"That doesn't explain why there were no signs of struggle," Detective Hutchins says. "And these two"—he gestures toward Christy and James—"are not big people. Even together I doubt they could have killed Ms. Rollins without her putting up a good fight . . . a struggle."

"There were no signs of struggle because . . . well, because

Raynell was already dead . . . or at least unconscious when Christy and James slammed her head against the bath tub."

Christy visibly tenses up. "That's ridiculous!"

"No, I'm afraid it isn't. And I'll tell you why. Word on the street is that someone stole Raynell's Escalade the day after she died—"

"Yeah . . . some hood rats must've heard Raynell croaked and figured they'll steal her car while there was no one home," Wavonne interrupts.

I eye Wavonne in such a way that tells her to cool it and let me do the talking. "But whoever stole the vehicle abandoned it on the side of the road when it ran out of gas only a few miles from her home."

"So?"

"That always struck me as odd. Raynell was very detailed-oriented and on top of things . . . and, like a Boy Scout, she was always prepared. She earned her living in her car and was hardly the kind of person who would let her gas tank get so low that her car would run out of gas before she could get to the nearest filling station."

"What does that have to do with anything? It means nothing," Christy says.

"It means we look for an explanation of why her gas tank was near empty the day she's found dead. Perhaps it was because *someone*"—I look at Christy as I say this—"left the car running all night with the garage door closed. Perhaps *someone* brought her home from the reunion and put her to bed. Then went into the garage and started the car, knowing that Raynell was so drunk she'd likely sleep through the carbon monoxide fumes coming into her house until they killed her or at least rendered her immobile."

"And not that anyone did, but let's just say that someone else entered the house shortly after you left." I move my gaze from Christy to Kimberly. "And let's just say this someone was there to . . . I don't know . . . switch out shampoo with hair removal cream. The running car in the garage would also explain why this person left Raynell's feeling light-headed and was so loopy that she had to pull over and get some rest in a parking lot. The house would have likely just started to fill up with fumes when she came to settle an old high school vendetta. While she wouldn't have been there long enough for the fumes to kill her, they could have made her feel unwell on the way home and caused the lingering headache she might have reported for days afterward."

"If you really think someone left the car running all night, what makes you think it was me?" Christy asks. "There were tons of people in town with motive to kill Raynell. From what I understand, half her former classmates hated her. Why not Gregory Simms . . . or her." Christy directs a finger toward Kimberly.

"Interesting that you're pointing to Kimberly. I went to see her today, and she was working with some spray paints. Did you know people wear masks when they work with spray paints? Funny thing, when she took the mask off, the straps that go behind her ears left some marks on her face—the same kind of marks you had on your face when I came to get my check from you the morning after the reunion. I thought they were sleep lines from a wrinkly pillowcase, but now I'm quite certain they were from a mask—a mask you wore when you went back to Raynell's after filling her house with carbon monoxide all night. It would have been necessary to wear one when you went around opening all the windows to let the fumes out.

"I thought it was odd that all the windows were open the morning we found Raynell. She was always complaining about how much she hated the heat—"

"Girl was a bigger sweater than Whitney Houston during her crack days."

I nod in agreement with Wavonne. "And why would she have all the windows in her house open when she was home alone? Let's face it, Christy, you went back to Raynell's the morning after the reunion, opened all the windows to clear the house of car exhaust. And, at some point, James joined you, and the two of you dragged Raynell's dead body out of bed into the bathroom and slammed her head against the tub. Shortly after you hastily created a bad reproduction of the Keckley painting and replaced it with the original, hoping it would go unnoticed."

"That's all speculation," James says.

Christy looks at him, and it seems that the stress of her actions and the lies to cover them have taken their toll. "So what if we did kill her? The bitch had it coming."

"Christy!" James calls, trying to get her to shut up.

"They've already got us on the stolen painting, James. It's over," she says to him, and then turns to the rest of us. "She was a horrible person. All she did was scream at me all day and complain about everything I did. She wouldn't have sold a single house if it wasn't for all of my work. But do you think that miser ever shared so much as a penny of one of her commissions with me? When she made a big sale, do you know what she would do? She'd give me some of her designer hand-me-downs in a plastic trash bag as some sort of warped thank-you. Like I was supposed to have undying gratitude for her leftover Manolos. Yeah, we killed her to keep her from finding out we tried to dupe her out of a hefty sum of money and to make sure we got the painting, but just ridding the world of Raynell Rollins was reason enough."

As Christy continues to unravel, I see Detective Hutchins approach the living room window and signal to the officers outside. Neither Christy nor James appears braced to make a run for it, so I'm surprised when Detective Hutchins flips his jacket back to reveal his gun. "I'm placing both of you under arrest," he says. "Don't make me take this out of its holster."

The words have barely left his mouth when two armed police officers open the front door, and quickly step inside with their guns drawn. Detective Hutchins directs them to cuff Christy and James and take them outside to read them their rights.

"I have to hand it to you, Halia, you did it again," Detective Hutchins says to me with a look of surprise. "But maybe from now on you should leave the detective work to the professionals. Or one of these days you may end up getting hurt yourself."

"I'll do my best."

While Wavonne and I watch him walk outside the apartment to check on his underlings, she leans toward me. "Think you can keep them distracted while I take a quick peek in Christy's closet for some of those hand-me-down Manolos?"

EPILOGUE

It's a crisp fall day, and I'm thankful to have a break from the heat we've dealt with all summer as Wavonne and I step out of my van and make our way to one of the event rooms in good old Rebirth Christian Church. I wasn't that eager to come, but Wavonne, for once in her life, has actually saved up money for the opportunity to bid on some of Raynell's things that are going to be auctioned off today, so I agreed to bring her.

It's been almost two months since Raynell's untimely death. I'm not sure if Terrence wanted to allow for a respectable amount of time to pass before putting Raynell's finer things up for sale, or if the lag time was due to Christy, the original curator, who was tagging everything and getting it ready for event, being hauled off to jail on murder charges.

I've been to Rebirth enough times now that I sort of know the lay of the land at this point; accordingly, it doesn't take Wavonne and me long to find the room reserved for the auction.

"I think I've died and gone to heaven," Wavonne says as we enter the space.

"They really didn't spare any expense, did they?" I take a look around. I guess I shouldn't be surprised by how grand the displays are. I should know by now that Rebirth does nothing on a small scale. Many of Raynell's outfits are displayed on actual mannequins just like you'd see in a department store. Some of her shoes and handbags are displayed in groups on long tables draped in silk fabric while others are displayed solo on individual pedestals. Jewelry, wallets, and scarves are displayed in glass cases.

"I wonder if Tiffany & Co. is as well-appointed as this place," I say to Wavonne as we begin to peruse the displays.

"I wonder if Tiffany is as expensive as this place." Wavonne looks at the bidding form for a pair of T-strap Valentino pumps. "The bidding starts at five hundred dollars. And they want at least four hundred for those Fendi beaded sandals." She sighs. "There're no bargains to be had here. I saved two hundred and fifty dollars for nothin'."

"Let's keep looking. I'm sure there is something you can afford."

I pick up a glossy color booklet from one of the tables and begin to thumb through it. It has a complete description of all the items up for auction, a brief bio about Raynell with her photo, and some information about her foundation. Once again I should not be surprised, but I find myself taken aback when I read the fine print at the bottom of one of the pages. It reads: "A portion of the proceeds from the event will go to the Raynell Rollins Foundation for Children in Need." *A portion?* I think to myself. The idea that *all* the proceeds will not go to the foundation seems a little shady, not to mention tacky, considering the auction has been heavily promoted as an event to benefit charity. But given that Raynell was likely the major bread winner in the Rollinses' household, Terrence may be hoarding earnings from her estate auction to meet the shortfalls he's bound to face without her income coming in.

"Halia and Wavonne," I hear come from behind as we move toward the jewelry display cases.

"Alvetta," I say. "How are you? Clearly you've been very busy," I add, looking around me.

She gives Wavonne and me a quick hug. "I'm fine," she says. "Yes, I've been busy getting everything ready for tonight. We've attracted a good crowd. I think we'll raise a lot of money for Raynell's foundation. It's a great way to honor her memory."

I'm tempted to ask exactly how much of the money made tonight is actually going to charity, but I decide to let it go. I'd rather just assume that most of it is slated for people in need.

"Yes. It looks like lots of people are placing bids." I take another look around and notice a few somber-looking people seated in the rows of chairs positioned in the middle of the room. "I guess those folks have already placed all their bids?"

"No." Alvetta laughs. "Those are the *serious* bidders. I doubt they are taking part in the silent auction at all. They are here for the live auction."

"Live auction?"

"Yes. For the Sarah Vaughan painting. It's been officially authenticated as an Arthur Keckley original." Alvetta points to the far side of the room, and I see the painting on display. Wavonne had me so caught up in Raynell's clothes and accessories I hadn't looked in the direction of the portrait.

"It really is stunning," I say as the three of us begin to approach the portrait. "It looks even more exquisite now that it's displayed with the appropriate lighting."

"And what do we have here?" Wavonne says when we reach the painting, and she takes note of a nicely built armed security guard standing next to it. "Mm-hmm," she adds, looking him up and down.

"We're here to look at the *painting*, Wavonne."

"Speak for yourself," she replies as the guard cracks a smile.

"Is an armed guard really necessary?" I ask Alvetta.

"We're starting the bidding at a hundred thousand dollars,

so yes, I'd say so," she replies. "Sotheby's did the valuation, and they are handling the live auction. It should be starting soon. We're about to close the silent auction, so you two should get any final bids in."

"I guess we should. It was nice to see you, Alvetta."

"You too," she says. "I hope you'll come to service again sometime soon." She gives us each a quick peck on the cheek and darts off to speak with a gentleman near the podium, the auctioneer, I assume.

Wavonne and I continue to walk the room, and it's not long before we are both thoroughly frustrated at the starting bids on most of the items.

"There's nothin' here for me," Wavonne says, defeated.

"They really did price things quite high." As I say this I try to think of some of the less expensive items we've seen tonight. There was a very small Coach wallet that started with a bid of two hundred dollars, but it was a simple leather piece and way too conservative for Wavonne. Some of the scarves and belts had starting bids under one hundred dollars, but I think Wavonne really had her heart set on a purse or a pair of shoes.

"What about those Fendi pink sandals we saw when we first came in?" I ask. I'm sure they have a smaller heel than Wavonne would like, but they are florescent pink with a wide beaded toe strap. I don't think Wavonne has ever turned down a florescent anything.

"Those started at four hundred."

"If no one has placed a bid on them, and they are still going for four hundred, I'll throw in the other one fifty," I offer, hating the idea of Wavonne having actually behaved like a mature adult and saving some money amounting to her leaving empty-handed.

"You would?" Wavonne's face lights up, and she leads us back over to the sandal display. Fortunately, no other bids have been placed, and with the silent auction about to close, I think it's safe to say Wavonne will be the winner.

"Looks like I'll be leaving with these babies."

"I think they have to reconcile everything tonight. You'll probably have to come back and pick them up tomorrow or another time."

Only slightly deflated, Wavonne writes down her bid, while, from the corner of my eye, I see someone approaching carrying a flat package wrapped in brown paper. I turn my head to bring the individual into full view.

"Kimberly!"

"Hi, Halia," she says while Wavonne is still distracted by the shoes. "I just came back for a quick visit to see my parents and to give you this." She nods toward the package. "I went by Sweet Tea to surprise you, and they said you'd be here."

"What is it?" I ask, intrigued.

"You'll see."

I take the package from her and set it on one of the display tables, so I can unwrap it. My excitement builds as I gently remove the packing paper, and it becomes clear that Kimberly's gift is a portrait—*the* portrait that we discussed her painting of my grandmother.

"I have no words," I say, smiling from ear to ear as I take in the painting of my hero and mentor and namesake . . . and all around special lady, Mrs. Mahalia Hix. "I love it!"

"Girl can throw down with a paint brush," I hear Wavonne say behind me as she takes in the painting.

"Hi, Wavonne," Kimberly says.

"Hey, girl. That painting's dope!"

Kimberly laughs. "Thank you," she says to Wavonne, and then turns to me. "I figured I owed you one. If you hadn't put all the pieces together and figured out who killed Raynell, I could have been in a lot of trouble if the police figured out I was there the night she was murdered. It's the least I could do."

"Well, I still insist on paying you."

Kimberly lifts her hand at me. "I won't hear of it. How about just the occasional complimentary meal at Sweet Tea when I come to town?"

"You've got yourself a deal."

"Perfect."

"I can't wait to take this back to Sweet Tea and get it on the wall."

I'm still gushing over the painting when Alvetta steps to the microphone and announces that the bidding has closed on the silent auction items, and that the live auction for the Keckley painting is about to begin.

"Can I entice you with one of those complimentary meals now?" I ask Kimberly. "You can help me hang the painting and see how perfect it looks at Sweet Tea."

"You don't want to stay and see how much the Sarah Vaughan painting goes for?" Wavonne asks.

I look past her at the portrait, and, while it is lovely, I can't help but think how it ultimately played a role in the death of Raynell and the incarceration of Christy. In my mind it's hard to separate the beauty of the artwork with the dreadful series of events that unfolded because of it.

"You know," I say to Wavonne as I pick up the painting of Grandmommy and gesture for her and Kimberly to follow me out the door, "the only painting I really have any interest in at the moment is this one. Let's get it back to Sweet Tea and admire it over a tall glass of iced tea and a few slices of whatever Momma has whipped up for dessert."